TO THE DOGS

Also by Louise Welsh

TO THE DOGS

Louise Welsh

CANONGATE

First published in Great Britain, the USA and Canada in 2024 by
Canongate Books Ltd, 14 High Street, Edinburgh EH1 1TE

Distributed in the USA by Publishers Group West and
in Canada by Publishers Group Canada

canongate.co.uk

1

British Library Cataloguing-in-Publication Data
A catalogue record for this book is available on
request from the British Library

ISBN 978 1 83885 981 7
Export ISBN 978 1 83885 982 4

Typeset in Perpetua Std by
Palimpsest Book Production Ltd, Falkirk, Stirlingshire

Printed and bound in Great Britain by Clays Ltd, Elcograf S.p.A.

To Jude Barber

One is dreadfully vulnerable through those
one loves.

The Masters, C.P. Snow (1951)

Semester One 2017–18

One

THE RECEPTION AREA had been designed with an eye to vomit and violence: wipe-clean surfaces, plastic chairs bolted to the floor, the counter shielded behind a Perspex screen. A cracked digital clock high on the wall clicked through the seconds, calculating time wasted. It was five past four. Dark outside, stark inside. Off-peak time for crime.

Jim sat in the seat furthest from the door. He glanced at his watch, confirming again that it tallied with the clock. Over an hour had passed since he had been told to *wait there*. He rubbed his face, felt the rasp of bristles against his palm. The sleeping pill he had taken in Beijing had towed him under before his (delayed) flight had lifted from the runway. He had slept through the in-flight service and was not quite free of the pill's effect, despite the changeover in Schiphol and the drive from the airport into the city.

He braced his palms against his lower back. His spine clicked, and he sighed. His last meal had been a bowl of noodle soup, twelve or thirteen hours ago, but worry about Eliot filled the gap with nausea where hunger should be.

A policeman stepped from the backroom, peered through the screen and went away. Jim looked at his phone, saw another missed call from Maggie. He texted *still waiting* and pressed send. The phone buzzed alive. He slipped it into the inside pocket of his suit jacket, felt it shudder and die against his heart. He would not survive another conversation with his wife, the round of questions for which he had no answer.

Paddy Kennedy walked into reception. The lawyer's mouth was set in the smile-that-was-no-smile he wore when he was on the losing side.

Jim sprang to his feet. 'What's happening?'

Paddy put a hand on Jim's arm and steered him back to the row of chairs. 'In the cells over the weekend, in court Monday.'

A pickaxe chipped at Jim's skull. 'Nothing we can do?'

Paddy shook his head. 'There were more pharmaceuticals in his flat than a Boots warehouse. You and Maggie will have to brace yourselves. Eliot's looking at a custodial sentence.'

Jim knew how the law worked but he had been hoping for a miracle. He exhaled. 'Jesus Christ.'

The policeman was back at reception. He stared at Jim and Paddy, as if sizing them up for a cell. Jim was aware of his rumpled suit, the scruff of new beard, and felt an urge to slide his last remaining business card, survivor of the Beijing graduation ceremony, onto the reception desk: *Professor James Brennan, FRSE, FRSS*. But it would change nothing, and the man might scent an opportunity to tip off the press.

'How long can he expect?'

Paddy shrugged. 'I'm no good to you this time, except as

a friend. You need a criminal lawyer. I'm guessing you know a few of those.'

'None I'd want to engage for this.'

Paddy took his phone from his pocket and scrolled down the contacts. 'I can recommend a couple of names.'

'I'd appreciate that.' If Paddy said they needed someone new, then they needed someone new, but Jim wished his friend had offered to act for them.

Paddy stared at the list of names on his mobile, selected a couple and tapped out a quick message. 'It'll be pricey.'

'No doubt.' They both knew he would pay whatever it took.

Jim's mobile chimed in his pocket, acknowledging receipt of Paddy's recommendations, and then buzzed urgently. He dug it out. *Maggie*. He pressed *reject*. The desk sergeant had started to sort through some paperwork. Jim wondered if it related to Eliot.

'How is he?'

Paddy softened his voice. 'Scared, but trying not to show it.'

'No chance I can see him?'

Paddy shook his head. 'Not a snowball's.'

Jim felt a wash of sorrow and relief. He wanted to hold his boy. Did not want to see the state he had got himself into this time. 'Maggie's going out of her mind.'

'And you?'

'Ditto.'

Paddy nodded. 'Don't blame yourselves.'

Jim said, 'I don't.' But he did. It was his own fate the boy was playing out, a generation delayed.

Paddy got to his feet. 'Let's get you home.'

Jim followed him, through the station door, into the street, not bothering to nod goodbye to the desk sergeant. They were on opposite sides now.

Outside, the air was harsh, the pavement busy with Friday afternoon shoppers and workers heading home or to the pub. Streetlights were glowing awake, the road choked with traffic. Jim felt like an actor walking onto the set of the wrong movie, everyone else costumed differently.

Paddy was at his elbow. 'Leave your car here. I'll drive you home.'

Jim made a face. 'I need to get my head round this before I break the news to Maggie.'

'You're dead on your feet. I know you think things can't get any worse, but they will if you're pulled over for dangerous driving.'

'I'll take it slowly.'

Paddy started to say something, but he charged by the hour and knew when he was wasting precious breath. 'Sure?'

Jim shook his hand. 'You're a good pal, Paddy.'

The lawyer put an arm around Jim and patted him on the back. They had never embraced when they were students, but they were getting older and more prone to wet-eye.

'Take care of yourself, Jim. Lots of boys do stupid things – Eliot was unlucky. He got caught.'

'He's twenty-three, and it's not the first time.'

Paddy looked away. He had a daughter studying aeronautical engineering at Imperial College, a son specialising in paediatrics at Ninewells. 'Kids grow up more slowly these days.'

Jim gave the lawyer's shoulder a brief squeeze. 'They grow at the same rate they always did.'

He turned his back and walked in the direction of the car park where he had left the Audi. It started to spit with rain.

Two

JIM PULLED INTO a parking space outside the Fusilier and killed the Audi's engine. He took in the familiar red sandstone tenements, the curve of the road, the high flats in the near distance. The tower blocks' exteriors had been refaced, but he supposed they were the same shitholes inside. Colleagues complained about the gentrification of the university district: the death of old-man pubs and the rise of student accommodation. There was no hint of the improvements that irked them here, but he doubted they would be beating a path to the Fusilier for post-lecture drinks.

A man ambled across the road, from the bookies towards the pub, his hips pitching in a lazy, Elvis swagger. Jim watched his progress. The gambler looked to be in his late fifties or early sixties, but Jim had a practised eye for poverty and reckoned you could shave a good ten years off. That would put the man somewhere around his own age. He wondered if their paths had ever crossed. The gambler turned and gave the Audi an appraising look. Their eyes met through the windscreen. The man nodded, spat on the pavement and continued on his way.

Maggie teased Jim about being flash with his cash: the expensive car, sharp haircut, designer suits. He had not minded, just as he had not minded colleagues calling him the Enforcer behind his back. Maggie liked his dandyish edge, and colleagues knew he was a good ally and worthy rival. Now Jim suspected his wife and colleagues recognised the same quality in him that the stranger had just marked. A willingness to go further than other men.

He took his phone from his pocket. A screed of missed calls, all of them from Maggie. She picked up straight away. 'Is he all right?'

Jim heard a faint chatter of starlings on the other end of the line and knew she was in the garden smoking, wrapped in the coat she wore when she walked Benji. There was no point in sugarcoating things, but he tried.

'He's all right. But they're keeping him in.'

'Are they allowed to do that?'

'He broke the law, love. He'll be in court Monday morning.'

He heard Maggie take a deep pull on her cigarette, the rush of breath as she exhaled. He knew what her next question would be and tried to deflect it with one of his own. 'How's Sasha?'

'Asleep. She guessed something was up. I told her Eliot was playing silly buggers again and she lost interest.' Maggie took another drag on her cigarette. 'We're not paying his fine this time, Jim.'

For a moment he was tempted to leave his wife in the happy land where serious drug charges could be wiped out by cash. 'It's gone beyond that, Mags. Paddy reckons Eliot will get a custodial sentence. He told me to hire a good criminal lawyer.'

'Shit.' The word was breath and smoke. There was a pause, and Jim wondered if Maggie was crying. 'How long?'

'He didn't know.' It occurred to Jim that Paddy might have had an idea of the length of sentence Eliot could expect but had not wanted to say. 'He gave me the numbers of a couple of criminal briefs.'

A tiny dog with oversized ears, whose ancestors hailed from somewhere in South America, trotted past the car. When he was a boy, dogs had been Yorkies, Alsatians, greyhounds or Heinz 57 varieties. Now, there were supposedly hypoallergenic breeds like Benji and types he could not identify. A small girl in a puffer coat followed the dog, hood up, a bag of messages in her hand.

Maggie's voice was husky with tears. 'Did you see him?'

'They wouldn't let me.'

'Did you ask?' Maggie had never been good with grief. Her tone was already hardening.

'Of course I bloody asked.' Jim took a deep breath. 'He's my son too. I love him.'

A fizzle of burning paper and tobacco reached down the line as Maggie inhaled. 'Prison's a nightmare for people with drug problems. They go in with a cannabis habit and come out crackheads.'

'Eliot's not a victim. He's the guy parents warn their kids to stay away from.'

'Whose side are you on, Jim?'

'Do you really need to ask? People get through worse than this. In a few years we'll look back and think, that was a horrible episode, but we got through it.'

'Right now I can't think of anything worse than my child being incarcerated.'

'It could be much worse, love. He didn't kill anyone.'

That was where they were, at the point where Eliot not having committed murder was good news.

He heard the whoosh of the glass door as Maggie stepped from the garden into the lounge. The faint thud as she slid it shut. 'Perhaps prison isn't such a big deal to you.'

'It is a big deal, but I'm not going to pretend Eliot's a choirboy.' He closed his eyes. 'I'm tired.'

Maggie's voice softened. 'Are you okay to drive?'

'I don't know.' Jim stared out at the Fusilier. Its flat roof was bereft of the coiled edging of barbed wire that used to protect it, though the windows were still guarded by metal shutters. He heard another door shut on the end of the line. 'Where are you?'

'The studio. Newlands' drainage system needs some modifications.'

He imagined Maggie in the office space she had designed for herself, light pooling on plans pinned to the drawing board, the fine lines around her eyes that she concealed with make-up during the day illuminated by the glow of her computer as she leaned in to make some adjustment to the design. He had always loved to watch her draw.

She said, 'Leave the car. Get a cab.'

'Maybe. There's something I've got to do first.'

'You just said there was nothing we can do. Text me the numbers Paddy gave you. I'll phone the lawyers.'

Jim released the buckle of his seatbelt. 'Thanks. I'll be home as soon as I can.'

Maggie sounded exhausted. 'Just come home, Jim. I've got enough to worry about without you going walkabout.'

'Go to bed. Get some rest. I'll be back before you wake up.' He meant the bed they shared in the master bedroom overlooking the front garden, but suspected Maggie would spend the night on the futon beneath the eaves of her studio. 'Eliot screwed up. He has to face what's coming to him, but I'm damned if he's going to carry the can for anyone else. He wasn't in this on his own. I'm going to talk to a few folk and see what I can find out.'

Maggie sighed. 'It isn't your world any more, Jim. You wouldn't know where to start.'

'Don't worry, love. I'm a criminologist, remember.'

'Yes, but this isn't your kind of crime. You're not going to be analysing statistics, debating ethics. Drugs are big money, and big money leads to violence.'

He told her not to worry again, hung up and texted the numbers Paddy had given him. Then, because he read crime reports and knew how these things worked, he forced the SIM card from his phone and put it in his wallet.

Three

IT WAS A poetic irony that his son had been arrested in his grandfather's local. When Eliot was a baby, Jim had noticed how the set of his eyes resembled Big Jim's. He had trained himself not to mind, though the similarity had grown stronger as the boy developed. He wondered if anyone in the pub had observed Eliot's resemblance to his grandfather and marked it. Big Jim was almost twenty years dead, but he had been a well-kent force and memories could be long.

The Fusilier had changed. In Big Jim's day, the interior had been shelved with layers of cigarette smoke, solid as ectoplasm, every table graced by a massive ashtray advertising Capstan Full Strength, Carlsberg Special, Whyte & Mackay, whose slogans vanished beneath tides of douts. Now, smokers were exiled outside, the fug of cigarettes replaced by sweat, spilled beer and Glade.

The lone one-armed bandit, with its promise of synchro-nised fruit and cartoon cut gems, had been conquered by a bank of electronic puggy machines. Four flat-screen TVs had replaced the black-and-white portable that used to relay snowy images from Goodwood. Two were tuned to WWF wrestling, the others to a pick 'n' mix of American Football matches between teams Jim did not recognise.

The most striking change had nothing to do with cigarettes or décor. When Jim's father was a regular, a woman's place had been behind the bar. Men were still in the majority, but some were accompanied by wives or girlfriends. A couple of women sat in a corner, sharing a bottle of white wine. A hen party had pushed three tables together and were goading a girl in a sparkly plastic tiara to slam through a line of shots.

Jim was already drawing stares. He stepped up to the bar and ordered a pint of lager. He had schooled himself not to see the world through his father's eyes, but it was easy to imagine Big Jim's reaction to a man in a designer suit and navy Crombie entering the Fusilier. The scent of success and hint of a world beyond the bar would have been a challenge that bunched his father's fists.

Jim meant to merely touch the pint glass to his lips, but he took a deep, head-cleansing swallow and then wiped his mouth with the back of his hand. It was the first beer he had drunk in months.

His old man's seat had been in the corner nearest the bar. Big Jim had spent so many nights there, sat in state amongst his cronies, his DNA probably lingered on in the walls. Jim raised the glass to his lips again. A group of young lads dressed in sports gear were crowded round his father's table, casting glances at the hen party. They were around typical third-year undergraduate age, but their fade cuts were sharper, their JD Sports tracksuits box-fresh. A couple looked in Jim's direction. His father had taught him that one word, a meeting of the eyes, could light a touch paper. Part of him would welcome the chance to beat out his frustration and take some blows in return, fists on flesh. But ambition had tamped that side of him. He had his own fiefdom, one that depended on a different type of muscle.

The futility of his half-plan hit Jim. His was a small city ringed by pockets of deprivation where drugs were grown, synthesised, bought and sold. Eliot had been arrested in the Fusilier, but the people who had connived with him might come from elsewhere. Maggie was right: he did not know where to start.

He was a university professor, a respected member of the senior management group with ambitions for the top post. This was no longer his world. The Audi was parked in full view on the street, his suitcase, containing his laptop and confidential university papers, in the boot. It was time to go home.

A hand touched his shoulder. 'Jimmy?'

The man was somewhere around Jim's age. A few inches shorter, broad-shouldered, and dressed in a grey suit with a faint silver pinstripe. His nose had been broken and reset at some time in his youth. It gave him the look of a rough-and-tumble sportsman. 'I thought it was you.'

The ghost of a memory lurked in the stranger's features. Jim tried to see beyond the salt-and-pepper hair, the blurred jawline. Some faint recollection called to him and vanished, leaving a mild feeling of unease.

'I'm sorry . . .'

The stranger grinned. His teeth had been bleached at some point, but there was a dullness to the enamel that suggested red wine, black coffee and cigars.

'Well, that's a dunt to the ego. Eddie – Eddie Cranston.

We went to the same school.' The face resolved itself, like one of those optical illusions hidden in a picture, impossible to unsee once it had been detected. The man held out a hand. After a beat of hesitation, they shook. 'Revisiting old haunts?'

'Something like that.' Cranston had been in one of the years above him, Jim recalled. A stocky midfielder who had got a trial at one of the local football clubs. There was something else too, something he had heard, or read, more recently; it flittered on the edge of his mind and evaporated into a fog of jetlag. He set his pint on the bar. 'Good to see you again, Eddie. You've caught me at a bad time. I need to hit the road.'

'I shouldn't have interrupted. I just wanted to say hello and congratulate you on your successes. I'll leave you to your thoughts.'

Jim should return the compliment, tell Eddie he was looking well and ask him something about himself, but it was too much. 'You did me a favour, interrupting me. It's been a long day – a long week. I'm not sure what I'm doing here.'

Cranston caught the barman's eye. 'Same again, please, Billy.' He turned his attention back to Jim. 'You're wondering how it came to this.'

'To what?'

Cranston gave an apologetic grin. 'Sorry, that was clumsy. I heard about your boy.'

'What did you hear?' Shades of his father's voice lurked, dangerous, in Jim's tone.

Cranston sucked the froth from a pint of Guinness, reached into his jacket for his wallet and drew out a business card. 'I was at the station when your son was brought in, three sheets to the wind and screaming blue murder.'

Jim took the proffered card. An evenly balanced set of

scales – one side black, the other white – set against a cream background, *E. Cranston & Co., Solicitors & Notaries* embossed below. 'Touting for business?'

The lawyer straightened his shoulders. 'Crime's a growth area – you of all people should know that. I don't need to tout, but, as it happens, I did offer Eliot my services. He told me to fuck off, that his father was a big-shot professor who would get him a better brief than me.'

Jim took another inch from his lager. Eliot, he reflected, had succeeded in driving him to drink. He would have to stop soon or get a taxi home.

'You were in the police station when he was brought in. Now you're here. Bit of a coincidence?'

'Not really, my office is just around the corner.'

'All the same, you strike me as more of a wine-bar man than a Fusilier regular.'

The barman placed a rum and Coke amongst the dozen drinks he had lined up on the bar. 'That's thirty-seven sixty, Eddie.'

'Thanks, Billy.' Cranston peeled four notes from a neat fold in his wallet. 'Have one yourself.'

'Cheers.'

Cranston nodded to the barman, then met Jim's eyes. 'I make a living defending young guys who've hit a bump in the road. I got sick of seeing generations making the same mistakes, so I started a boys' club.' He nodded towards the group of youths Jim had noticed earlier. 'The football team just lost 3–2. I'm buying them some consolation.' He raised his voice and turned towards the table. 'Do yous lot want your drinks or not? I'm your coach, not a bloody waitress.'

A couple of the youths stood up slowly and ambled to the bar.

'Awright, Mr Cranston,' one of them said in the nasal whine Jim associated with heroin and panhandling. 'We didnae want to interrupt your conversation in case it was confidential, like.'

'Very thoughtful of you, Jordan.'

The barman passed a couple of trays to the youths, who loaded them and ferried the drinks to the table.

Jim waited until they were out of earshot. 'I would have thought you'd get enough of bad boys during your working day.'

Cranston took a swig of his Guinness. 'I'm not a poof, if that's what you're getting at. Some people walk away from their roots first chance they get, others stick around and try to make a difference.'

Jim frowned. Less than twelve hours ago he had been at the university's Beijing campus, representing the principal at graduations. He had deliberately conjured memories of his own graduation and shaken each student's hand with a warmth he wished on his younger self. 'You don't have to stay where you came from to make a difference.'

'True.' Cranston gave a sudden grin; laughter lines crinkled his face. 'I came over to wish you well and commiserate with you on having an idiot for a son, but we seem to have got off on the wrong foot. Come and say hello to some of my idiots. It'll do them good to meet someone from the neighbourhood who's done well, and it might cheer you up to know your boy isn't the only dafty in town.'

Jim glanced at the youths. They were around Eliot's age. 'Okay, just for a minute.'

'Good man.' Cranston pointed at Jim's glass. 'Let me freshen that drink for you.'

Jim saw that his pint had dipped below the halfway mark.

He would have to get a taxi after all and trust the Audi to the fates overnight. He made a mental note not to forget his suitcase.

'Just a half, thanks. I promised my wife I wouldn't be late.'

Cranston raised a hand in the air to attract the attention of the barman and then pointed at Jim's glass. 'Billy, another one of these, please.' He put an arm around Jim's shoulder and gently ferried him towards the corner table. 'You're a wise man. If I'd taken more care to get home at a decent time, I might still have a wife to go home to.' Cranston switched his attention. 'Shift up, lads, we've got a visitor. Professor Brennan's a big shot at the university, but once upon a time he went to the same school yous lot used to dog.'

The boys nodded politely, and Cranston galloped through the introductions. Jim repeated each name in turn. Remembering who was who had stood him in good stead over the years.

Jordan asked, 'Is that your motor outside, Mr Brennan?'

'Professor Brennan,' Cranston corrected.

'Sorry, is that your motor outside, *Professor* Brennan.'

'The Audi? Aye, that's mine.'

Jordan gave a puckish grin. He was smaller than the others, with features that hinted at foetal alcohol syndrome.

'Nice wheels. Nice threads too.' Jordan nodded at Jim's suit. 'I'm guessing they pay well at the uni.'

'Well enough.'

Cranston said, 'The professor worked hard to get where he is.'

A black-haired youth called Sammy made a sound like a deflating balloon. His father would have cuffed the boy around the ear and sent him packing, but Jim merely raised an eyebrow. 'What's so funny about hard work?'

'Nothing, mate.' Jim saw there would be no 'professor'

from this quarter. 'It's the idea of a fair day's pay for a fair day's work that's cracking me up.'

Cranston said, 'Sammy's the team's shop steward.'

Sammy wiped a sheen of sweat and alcopop from his upper lip. 'Aye, well, I'm sick of folk talking to me like I'm a lay-about. I work my arse off, five in the morning till twelve midday, for buttons. I may as well be on the brew for all that's left after I give my mum my bed and board.'

The barman set a full pint of lager on the table. Jim took a sip and asked, 'Where do you work?'

'Greggs the fucking Bakers. Before that it was Krispy-crappy-Kreme. McJobs – real work for a muppet pay packet. Then when your six months are up, you're out the door and another bastard's wearing your uniform.'

Jordan grinned. 'That's what gets to him. He thought he looked good in that Krispy Kreme hat.'

Sammy leaned across the boys sitting beside him to bat a half-hearted shove at Jordan. 'Least I'm working, not sucking spliffs in front of *Homes Under the Hammer* all day.'

Jordan returned the shove. '*Homes Under the Hammer* is only on in the morning, wankstain.'

Jim looked at his watch. Nine o'clock. He pictured Maggie standing at the window of her studio, staring out into the darkened garden.

Their son had been a cheeky child, full of energy and good to be around. The trouble had started somewhere around the last year of primary. There was no obvious reason for the boy's altered personality: no change of school or death in the family, no sudden illness or head injury. Maggie had accused Jim of not giving Eliot enough attention, and so he had initiated a series of father-and-son Saturday after-noons that had made him sympathise with divorcees.

They had tried football matches, museums, the zoo, art galleries, swimming, climbing walls, matinees at the theatre. The boy had been a surly companion, uninterested in anything except shoot-'em-up computer games and Netflix.

Maggie blamed their son's problems on drugs, but Jim thought they had started with a growth spurt. Eliot had misused his new strength and become a bully – a swaggerer, unpopular with his classmates. Jim suspected cannabis had initially been a bid to buy friends.

He took a sip of his pint. 'Are drugs easy to get round here?'

A boy in a funnel-necked Nike sweatshirt leaned across the table. His eyes were red, as if he was struggling with some allergy. 'Aye, what are you after?'

Cranston flapped his hands laconically, like a man putting out a not very urgent fire. 'Okay, lads. Not in front of visitors, remember.'

Sammy swigged his drink straight from the bottle. 'The likes of him think we're all toking and smoking.' He stared at Jim. 'We've just been playing football. We're into healthy living, mate.'

'I'm not accusing you of anything. My son was arrested in this pub earlier today on a drugs charge. His name's Eliot. I thought one of you might know him.'

Jordan said, 'That fud's your son?'

Jim kept his face gangster-straight. The boy in the funnel-neck whose name was Ally set his drink on the table. 'It's like Sammy said – we might not have been good at exams and the like, but we steer clear of trouble. No offence, but we give guys like your son a wide berth.'

Jim took another ill-advised pull of his pint. 'What do you mean, guys like my son?'

No one answered.

Cranston said, 'If you know something, tell the professor.'

Sammy's expression was serious. 'We might look like fuck-ups to you. We didn't pass exams or go to uni, but we grew up around here and we know who to avoid.'

Ally said, 'I'm not a fuck-up. I got my Duke of Edinburgh Award.'

Jordan's grin returned. 'That's right. He's a fucking Boy Scout.'

Ally gave him a friendly cuff to the head. 'I'm joining the army. You'll be calling me Sergeant Ally soon enough.'

Sammy said, 'If you dinnae get your balls blown off.'

Jordan adopted a falsetto voice. 'Then it'll be *Sergeant Ally*.'

Jim said, 'How did you know to avoid my son?'

Sammy's smile died. 'He wasn't exactly subtle. I don't know who dobbed him in, but no one likes posh wankers, especially not one who thinks he's the next Pablo Escobar.'

Jim got up and went to the toilet. It was time to head home. The gents was blue-lit to prevent injecting into veins. He washed his hands, took out his phone, slid the SIM card back in place and texted Maggie: *Home soon x.*

There was a fresh pint waiting for him at the table. Jim wondered what his colleagues would think if they could see him in a scheme bar drinking with a bunch of boys barely out of their teens. The thought made him shake his head. Every move he made to help his son diminished him.

Jim sank into his seat and tipped the pint to his lips. There would be no more after this one. 'Does anyone have a taxi number?'

A thin boy who had not spoken before piped up, 'I can drive you.' A blameless tin of Coca-Cola garnished with a plastic straw sat in front of him.

Jim rubbed a hand across his face. The tiredness the alcohol had initially held at bay crashed down on him. 'You're all right, son.'

'It'd be nae bother. My da's got a garage. I'm insured to drive any car.'

Jim realised the boy was proposing to drive the Audi and laughed. 'You're still all right.'

Cranston said, 'Marky's a good driver. I trust him with my own car, and you're looking more than a wee bit peaky.'

Jim took out his mobile, ready to search for a taxi firm online, but his fingers felt like mattress foam. The phone slipped from his grasp and landed beneath the table. He said, 'Did one of you wee bastards put something in my drink?' But the words came out slurred and nobody answered. He leaned beneath the table to retrieve his phone. The movement unbalanced him, and he toppled, jarring the table and knocking over freshly charged glasses. Beer, spirits and sticky mixers soaked Jim's smart suit, his hair, his face.

Cranston bellowed, 'There he goes,' in a voice that suggested shipwrecks on stormy seas. The youths laughed, and the rest of the bar joined in, the hen party's screeches rising high above the rest.

'Let's get you some fresh air, Jimmy.' Cranston hooked an arm beneath one of his oxters, and the boy who wanted to be a sergeant lifted him by the other. Jim's legs were a stumble, the floor jouncing. He mumbled, 'I can manage fine,' but they half walked, half carried him across the floor and through the swing door. Cold air, steamy breath and cigarette smoke wrapped around them.

Marky reached into the pockets of Jim's suit jacket, searching for his car keys. The youth's breath was sugar-scented. 'Dinnae worry, professor. I'll take good care of your car.'

Jim tried to bat him away. Cranston patted his suit like a nightclub bouncer checking for weapons and then slid a hand into his breast pocket. Jim realised the lawyer was taking his passport and tried to punch him.

Sammy caught Jim's wrists. 'That's not very friendly, professor. We're trying to help you.'

Jim muttered, 'Get tae fuck or I'll set the polis on you.'

Jordan said, 'You're sounding like my da.'

Jim thought he heard one of the smokers ask, 'Is that Big Jim Brennan's laddie?'

But Cranston and his boys were folding him into the back of the Audi, and he did not hear the reply.

Four

JIM WOKE TO dazzling blindness. He was in the downstairs guest room of his own home. A shaft of sunlight had crept across the bed while he slept and then settled, a brilliant bar of pain, across his eyes. He rolled beyond its reach and looked at the bedside clock: 08.45. There was no glass of water on the bedside table, no aspirin left as a love token by his wife to ease the band of pressure in his head.

The bed smelt of sweat, alcohol and the familiar, fresh-laundry scent of clean sheets. His suit was folded on a chair in the corner, his shirt, tie and underwear a crumpled blastula of fabric on the floor. Jim tried to remember the journey home but could only recall his exit from the pub and a flash of streetlights streaming through darkness, which might have been a dream.

Somewhere beyond the guest room a radio was playing. Jim made out the cheerful voice of the Saturday morning DJ and guessed that Maggie and Sasha were together in the kitchen. Maggie preferred silence, but their daughter liked friendly chatter and pop music. The shame that had shadowed him in the days when he used to drink to excess was on him, souring his stomach. He imagined Sasha, woken by the sound of his stumbles, getting out of bed and witnessing his drunken homecoming. Jim groaned again.

His father had been the kind of drunk dogs crossed the street to avoid. Jimmy had dreaded the sound of Big Jim's key scraping against the keyhole, the eventual turn of the lock, the noise of his boots being discarded, thud-thud, on the floor. The unpredictability of his returns had been excruciating. Some nights he would be accompanied by a merry crew and a carryout, and Wee Jimmy would be called from bed to show off his cleverness by reciting some poem or other. He had hated these command performances, his father's jealous pride, manifested in sly shoves and put-downs. Jimmy had been embarrassed by the bored expressions on the drinkers' faces, their laughter at Big Jim's jibes, the sympathy of shillings they shoved at him, and the women's calls to 'let the laddie get to his bed'.

Bad as they were, these impromptu parties had been preferable to evenings when his father returned alone and angry. On those nights his boots stayed on. They had work to do. There was no back door in a tenement, nowhere to run to, once Big Jim was home.

The radio burble stopped. Jim heard the voices of his wife and daughter in the hallway, then the sound of the front door shutting followed by the slam-slam of car doors. The Range Rover growled awake. There was a crunch of gravel, and the engine faded into the distance. Jim wondered where they were going and then remembered that Sasha was starting Saturday morning ice-skating classes. He had promised to take her.

'Shit.'

He slid naked from bed, walked to the window and peeked through the curtains. The Audi was neatly parked on the drive. He went to the chair where his suit lay abandoned. His wallet was in the breast pocket of his jacket, his credit cards and driving licence snug inside. His mobile phone and passport were tucked in another pocket. He flipped the cover of his phone open. Eddie Cranston's business card fluttered to the floor. Jim picked it up and regarded the perfectly balanced black-and-white scales.

He had drunk two pints of lager – or was it three? – in the Fusilier. Beijing was seven hours ahead. It had been a long journey, followed by the stressful visit to the police station. He had barely eaten in the preceding twenty-four hours and was not much of a drinker these days. It had been unwise to sink the beers so quickly, but their effects seemed out of proportion. He remembered his accusation to the boys and wondered if he had hit on the truth: that they had spiked his drink while he was in the gents. It seemed ridiculous – why would they? – yet these things did happen. A case had been brought to the attention of the University Senate only a few months ago of an undergraduate who claimed to have been drugged and sexually assaulted. The young woman had been left with no memory of the event until photographs of her appeared online. Jim crushed Cranston's card in his fist and pulled on the dressing gown hanging on the back of the door.

His car keys sat in a dish on the hall table; his suitcase and briefcase were tucked neatly by the stairs. Benji ran from the lounge to meet him. The dog's paws lost purchase on the parquet floor, and it slid the final yard, front legs splayed, and bashed against his bare feet, tail wagging. Jim paused to scratch the dog's ears and then climbed the stairs to the main bathroom. He locked the door, relieved himself and stepped into the shower. Turning the water pressure up to max, he raised his face to meet the needle cascade.

The Procurator Fiscal had regretted the gap between the assault on the undergraduate and her complaint to the police. There had been no forensic evidence and nothing to prove the student accused of posting images of her online was lying when he said the girl had been a willing partner. Jim had believed the young woman. He argued for her assailant to be charged, but in the end had to concede the evidence was not strong enough. Both students had remained at university, both tainted with rumours.

Perhaps it was the memory of the woman he had been unable to protect that had made him think of spiked drinks. Jim soaped his body. Except for a sore head and the flu-like ache in his limbs he always experienced after long-haul flights, he felt okay. He remembered the sleeping pill he had taken as the plane lifted into the sky from Beijing Capital and wondered if it could have played a part.

Jim turned off the shower and heard the landline ringing. He wrapped a towel around his waist and jogged to the bedroom. The ringing stopped as he lifted the handset.

'Fuck.'

He set the phone back on its cradle. Water dripped from him onto the kilim by the bed. Jim tugged the towel from his waist, rubbed his hair and began to dry his body. He picked up the phone again and dialled 1471. The number was withheld; the caller had left no message.

Benji bustled into the bedroom, a ball in his mouth, his ridiculous tail wagging.

Jim pointed at the door. 'Out! Ye ken you're not allowed in here.'

The dog heard the business in his voice and scooted from the room, leaving its ball behind. Jim sat on the edge of the bed and put his head in his hands.

'Is that how you speak to him when no one's around?'

Jim raised his head. Maggie was standing in the doorway, car keys still in her hand. 'I usually baby-talk the wee fucker. I missed the phone. It might have been Eliot.' He cast his towel aside, went to the chest of drawers and rooted around for underwear. He wanted to ask her what had happened the previous night, but the urge to know his son was okay was stronger. 'Did you manage to get a lawyer?'

'It wasn't easy. In the end your friend Eddie agreed to act for him.'

Jim had pulled on a pair of boxers and his right sock. He paused and looked at his wife. 'Eddie Cranston?'

Maggie nodded. 'He stayed for a drink, after he brought you home last night.'

'Cranston's no friend of mine.' Jim felt a pulse of anger he was surprised to realise was jealousy. He pulled on his other sock. 'What was wrong with Pat's recommendations?'

Maggie was wearing slim-fit jeans, sneakers and a mannish white shirt. She leaned against the doorframe, watching him dress. 'Nothing, except none of them picked up when I rang, and I didn't feel like confiding in their answer services. Eddie's the right choice. He has a good record of defending the young men juries might not be inclined to empathise with.'

Jim took a tracksuit from his side of the wardrobe. Under other circumstances his semi-nakedness and Maggie's Lauren Bacall pose might have turned him on.

'Sounds like he gave you a good spiel.'

'He didn't need to. I looked him up online.' Benji peeked round the bedroom door. Maggie picked the dog up and cradled it like a baby. 'Don't mind Daddy. He didn't mean to shout at you.'

Jim heard the forgiveness in her voice. 'I've told you before, I'm not that mutt's father.' He went to the door, and they kissed, the dog an impediment between them. 'What time did I get in last night?'

'Around ten thirty.'

Eddie Cranston and his boys had been true to their word and driven him straight home. One of the knots in Jim's spine loosened. 'What happened?'

'You were tired and emotional.'

He took the dog from his wife and put it on the ground, so he could hold her closer. 'What does that mean?'

Maggie's breath smelt of fruit pastels. 'Drunk and morose. Eddie helped you up the front steps. I asked you if you were okay, you told me to fuck off and lurched into the guestroom like a sweary robot.'

He rested his forehead on her shoulder. 'I'm sorry.'

'Eddie already apologised for you. He said you barely drank anything. One minute you were talking about Eliot, the next you were on the floor.' Maggie placed her palms on either side of his face and took a step backwards so she could look at him. 'You should see the doctor. You're under a lot of stress. It's not just Eliot. All that work on the new research building is taking its toll. You're reaching the age when men suddenly drop dead of heart attacks.'

His laugh was harsh and unexpected. 'Thanks for trying to cheer me up.'

Maggie stroked his face with her fingertips. 'It's true. I love you. Me and the kids need you to stick around.'

*

They sat on stools at the kitchen island, each of them cradling a cup of tea in their hands.

Maggie looked at her watch. 'I need to collect Sasha in half an hour.'

'I'll do it.'

She gave him an apologetic smile. 'I promised her a girly afternoon. We're going to get our nails done, then go for pancakes.'

'She's eleven years old. Isn't that a bit young for a trip to the beauty salon?'

'It's a manicure, not Botox. You warned me you had a lot of work to do over the weekend. I thought you'd be glad of an empty house.'

'That was before . . .'

Maggie made a face. 'I know. I can't stop thinking about it either.'

They had not discussed Eliot's misdemeanour, only how to deal with it.

Jim sipped his tea. 'What you said earlier, about Cranston having a good record of defending young men . . .'

'Eddie thinks juries are harsher on them than on other demographics. He has a thing about it.'

Maggie had always been clear-sighted in her feminism. Jim raised his eyebrows. 'And you agree?'

She rubbed a hand over her face, and he realised how tired she was. 'Not necessarily, but I think his motives are good and he might help Eliot.' Maggie got to her feet and took her cup to the dishwasher. 'I googled him. Some of the boys he's defended did far worse than sell drugs. One lot set a building on fire, killed a homeless couple sleeping there. They had records as long as your arm, but Eddie got them a low sentence.'

It was the case he had almost remembered the night before.

An act of vandalism had got out of hand and become a murder inquiry. A gang of unemployed youths were charged. Cranston had defended them, and the boys had received custodial sentences. One had broken ranks as he was about to be taken to the cells and shouted that the building's owner had paid them to burn the place down. Cranston had called for an immediate appeal, but the evidence was conclusive, the boy alone in his allegation.

Jim said, 'If it's the case I'm thinking of, it was a shit storm.'

'You're remembering the headlines. If you looked more closely, you'd see Eddie got the charges reduced from murder to culpable homicide. He convinced the judge to give those boys lower sentences than they could have hoped for.'

Jim took out his phone. The case was easy to find. Maggie was right. The youths' sentences had been so lenient there had been a campaign to get them extended.

'He's a blowhard.'

Maggie was at the sink, refilling Benji's water bowl. She set it back on its plastic mat. 'Isn't being a blowhard one of the essential qualifications of being a lawyer?'

The thought of Cranston and his entourage in his house made Jim cringe. 'Did the boys come in for a drink too?'

Maggie smiled. 'They were too shy. Eddie got them an Uber.'

'Cranston isn't shy.'

'He was kind. I told him all about Eliot. He wants to help.' Jim looked away. Maggie's voice sharpened. 'You make a face if you want to, but where were you?'

'Trying to help.'

'By going back to your roots and getting pissed? Very helpful. Who knows what would have happened if Eddie hadn't taken charge?'

The discussion was looping towards a row.

Jim said, 'Was Sasha disappointed I didn't take her ice-skating?'

Maggie took a deep breath. She was still standing by the sink, the length of the kitchen between them.

'She knows you're tired. Beijing and back in three days? It's less than a month since you were in Mumbai. You put yourself under too much pressure.'

'It was the only way to make my schedule work.'

Benji was whining at the kitchen door. Maggie opened it and let him out into the garden.

'It wasn't exactly ideal for my schedule. I had to rearrange a site visit.'

'I know. I'm sorry. I couldn't get out of it.'

'You didn't want to get out of it.' Maggie went into the utility room. He watched her through the open door as she transferred wet laundry from the washing machine to the tumble dryer. The hum of the dryer reached into the kitchen. She emerged from the room, brushing hair from her eyes. 'Eddie said we should be at the court for nine, Monday morning, but there's no guarantee of when Eliot's case will come up. We could be there for hours.'

Jim turned his phone in his hands, catching sight of his reflection, a pink blur in its silvered surface. 'The building procurement meeting is at ten thirty on Monday followed by lunch with potential funders. It took weeks to set up. Put him on the case if you think it'll help, but I'm not cancelling. I don't think you should disrupt your day either.'

Maggie closed the door to the utility room, shutting out the noise. Her voice was dangerously calm. 'We're talking about our son.'

They must have argued before they had children, but Jim

could not remember what they had argued about. It seemed to him that every dispute centred on their son. 'Eliot's a grown man. Let him stand on his own two feet for once.'

Maggie took a step towards him. 'What if he goes to jail?'

'It's a preliminary hearing. The sheriff will grant bail and set a court date. Eliot will slink home with his tail between his legs. He doesn't need us there to hold his hand, and I'm damned if I'm going to upset a lot of important people because of his idiocy.' Jim's phone chimed. He flipped it open. One of the comms team had WhatsApped him a photo of the Beijing ceremony to approve for social media. Smiling graduates dressed in robes, gathered around him on the steps of the university. He looked small in their midst: a middle-aged man dwarfed by the future. He sent a thumbs-up emoji and clicked the phone shut. 'I knew Eliot lacked direction, but I thought the DJing thing was working out.'

Maggie opened the door and let Benji back in. The dog trotted to its water bowl and started lapping noisily. She picked up her car keys. 'I'll get something for supper on my way home.'

Jim sensed some avoidance in his wife. 'Did you suspect anything?'

'Of course not, but . . .'

He took her hand, unsure if he was encouraging or detaining her. 'But what?'

'But maybe I should have. He'd stopped asking me for money.'

Jim raised his eyes to the ceiling and let out a sigh. 'We agreed not to sub him beyond the flat and utilities.'

Maggie pulled her hand away. 'I know, but he'd text me saying he was short of food, or needed a bit extra to pay a bill on time . . .'

'. . . and you always gave in.'

'Not always, but I'm his mother. I found it hard to say no.'

The appeal to her motherhood irritated Jim. 'When did he stop asking for money?'

Maggie took the cup from him and put it in the dishwasher. 'About a month ago. I thought the same as you did, that his DJing was taking off. His style changed – did you notice? It got more hip-hoppy.'

Jim was not sure what 'hip-hoppy' looked like, beyond a vague impression of gold chains and baseball caps. 'How much did he sting you for?'

Maggie picked up her handbag. 'What does it matter?'

'Eliot sent me a screenshot of a bill from a garage around six weeks ago. That old Volvo Estate I gave him was dead. He said he needed a new van, or he wouldn't be able to transport his gear. He stung me for five grand.'

Somewhere outside, a bird started to whistle.

Maggie took a pair of sunglasses from her bag and slid them on, but not before Jim saw tears spring to her eyes. 'He knew the odds of us telling each other were low.' She gave an upside-down smile. 'He told me someone had stolen his speakers. He couldn't afford to replace them. I gave him two thousand pounds.'

Jim tried to smile. 'I guess that answers the question of who set our son up in the drug-dealing business.'

Maggie nodded. 'It was us, his loving parents.'

Five

THE DEMOLITION MACHINE resembled a long-necked, mechanical dinosaur with a tiny head and grasping jaws. It juddered towards what remained of the Adult Education building and took a bite. Plaster crumbled and bricks dislodged and tumbled to the ground, raising plumes of dust. The machine pressed its forehead to the ruined structure and pushed. The wall bent and bulged, then the last of the bricks fell, revealing a skeleton of metal supports. A view of grey sky and distant tenements appeared where Adult Ed had stood for decades. A small crowd of students cheered. The hungry machine snapped and shoved. Metal quaked, yielded and, finally, broke. The students cheered again.

Jim glanced at his phone. It was twenty past ten. Maggie would have been at court for over an hour. He texted: *Call me as soon as you hear anything, love you both x.*

Ronald Fergusson joined the edge of the crowd. Jim looked away, but Fergusson was already coming towards him. The demolition machine picked through the wreckage, crunching at the remnants, as if not quite certain it had brought the building down.

Fergusson was a physicist prone to exacting parameters and flights of fancy. He nodded at the mountain of rubble and twisted metal. 'Good metaphor for an academic career. Decades of hard work, and one day it's all over.'

Vibrations from the machine's engine reached up through the soles of Jim's feet. He felt his bones judder beneath his flesh. He turned his back on the building site and walked towards the quadrangles. Fergusson fell into step beside him. The wind was rising. Demolition dust powdered Jim's face and tickled the back of his throat. He repressed an urge to hoick and spit.

Fergusson gave him a sly look. 'Whose design do you favour?'

Jim had read the various architects' bids for the new learning and teaching hub on the flight back from Beijing. He had hoped to discuss them with Maggie, but Eliot's antics had got in the way.

'Let's save that discussion for the meeting.'

They passed through the gate to the old part of the university. Once, this had been the entire campus, but the university had long outgrown it. The picturesque buildings, which featured in so many promotional videos, were now home to admin offices and a business school.

Fergusson raised a hand in silent greeting to some passing colleagues Jim did not recognise. 'You're a cautious man, James.'

'It's a lot of money.'

'It is, and not all of it in the bank yet.'

It started to spot with rain. They entered the cool damp of one of the stairways and climbed upwards towards the quads. Fergusson was almost two decades older, but he took the stairs at a swift pace. The rain was getting heavier. Fergusson held his folder over his head as they crossed the quads to protect his thinning fluff. He nodded towards the lawns, lush from frequent drenchings, the turreted buildings and the cloisters beyond.

'Health and safety has put paid to truly magnificent European buildings. The best architects head for Shanghai or Dubai where they can realise their visions, free of petty bureaucracy.'

Jim resisted an urge to mention mortality rates on construction sites free from health and safety restrictions. 'The old buildings are iconic, but they're no longer fit for purpose.'

Fergusson tucked his folder under his arm. 'That's already been established. My point is, we have a responsibility to choose a structure that reflects the distinctiveness of our city.' He touched Jim's arm and paused, holding him there. 'Your wife's an architect – what does she make of our plans?'

Fergusson's reference to Maggie surprised Jim. 'She hasn't seen them in detail, but I'm sure she'll be behind them.'

'We discussed architecture at one of the Senate dinners. She's a sensible woman.'

'I know. I was surprised when she agreed to marry me.'

Fergusson acknowledged the feeble joke with a brief smile. 'What I'm saying is, balance sheets are important, but this building will represent our generation of scholars. Let's not settle for an anonymous white box with a thirty-year lifespan.'

The university tower struck the half hour. Fergusson let go of Jim's arm, and they resumed their progress at an increased pace. They entered the admin building and climbed its carpeted stairs to the meeting room in silence. Fergusson's talk of the distinctiveness of the city irritated Jim. A building that reflected the place he had come from would be piss-stained and tagged with graffiti. Fergusson wanted to immortalise his own breed: members of Royal Societies and civic trusts.

Their discussion had made them late, but Jim paused outside the meeting room to check his phone. There were no messages. Eliot must still be locked in the cells beneath the courthouse, Maggie still trapped in one of its waiting rooms. He switched off his mobile and followed Fergusson into the building procurement meeting.

Six

JIM KNEW THAT his son was in the house as soon as he opened the door. There was no blast of music as there had often been when Eliot had lived at home, no particular smell, no extra jacket in the entrance lobby where they kept their outdoor gear, but Jim could feel his presence. It sparked the same sixth sense that had told him Ronald Fergusson was crossing the quads.

Jim hung up his coat, took off his shoes and slid them into the rack by the door. He had resisted making a habit of a consoling, homecoming drink, but felt an urge for something strong and alcoholic now, to erase the day and fortify him for whatever was to follow.

Sasha was coming down the stairs as he entered the hallway, Benji trotting in her wake. A small pink bow between the dog's ears gathered a fluffy fringe from its eyes. Sasha had changed out of her school uniform into a banana-yellow sweatshirt, blue jeans and stripy slipper socks. She was growing her hair, which had just reached a length where she could tie it back in a ponytail.

'Hi Dad.'

Jim reached over the banister and ruffled her hair. 'Hello princess.'

Sasha made a face. 'I just brushed it. I'll have to do it again now.'

'It looks fine. Very Ariana Grande.'

'Daaaaad.' She dragged out the word, his other, better name. 'I like it tidy.'

She turned and climbed the stairs she had just come down, exaggerating the effort, her chin high, ponytail swinging. Benji scampered after her. The dog's legs were too short to climb the stairs comfortably, and it took each one at a hop.

Jim wondered what it would be like not to have the awareness of his children within him. Sometimes it was a barely noticed vibration on the edge of his consciousness, other times so painful it made him catch his breath.

Monday was usually a meat-free day, but the kitchen smelt of roast lamb and fried onions. Maggie was at the stove, Eliot leaning against one of the kitchen units, a bottle of beer in his hand. They stopped talking as he entered the room. Jim noted a new tattoo on Eliot's neck: a skull wearing a jaunty top hat decorated with an ace of spades. The tattoo would reach beyond the confines of a shirt and tie. He wanted to ask his son why he was so intent on advertising himself a fool, but merely raised his eyebrows at the skull's crazy grin.

'Smells good.'

Maggie's smile was tense. 'How was your meeting?'

Normally he would have lain it all out before her, like a general reliving a battle. Instead, he opened the fridge and helped himself to one of the five beer bottles ranked across the top shelf, neat as soldiers on parade. They had not been there that morning.

'Fine. I'll tell you about it later.' Jim grasped Eliot's free hand and pulled him into an embrace. 'I was worried about you.' He smelt his own shower gel and shampoo on his son's skin. Eliot returned his grip and clicked into the kind of complex handclasp beloved of TV gangsters. Jim pulled away. 'What's with the funny handshake? Did you join the Masons while you were inside?'

Maggie's voice was low and warning. 'Jim . . .'

Eliot raised his bottle. 'I'm not sure two nights over a weekend counts as *being inside.*'

His hair was newly cut. His clothes and trainers had a fresh look that made Jim suspect Maggie had taken him shopping on their way home from court.

'It certainly doesn't count as being at liberty.' Jim lifted a bottle opener from the worktop and prised the cap of his beer free. He would have preferred a whisky, but he had work to do later: the report about the China trip was yet to be written, and there were expenses to file, a reference for a student to compose. He raised himself onto one of the high stools at the kitchen island and lifted the bottle to his lips. 'How are you?'

Eliot gave the grin that reminded Jim of his father. 'Okay . . . relieved . . . embarrassed.'

'When are you due back in court?'

Maggie opened the oven door and spooned meat juices over the joint. 'Let's talk about it later.'

Jim kept his eyes on his son. 'It's a simple question, love.'

Eliot tipped back the last of his beer. He reached into the fridge for a fresh one and popped its cap. 'A fortnight. Eddie reckons I'll get a custodial.'

Jim noted his son's ease with prison vocabulary. 'How long a custodial?'

Maggie replaced the lid on the casserole dish, turned down the gas and untied her apron. Underneath she was wearing a black dress usually reserved for dinner parties or nights at the theatre. 'Eddie's due round in half an hour to discuss it.'

Eliot had taken out his mobile phone and was scrolling through his messages. He stretched, like a cat getting to its feet after a long sleep in the sun, and laid his beer on the counter. 'Sorry, Mums, you'll have to count me out.'

Sasha came into the kitchen, her hair restored to sleek smoothness, and peered through the glass oven door at the sizzling joint. 'I meant to tell you this morning, I'm a vegan.'

Eliot snorted, 'Good timing, sis.'

Maggie touched her daughter's shoulder. 'Can you set the dining-room table, please? Get the nice cutlery and glasses from the cabinet.'

Sasha sent Eliot a look that indicated she judged him to be as useless as the rest of the grown-ups. 'It means no meat, no fish, no eggs or dairy.'

Maggie gave a tight smile. 'I know what it means. Go and do what I asked, please.' She waited until the girl had left the room and then turned to her son. 'All this is for your benefit.'

Eliot slid a hand inside his T-shirt and scratched his chest. The fabric rode up, revealing a delicate line of body hair trailing from his navel down into his Calvin Kleins. 'I don't have to eat it to appreciate it. Your lamb is world-famous, tastier than Nigella, but I'm due elsewhere.'

Jim placed the tips of his fingers on the kitchen island and silently counted to ten.

Maggie shook her head. 'I'm not talking about the food.'

Jim counted to ten again, then looked up. 'He doesn't have to meet with Cranston if he doesn't want to.'

Maggie turned on him. 'This is important, Jim.'

'It's his future, his decision. If Eliot doesn't like the lawyer we engaged, he can find one for himself.'

Eliot looked at his phone again. 'Eddie's all right, but I'd rather do this in office hours.'

'Your father and I work *office hours*.' Maggie snatched the phone from him. She turned it off and dropped it into the cutlery drawer, which she slammed shut.

Eliot gave a cry of protest. 'No, man, you work all the time, night and fucking day. You ask me, that's why Sasha's turning vegan – to try and get a bit of attention.'

He opened the drawer, took the phone from it, and examined it for scratches.

Jim said, 'Is that why you got that monstrosity tattooed on your neck? For attention?'

Eliot gave a grin that showed his Ken Doll-white teeth. He touched the skull with his fingertips. 'That was a style decision. What do you think?'

The peal of the doorbell saved Jim from having to answer.

'That'll be Eddie.' Maggie looked from her husband to her son, and when neither of them showed any sign of moving muttered, 'For God's sake,' and left the room. Jim heard her open the front door and then Cranston's voice, deep and indistinct in the hallway.

Eliot stuffed his phone in his pocket and sank the last of his beer. 'I'm out of here.'

Jim said, 'Out of interest, what kind of drugs were you dealing?'

Eliot met his gaze and grinned. 'Good ones, Dad. Top of the range. I'm my father's son. When I do things, I do them well.'

He opened the kitchen door and slipped into the garden.

Jim had expected Maggie to take Eddie Cranston into the lounge, but she brought him through to the kitchen. 'Where's Eliot?'

'He bailed.' Jim had not seen the lawyer since his collapse in the Fusilier. He met Cranston's eyes, determined not to be embarrassed. 'Sorry Eddie, looks like you had a wasted trip.'

'Couldn't you stop him?' Maggie opened the kitchen door and stepped into the back garden. She returned a moment later, her cheeks flushed. 'For Christ's sake.'

Jim rubbed his face. 'I tried, but you know what he's like.'

Eddie Cranston was wearing the same pinstripe suit. It looked crease-free, as if it had never seen the inside of a flat-roofed bar. 'It happens, especially with boys who haven't been in trouble before. They seem to think it'll go away if they ignore it.'

Maggie opened the oven door. The sizzle of roast lamb filled the kitchen. She prodded the meat with a knife, her gestures tight and angry. 'Eliot's been in trouble before, but never to this degree.'

Cranston was still standing in the middle of the kitchen floor. 'Always for drugs?'

Maggie closed the oven door and turned to look at him. 'He was caught with cannabis twice, and I'm afraid he was arrested once for getting into a fight after a party. Nothing came of it.'

There was more she could have said, much more: the exclusion from the local state school, the complaints from parents of boys Eliot had bullied, the ban from the local newsagents, the speeding tickets, the drunk and disorderlies and failed college courses.

Jim got to his feet. 'There's not much point in going over

things without Eliot. Thanks for your help and sorry to have wasted your evening. I'm assuming you'll send us a bill for your time?' Maggie came to Jim's side. He put an arm around her. 'I'll see Eddie to the door, love.'

He wanted to be alone with the lawyer, so he could tell Cranston personally that his services would not be required.

Maggie pulled free. 'Don't be so antisocial, Jim.' She turned to Cranston. 'Why don't you join us for dinner? Eliot's deserted us and our daughter Sasha decided to become vegan exactly three minutes ago, so we've plenty to go round.'

Cranston smiled. 'It smells wonderful, but someone's waiting for me.'

'Your wife?'

It was unlike Maggie to probe. Jim gave her a look. 'Maggie, love . . .'

Cranston brushed his objection aside. 'A date. As a matter of fact, she's waiting in the car. I'd better get back, before I blow things.'

Something about the way he smiled invited Maggie to extend the offer. 'She's welcome to join us – unless you already have somewhere booked?'

Cranston looked from one to the other. 'Are you sure? You wouldn't prefer space to talk things over?'

Maggie touched his arm. 'I wouldn't have got through this morning without your support. It'll be an opportunity to say thanks and get to know you a little better. After all, it looks like we'll be seeing a fair bit of you until Eliot's trial is over.'

Cranston looked at Jim. 'All right with you, prof?'

Jim forced a smile. 'Of course.'

Cranston grinned. 'I'm always happy to lend a hand where a lamb is involved.'

Seven

CRANSTON'S DATE WAS called Becca. She was somewhere around Eliot's age with shoulder-length blonde hair and the kind of figure that used to grace the painted covers of pulp magazines. She appeared content to have her evening relocated to a stranger's house, just as she had apparently been content to wait in the car.

Jim's eyes met Maggie's. She looked away and bared her teeth at the girl, in a grin that on another species, a gorilla for example, might have looked threatening. 'Come away in, let me take your things.'

'Thanks.' Becca slipped off her coat to reveal a red wraparound dress Jim guessed men would appreciate more than women.

Cranston took a bottle of red wine from behind his back. 'Luckily I had this in the boot.'

Becca smiled at him. 'In case of emergencies.'

Cranston peered at the label. 'A present from a grateful

client. It should be all right.' He presented it to Maggie, with a flourish. 'A step up from Buckfast at any rate.'

Usually, when they had dinner guests, they started with drinks in the lounge, but Jim ushered the couple straight through to the dining room. The sooner they ate, the sooner he could get rid of them.

Sasha slid into her seat, looking with frank interest at Becca. 'Are you vegan?'

Becca leaned forward and stage-whispered, 'I'm a fully fledged omnivore. I'm not even gluten-free.'

'Thank goodness for that. One vegan at a time is enough.' Maggie passed Cranston's bottle of wine to Jim. 'Can you take care of this, please? The food's just about ready.' She touched her daughter's hair lightly. 'Come on, Trouble, you can carry something through for me.'

Sasha got down from her seat. 'You shouldn't call me names in front of guests.'

'I think they'll realise it's a term of endearment.' Maggie turned to go through to the kitchen.

Cranston jumped to his feet. 'Let me give you a hand.'

Maggie had seated Becca opposite Jim, in what had been Eliot's chair. Jim examined the wine label. It was a good New Zealand Pinot Noir from a vineyard he and Maggie had visited when he was on exchange to Victoria University, years ago, before the kids came along. On another evening he might have exclaimed at the coincidence and told some stories from those days, but this was not a night for reminiscing. He took a corkscrew from the credenza and started to peel the foil from the neck of the bottle. Becca watched him. She was too young, too good-looking for the lawyer. He screwed the foil into a ball. 'How long have you known Eddie?'

'Not long. How about you?'

Jim unscrewed the bottle and filled her glass. 'He was a year above me at school. We reconnected over some trouble my son's involved in. Eddie's representing him. How did you meet?'

Becca smiled, showing teeth as white and even as Eliot's. 'How does anyone meet these days?'

'You both swiped right?'

'Something like that.' Becca took a sip of her wine. 'You don't remember me, do you?'

Jim had nothing to worry about – no blacked-out drunken sprees, no infidelities or massage parlour jaunts – but his smile froze. 'I'm sorry, should I?'

'I was in one of your seminar groups. You advised me to stay on and do a masters, but the thought of more debt didn't turn me on.'

He looked at Becca again. The effect of her red dress, blonde hair and swooping figure had distracted him from seeing her. Careful make-up had flattened out her features, obscuring the fact that her nose was slightly too long for her face, her chin a trifle blunt.

He grinned. 'I do remember you. You wrote that essay on deviant leisure and crime. I was disappointed when you decided not to apply for a postgrad. What are you doing now?'

Becca shrugged. 'This and that.'

Back then, she had dressed in tracksuits and trainers, as if she was always on her way to or from the sports building.

'It's not that surprising I didn't recognise you. You look different.'

Becca showed him her expensive dental work again. 'I graduated two years ago. I guess you've processed a lot of students since then.'

'Processed makes us sound like a sausage factory.'

Cranston entered the room, laughing at something exchanged in the kitchen. He had a dish of couscous in one hand, a bowl of green salad in the other. He was followed closely by Sasha, concentrating on a jug of harissa sauce she clutched with both hands. Maggie was laughing too. She had already carved the lamb into neat slices and arranged them in a circle on the plate. Maggie added couscous and salad to the veggie burger on Sasha's plate and handed it to her. 'You can take yours through to the TV room if you like, love.'

Dinner in front of the television on a weeknight was an unexpected treat. Sasha smiled politely at the guests. 'Enjoy your dinner.' She left her seat and slid across the wooden floor, her plate balanced precariously shoulder high, on one hand. Benji scrabbled from beneath the table and scampered after her.

Maggie got up and shut the dining-room door. 'Her friend Isla had a birthday party in an American hamburger joint, complete with roller-skating waitresses. It's Sasha's new ambition.'

Becca laughed. 'I went through a phase of wanting to be a majorette. I fancied the costume.'

Cranston grinned. 'Don't let the dream die.'

Maggie refreshed their wine glasses and turned to Becca. 'What do you do?'

'I work in corporate entertainment.'

'Sounds glamorous.'

Becca cut a slice of lamb into slivers. 'Not really. It's mostly making sure guests are happy, the wine's flowing freely, but not too freely, canapés circulating – you know the kind of thing.'

Cranston said, 'Tell them about the comedian you hired to entertain that bunch of accountants.'

Becca rolled her eyes. 'Such an old story.'

'Maggie and Jim haven't heard it.'

Becca sipped her wine and smiled at them, readying herself for the tale. 'Okay . . .'

Jim's mobile buzzed in his pocket, indicating a new text message. He resisted the urge to check it at the table. 'Excuse me, I'll just make sure Sasha's okay.' He got to his feet. Maggie gave him a look, but Becca had embarked on her anecdote and his wife was already laughing at the antics of the comedian, who had turned up at the accountants' charity ball, drunk and belligerent, despite being dressed as a chicken.

Jim stood by the window of his study. It was dark outside, but he did not bother to put a lamp on. The text was from Eliot: *soz couldnt hang about electrix out in apt need £50 to get it turned on Ur the best* ☺ .

Jim deleted the message. He guessed Eliot had sent a similar one to Maggie. It crossed his mind that he could find her phone and delete it from there too, but he dismissed the impulse.

He opened his internet browser, logged into his university webmail account and scrolled quickly down his inbox, looking for any marked high priority. He almost dismissed the message from an unknown sender with a Chinese name as a phishing scam, but his Beijing visit was still in his mind, and he clicked on it.

Li Jie who you met at graduation has vanished. He has been disappeared. Please, Professor Brennan, can you help?

There was a photograph at the bottom of the email of a young Chinese man, pale-faced and handsome with high cheekbones and a serious expression.

His memory of most of the Beijing students had been

absorbed into a general impression of earnest faces and graduation robes, but Jim remembered Li Jie. He was shorter than the others, and despite his stature and easy smile gave the impression of being a little older than the rest. Li Jie had introduced himself, and a young woman whose name Jim could not recall, after the ceremony. They had talked of possibilities for overseas students in Scotland. Jim had made the usual joke about the country's weather, and Li Jie had said his home province was also prone to rain. The wet weather was a good thing because it encouraged pandas. Jim had asked if Li Jie had ever seen one in the wild.

The young man had grinned and shook his head. 'Only in the wildlife centre, but one day, I hope.'

'You're an optimist.'

'A pragmatic optimist. People must see clearly in order to realise their dreams.'

The girl had given him a stern look that had made Jim smile. He had not thought much about the young man's statement. Now he wondered if Li Jie's desire to 'see clearly' had resulted in trouble.

Maggie was standing in the doorway. 'What are you doing?'

Jim held his phone out to her. Maggie stepped into the room and took it from his hand. She read the message and stared at the picture. The young Chinese man stared back. His face shone in the darkness, illuminating Maggie's features, her worried expression. 'What will you do?'

Jim shrugged. 'He's graduated. Strictly speaking, he's no longer our responsibility.'

'That feels a bit harsh.'

He nodded. 'I'll forward it to Grace McCann in the Centre for Refugee Studies. She'll know if there's any action we can take.'

Maggie gave the image a last look and handed the phone back to Jim. He put it in his pocket and touched her cheek with the tips of his fingers. A cough sounded outside, and she pulled away. Eddie Cranston stood in the doorway, his stocky frame silhouetted in the hall light.

'Sorry. I didn't mean to interrupt. I was looking for the bathroom.'

Maggie laughed. 'Don't apologise. We're the bad-mannered ones. Jim's got a bit of a crisis on the Beijing campus.' She smoothed her hair, though Jim had not touched it. 'The bathroom's down the hall.'

They had Jaconelli's ice cream and defrosted summer berries for dessert. Jim was still worried about the incident in the Fusilier and had gone easy on the wine. Cranston was driving and stuck to water after his first glass of pinot. Maggie and Becca finished the bottle and embarked on a second.

Cranston had praised the lamb, the couscous, harissa and flatbreads. He complimented Maggie and Jim on the intelligence of their daughter, the cuteness of their dog and their taste in décor. Now he praised the dessert.

'Nothing beats proper Italian ice cream.' He widened his eyes in pleasure and then turned his gaze on Jim. 'A crisis in Beijing. Must be challenging working at such long distances?'

Jim pushed his dessert aside, mindful of the Madeira cake and cream that had rounded off the funders' lunch, the petits fours that had accompanied post-prandial coffees. His phone buzzed in his pocket. He guessed it was Eliot repeating his appeal for money and ignored it.

'Not really. We've good people running things over there.'

Becca touched her spoon to her lips. 'What kind of crisis?'

Maggie lifted Jim's untouched bowl and passed it to

Cranston. 'A Chinese student has disappeared. Jim thinks it might be something political.'

Becca put her spoon down. 'I guess that kind of thing is to be expected.'

Jim looked at her. 'What do you mean?'

She sipped her wine. 'When you get into bed with a repressive regime.'

'The only person I get into bed with is my wife.' Jim tried to soften his words with a smile. 'The Chinese system is different from ours. Aspects of it are challenging, but what better way to change a system than through education? Our Chinese students gain a knowledge of democratic values.'

'Values that may get them into trouble.'

Maggie said, 'Jim's concerned about this young man.'

Cranston's spoon rattled against his bowl as he finished his second helping of ice cream. 'That was the best meal I've had in a long while. Thank you, Maggie.' He touched Becca's hand. 'I think it's time we hit the road.'

Becca nodded but did not move. She replaced her wine glass on the table. A red ring settled around the base, staining the white tablecloth.

'It comes down to money, doesn't it? We dress it up in different ways – education, entertainment, new housing, the law – but we're all trying to make a buck. China's rolling in the stuff so we coorie up to them and damn the consequences.'

Maggie stacked the dessert dishes and arranged the spoons inside the upper bowl. 'Jim has dedicated his life to education, I'm choosy about the buildings I design, and the small contact I've had with Eddie tells me he does a lot of good work for young people. I don't know much about corporate entertainment though, so I couldn't say if it's clean or not.'

Becca gestured with her hand, indicating the room with its cool off-white walls, the solid wood dining table and credenza, the sparkling crystalware, the series of watercolours of Highland views by an artist Maggie admired. 'I don't mean to insult anyone. I'm including myself in this. We're all sincere about what we do, but profit is always at the heart of it.' She smiled at Jim. 'The reason your university is in China, India and wherever else they've spread their net is because there's money to be made. If a few students get the wrong end of the stick, think they can talk freely and end up in jail as a result, it's their own lookout.'

Jim got to his feet. 'I disagree, but this is a discussion for another day.'

Becca got to her feet too. Cranston put a hand on her elbow, but she shook him off. 'All universities think about is more — more students, more money, more buildings.'

Jim felt too tired to argue. 'The university is a not-for-profit charity . . .'

Maggie lifted the pile of dishes. 'You'll have to excuse me. It's been a long day and I'm ready for bed.'

Cranston stood up. Now they were all standing, an awkward tableau around the table. The lawyer touched Becca's arm. This time she did not shrug him away.

He looked at Maggie. 'We shouldn't have stayed for dinner. It was lovely, but it was an imposition. I'll call you tomorrow, and we can talk about what happens next where Eliot's defence is concerned. Try and get some rest. Your boy's out and sleeping in his own bed. You don't have to worry about him for now.'

Maggie's features set in the grim expression that indicated she was trying not to cry. 'For now.'

Becca made a face. 'I'm really sorry. I didn't mean to be

rude. Eddie's right. That was a lovely meal. I hope I didn't spoil it.' She started to gather the empty glasses. 'Let me help you clear up.'

Maggie shook her head. 'No, thanks.'

Jim's phone buzzed again in his pocket. He turned it off and placed it face down on the table. 'We're not a hundred per cent sure that the student *is* missing, but rest assured, if he is, we'll do all we can to assist him. Meanwhile, I'd be grateful if you kept this to yourselves, until we know the facts.'

The landline sprang into life. Jim swore under his breath, excused himself and crossed the room. He lifted the receiver.

Maggie threw him a swift, worried look, but Cranston and Becca were leaving. Becca was apologising again, Cranston gushing about the meal.

Eliot's voice sounded on the other end of the line – slow, like a record playing at the wrong speed. 'Dad, they've lifted me again. I'm in the copshop. You need to come down and get me out.'

Jim repressed an impulse to slam the phone down. 'What did you do?'

'Why do you always assume I'm in the wrong?'

'Bitter experience.'

'What have you got to be bitter about?' Someone said something out of range, then Eliot named a police station on the far side of the city. He muttered, 'Just get here,' and hung up.

Maggie was standing at the front door, her hand raised in farewell to Cranston and Becca, who were halfway down the path.

She put an arm around Jim. 'Thank Christ that's over. I wonder what he sees in her, apart from the obvious.' She glanced up at him. 'Was that the uni calling about your student?'

Jim shook his head. 'No, it was Eliot. He's been arrested again.'

Maggie's breath caught in her chest. 'What for?'

But Jim was jogging after Cranston and Becca. He caught up with them on the street and grasped Cranston by the arm. 'I need your help.'

Eight

JIM AND CRANSTON bypassed the centre of town and drove fast along carriageways that only a few hours ago had been sluggish with traffic. They had taken Cranston's BMW, and the lawyer was at the wheel. His profile shone white in the dark. The car's interior was illuminated by the headlamps of an overtaking car, swiftly followed by another, the light sweeping through and then beyond.

'Boy racers.' Cranston took a pack of chewing gum from the cup holder and offered it to Jim, without taking his eyes off the road.

Jim shook his head. 'No, thanks.'

'Take it. One drink smells the same as twenty. It won't do any harm to let the desk sergeant know your boy's from respectable stock.'

Jim shook a pellet of gum free and put it in his mouth. The gum's sugar-shell coating was soft, its interior stale. He resumed the conversation they had been drifting in and out of since they got into the car.

'You're certain there's no chance?'

Cranston risked a quick glance at Jim, his eyes pouchy from lack of sleep. 'Eliot broke his bail conditions. I don't mind if you go elsewhere for advice, but it won't change anything. He's going to prison.'

Jim spat his chewing gum into a paper hanky. 'How long for?'

They had reached the roundabout that would take them from the dual carriageway onto a B road. A sign pointed the way to the hospital where Jim's mother had died.

Cranston waited until he had negotiated the junction before answering. 'Until he goes to trial. It could be up to ten months.'

A vein in Jim's forehead started to throb. 'And then?'

'And then we do our damnedest.'

A set of traffic lights up ahead shifted from green to amber to red. Cranston braked to a halt.

Jim asked, 'Couldn't he be tagged? Put on a curfew or something?'

An ambulance raced past them, lights flashing, siren muted. Cranston's face was briefly bathed in electric blue. 'I've more chance of becoming Pope.'

'No chance then?'

The traffic lights turned to green. Cranston drove on without bothering to answer. Fields stretched on either side of the road, sleeping cows black shapes in the darkness. Jim stared at his reflection in the passenger window. He saw nothing of his father, nothing of his son, in his features.

*

It was a different police station, but with the same wipe-clean surfaces, bolted-down chairs and blinding lights. Jim let Cranston do the talking and then waited while the lawyer was led to an interview room. This time there were no phone calls or frantic texts from Maggie. He wondered if she had managed to fall asleep, or if she was lying on the futon in her studio, staring at the mezzanine ceiling, almost within reach.

Jim hunched forward, mobile phone in his hand. He opened his web browser and typed *broken bail conditions on remand*. A depressing litany of misdemeanours, backsliding, recidivism and self-sabotage appeared. He scanned the articles, a metallic taste in his mouth. Cranston's assessment was dead-on. Eliot might easily be detained for ten months before being taken to trial.

It was nigh on thirty years since he had visited his father in prison, but Jim could still recall the smell of piss and bleach, the undertones of violence and sexual frustration. Slopping out had been abolished in the intervening decades, conditions improved, but Eliot was a cocky young swaggerer, ripe for beatings and exploitation. There was little prospect of him serving out his time quietly. He would push at boundaries, get in with the wrong crowd, or, worse, get up the wrong people's noses. The vein in Jim's head throbbed again. He touched it with his fingertips, felt the pulse of blood forcing its way through. Maggie was right: he was at an age where men suddenly dropped dead.

The desk sergeant had disappeared. Jim was alone in the waiting area. He looked down the corridor where Cranston had gone twenty minutes ago. It was stark and coldly lit, a CCTV camera high on the wall angled towards the bank of seats where he sat. Jim wondered if anyone was monitoring it, watching him.

He had forgotten how afraid he had been of prison when he was a boy. The building whose walls felt impregnated with ghosts, the men who resided behind the cold bricks, the atmosphere of violence. Studying criminology had smothered the nightmares of dark shadows and clanking metal that had haunted him in childhood. The memories returned now like a familiar smell.

There was nothing he could do for Eliot except wait. Jim lowered his eyes to his phone, clicked open his email and looked again at the photograph of Li Jie. He typed *Disappeared China* into his browser. A screed of articles appeared. Jim clicked methodically through them, reading of arrests, of forced confessions, sleep deprivation and solitary confinement, of imprisonments, televised show trials and genocide.

Appeals to the authorities by friends and families of victims of kidnapping immediately after their disappearance elicit no response. Families are left adrift, uncertain of their loved one's whereabouts. Meanwhile, the kidnapped person is subject to torture or other means of coercion, the object of which is to force a confession. The confession may be televised as part of a show trial, completing the detainee's humiliation and justifying any jail sentence imposed upon them.

He read about a Chinese publisher spirited away from self-imposed exile in Sweden; a bookseller who was released from prison and immediately retracted his confession; a businessman who filmed a video in advance of his disappearance stating he would never accept a lawyer appointed by the authorities unless he was tortured and who, shortly after his arrest, released a statement announcing he had fired his legal team and wished instead to be represented by a state-appointed lawyer.

Jim took his earbuds from his pocket and pressed play on a BBC interview with a disappeared lawyer's wife. The woman was elegantly dressed in a pink dress and pearls. She sat opposite a male British journalist in a quiet café, somewhere in Beijing. Jim recognised the aesthetics of the place, the wooden screen carved with Chinese characters, the western-style cups set on the dark wood table between them. He caught a glimpse of a busy road beyond the café windows and recalled the heat of the city, the sensation of smog gritting his lungs, the competing pitches of car and motorbike engines.

The lawyer's wife brushed away tears as she recounted her husband's detention and the local policemen who claimed to know nothing of his disappearance, although ten of them had taken him from their home before searching it. Beneath the English translator's voiceover Jim faintly heard the journalist asking the woman, 'Are you all right?' She dabbed her eyes with a paper tissue and nodded. The voiceover translated her reply: 'If I don't step forward, who will speak for him? I am his wife.'

Jim suspected that Li Jie's fate was as beyond his control as that of his own son, but he forwarded the email to Grace McCann with a covering note: *Anything we can do?* He skimmed his inbox. A plaintive appeal from Michael Peterson sat at the top, the subject heading: *Deadline for my application for Harvard Fellowship is tomorrow.* A red exclamation mark highlighted the email's importance.

Jim had promised the PhD student a reference and knew the exclamation mark would have cost his student more than a moment of anguish. He leaned back in the plastic chair and closed his eyes, wishing he'd had the foresight to bring his iPad with him. The fellowship was prestigious. Michael had a decent chance of winning it, but Harvard's electronic system would only accept the application once all references had been uploaded. Jim opened the attached CV and re-read the project statement, trying to compose the testimonial in his head, but it was as if the wires in his brain were overloaded, connections misfiring and burning out.

Eddie Cranston stood over him, his expression grim. 'We can go.'

Perhaps it was his imagination, but Jim thought the lawyer smelt different – the scent of sandalwood replaced by misery and perspiration. He got to his feet and glanced in the direction of the interview room. 'Can I see him?'

Cranston turned away. 'He's being processed.'

'How long will that take?'

'It doesn't matter. They're sending him to Linbarley, soon as there's a van free to take him there.'

It was the same prison that Jim's father, Eliot's grandfather, had been a guest of. The same prison his mother used to threaten him with when he misbehaved.

'When do I get to see him?'

'That's up to Eliot. Tomorrow or the day after, if he manages to get you a visiting order. I explained the process to him, and he said he would.'

The desk sergeant was back at his post. The lawyer nodded to him and headed to the door. Cranston looked at home in the police station, thought Jim, just as he had looked at home in the Fusilier and eating an extra portion of ice cream at his dining-room table.

It was dark now, but the car park was hemmed with arc

lights and Jim could see the dour set of Cranston's mouth. The lawyer was silent until they were both seated in his BMW.

'What do you know about Eliot's activities?'

Jim stared straight ahead. A fox trotted out of the darkness. It crossed the car park and vanished into the night.

He did not know where to start. 'Eliot was never an academic boy. He tried various college courses, a couple of internships, but . . .' He shrugged. There was no point in recounting the litany of wasted favours, broken promises and disappointments. 'Maggie and I gave him money to set himself up as a DJ. Eliot liked music when he was a boy – rap, grime, that kind of stuff. He was genuinely knowledgeable about it. I thought it might be a way out. Now it looks like he used the funds we gave him to buy drugs.' He shook his head. 'That's the sum of my knowledge. Most of it's guesswork. What did he tell you?'

'He wasn't very forthcoming.' Cranston rubbed his face with his hands and turned to look at Jim. 'Do you have keys to his flat?'

'Maggie might. She did his washing. Sometimes she delivered it.'

It had made him angry, the way Maggie ran about after the boy who was now a grown man.

Cranston turned the key in the ignition. The BMW's engine growled into life. 'The police will apply for a warrant to search Eliot's place. Any drugs they find will be taken as evidence. Given Eliot's previous form, they'll have no trouble getting the warrant.'

'Will they want our keys?'

Cranston smiled. 'The police don't need keys. I presume they've got Eliot's.'

'Why were you asking . . .' The penny dropped. Jim shook his head. 'If you think I'm going to Eliot's flat to start tampering with evidence, you're mistaken.'

'I didn't suggest you should.'

'You planted the seed.'

When they reached the slip road to the dual carriageway Cranston glanced in his wing mirror and put his foot down hard. A cattle lorry was rumbling up the inside lane. Cranston slid the car into the fast lane.

'It's my job to keep you informed. All I was doing was telling you what to expect.'

Jim took his phone from his pocket. 'Pull over. I'll make my own way home.'

Cranston accelerated beyond the lorry and cut into the slow lane. 'There's no need.'

'There is.'

'I can't stop here. You'll have to wait until we're past the roundabout.'

Jim found a taxi number. He called a cab and mentioned the name of the road up ahead. The operator asked for the number of the house where he was to be collected and he told her, 'Near the roundabout.'

'It'll be with you soon,' the operator said, as if it was an everyday thing to send a cab for a man wandering on his own along a dual carriageway after midnight.

Cranston steered the car towards their exit. 'This is stupid, Jim.'

Jim's rage was already dissolving into shame. He waited until Cranston pulled onto the hard shoulder and got out, slamming the door behind him. What could he say except yes, it was stupid, all of it stupid, and so he kept silent and walked to where his cab was waiting.

Nine

'FALLEN OUT WITH the wife?' The taxi driver met Jim's eyes in the rear-view mirror.

'I'm not in the mood for talking, mate.'

The driver nodded. 'You don't have to tell me how it goes. I got divorced three years ago. Best thing I ever did.' He drove on, through empty suburban streets. Most of the houses were in darkness, but now and then a light showed in a window. Jim remembered when the kids were younger. He had taken pride in leaving his warm bed to change a soiled nappy, sicked sheets, or to comfort them when the night horrors hit. Eliot had been plagued by a recurring nightmare of a man in a top hat, the source of which neither Jim nor Maggie could fathom. He wondered if his son recalled the dream, the nights when Jim had lifted his damp body from bed and walked up and down singing softly until the boy became limp as he fell back into sleep. Jim remembered how Eliot had clung to him, arms and legs wrapped around his body, like a monkey clinging to its mother. It was gone. All of it wasted.

The taxi stopped. His own house was in darkness, curtains drawn.

Jim fumbled for his wallet and realised he had left it on the hall table. 'Sorry, I need to go inside and get some money.'

The driver turned to look at him. 'Don't worry about it, pal. I hope you make it up with the missus.'

Jim was about to say it would only take him a moment to fetch the cash, but he remembered his house keys, abandoned in a dish beside his wallet, and there was something in the man's expression that told him this was an important gesture.

'Thanks, I appreciate it.' He glanced at the meter. 'I'll pass the favour on to someone else who needs it.'

The driver smiled. 'That's the thing to do. Us guys have to stick together. What goes around comes around.'

Jim took the back-door key from the fake rock by the step and let himself in. Benji was curled in his basket in the kitchen. The dog raised its head. Jim shushed it, and for once the dog obeyed, lowering its chin onto its front paws and closing its eyes.

Jim poured himself a glass of water and went through to his study, closing the door softly behind him. He switched on the desk lamp and woke his computer. The time glowed in the bottom right-hand corner of the screen: 02.03. He brought up the postdoc student's reference request and worked steadily through it. It was almost four before the reference and its attendant forms were complete. Jim knew he should write an email to Michael reassuring him all was in place, but the thought of his bulging inbox stopped him. It could wait until morning – until later in the morning.

Jim shut his eyes and leaned back in his chair. He wondered where Eliot was. Still in the police cell? Travelling along the motorway in a prison van, or lying awake in a bunk listening to the snores of some seasoned lag? He thought again of what Cranston had said about the longer sentence that awaited his son if the police found more drugs in his flat.

Jim closed his computer and clicked off the desk lamp. Maggie's handbag was hanging in the lobby by the front door. Jim opened it and caught the scent of his wife. He rifled through the bag's contents without looking at them, feeling for the hard clink of metal.

'What are you doing?' Maggie was wrapped in her dressing gown. She had run a hand through her hair; it sat electric around her face, as if transmitting the irritation in her voice.

'Looking for the keys to Eliot's place.'

'Is he here?'

'No, love, he's still at the police station. Eddie said the police are going to search his flat again. He'll get into more trouble if they–'

Maggie finished the sentence. 'Find more drugs.'

He nodded. 'Eliot deserves everything he gets but . . .'

'I know.' Maggie belted her dressing gown tighter and led the way to her studio. The room was in darkness, but she did not bother to turn a light on. Jim waited in the doorway. He heard the open-and-close slide of a desk drawer. Maggie returned and handed him the keys. 'What if the police are watching the flat?'

The thought had not occurred to him. 'It's unlikely. They only just lifted him. Eliot's small fry.'

'But what if they are?'

'I'll say I'm checking everything's okay.'

'At four in the morning?'

'I couldn't sleep. I was looking for clues to where we went wrong.'

Maggie shook her head. 'Tell them you went to collect a suit in case he goes to court.'

'At this time?'

'You're a busy man. You couldn't sleep. If you find anything, put it in the pocket of his suit. That way you can pretend you didn't know it was there.'

'What if it's too big to fit in his pocket?'

They were whispering, their voices soft and urgent, like Macbeth and his wife planning to do away with Duncan.

'I don't know. Use your imagination. Stick it in the pocket of a holdall or something.'

'What are you doing?' Sasha stood in the hallway, long hair tangled, eyes bleary.

Maggie smiled brightly. 'Eliot's locked himself out. Your dad's just going over with a spare set of keys.'

'Eliot's an idiot.' Sasha rubbed her eyes. 'Can I have a glass of water please?'

Maggie nodded. 'Of course you can. Pop back into bed and I'll bring it up in a moment.'

Sleep had shed Sasha of tween sophistication. The sight of his daughter pale and half-asleep made Jim feel ashamed.

He touched her hair. 'Give your old dad a cuddle before you go back to bed.'

Sasha held out her arms. He hugged her and she nuzzled her nose into his collar. 'You smell all sweaty.'

'That's the aroma of hard graft, kid.' He let her go, patting his jacket pocket to check the keys were there.

'Here.' Maggie handed him his North Face jacket. She put her hands on Sasha's shoulders, steering her in the direction of the stairs. 'Bed. You've got school tomorrow. I'll be up in a moment to tuck you in.'

'Don't forget my water.'

Maggie smiled, but the strain told in her voice. 'Don't worry.'

Sasha looked at her, more alert now. 'And Benji to keep me company?'

'Benji has his own bed and so do you. You can read your book until I come up.'

Jim watched their daughter climb the stairs. Maggie leaned into him and kissed his cheek. 'I love you. You've worked so hard to get to where you are. I don't want anything to spoil it. I'll go to Eliot's. You stay here with Sasha.'

'It's okay, love. You get to bed. I'll be home soon.' He patted his jacket pocket, checking again for Eliot's keys, although he knew they were there.

Maggie went with him to the front door. 'Park around the corner from the flat. Don't let anyone see you.'

'Don't worry.' He kissed her goodbye and stepped back into the night.

Ten

ELIOT'S FLAT WAS in a converted whisky bond that reminded Jim of an oversized barracks. He and Maggie had bought it three years ago, when Eliot had been accepted for a marketing course at one of the city's new universities. The course had not worked out, and the flatmates who they had intended to subsidise the mortgage had drifted away. The trendy shops, cafés, restaurants and bars the estate agents had predicted had not materialised, and the roads around the warehouse maintained an industrial feel, though the bottling plant and lorries that had once busied the district with workers were long gone. Jim had always had reservations about the apartment's location on the borderland of deprivation and gentrification. Maggie was convinced its time would come.

Jim parked the Audi in an adjacent street and walked the rest of the way, hood pulled up, hands in pockets, head down. He fumbled for the key to Eliot's block and let himself into the communal hallway. He ignored the lift and climbed the stairs to the third floor. The door to Eliot's flat was scuffed with muddy boot prints where someone had tried to kick their way in. The police had Eliot's keys. If they had not, they would have used the battering ram they called the big key. These marks had been made by someone else. Jim wondered what he would do if they returned.

The front door opened straight onto a large lounge-cum-kitchen-dining room from which three bedrooms with small en suites radiated. The flat was pitch-black, but enough light shone in from the streetlamps below to reveal the outline of the two couches Maggie had bought in the John Lewis sale and the glass coffee table set between them. There was a stale smell of cigarettes, unemptied bins and sour drains. Jim switched on an uplighter. The place was a mess, but it was the mess of an untidy person, a slob who did not bother to clean up after himself, rather than the chaos left by a break-in or police search.

Jim had blamed his mother's departure on a police raid that had turned their tenement flat upside down. He had long since realised it was not the reason, merely the final straw; but even now, from a distance of almost forty years, he could not understand why his mother had not taken him with her. His father dropped dark hints and darker accusations about another man. Later Jim discovered she had merely gone home to her family in Ireland, before returning to the city and settling in another district. He would not have thought it possible for her to hide from him, but she had, for decades.

He had been thirty, recently promoted to senior lecturer, when a neighbour of his mother got in touch to tell him she was in hospital and wanted to see him. He had armed himself with photos of Maggie and Eliot, who was still a toddler, and a picture of himself in his graduation robes. The woman in the hospital bed peered at the images, her eyes small and staring like a bird's.

Jim said, 'These are copies – you can keep them if you like.'

She handed them back to him. The neighbour, who he had never met before but had known how to find him when the time came, said, 'She's too far gone to know what she's doing.'

He wanted to ask if his mother had always been too far gone, if that explained her abandoning him to his father. Instead, he had slid the photographs into his pocket, left the ward and driven home. The neighbour had phoned him at his office a week later with news of his mother's death. Jim had been relieved by her offer to 'make the necessary arrangements', had refused the invitation to look through his mother's 'bits and pieces' for a keepsake, and when the funeral director's bill arrived in his university mail, paid it promptly, without comment.

The clock on the microwave in Eliot's kitchen glowed 04.33. Four hours before Jim was due at his desk. He pulled back the hood of his jacket and took in the room. The coffee table was covered in the detritus of indulgence. Lager bottles sat amongst half-full coffee mugs, a termite mountain of douts spilled from an ashtray, ripped Rizla packets, slivers of cigarette papers and frizzled strands of tobacco. A bong formed out of a plastic bottle that had previously held a litre of Irn-Bru sat beside one of the couches. Jim picked it up, marvelling that his son, who had never shown any aptitude for art or crafts, could be so resourceful. He rooted in the cupboard beneath the sink, found a bin bag and swept the bong and the contents of the coffee table into it.

The loneliness of his early years, the self-loathing that Maggie had saved him from was upon Jim. He had left his mobile at home, aware that the police could trace his movements retrospectively if they wanted to, but he wished he could call his wife. He needed her to tell him that this was not his fault – bad blood carried like an infection from him to his son.

Jim lifted the couch cushions and shook them. A pair of women's pants, white and patterned with cherries, fell out. He grimaced. They looked childish, like something Sasha might wear. He took a ballpoint from his pocket, hooked them by the side and dropped pen and pants into the bin bag. He replaced the cushions, resisting the urge to sit down, put his feet on the coffee table and close his eyes.

The kitchen area was furnished with slate-grey cabinets Maggie had selected from the estate agent's brochure. The cabinets' drawers and doors eased soundlessly back into place as he worked his way through them, finding clues to his son's life, a dependence on instant noodles and energy drinks, but no drugs.

Both guest rooms showed signs of recent occupancy. The stylishly masculine duvet covers Maggie had sourced were rumpled and untidy. Each bedside table bore a beer bottle and a saucer that had been used as an ashtray, the arrangements so uniform they might have belonged to a hotel keen on pandering to guests' needs. Jim shook the duvets and pillows, raising a tang of sweat and drunken sex.

The wardrobes were surprisingly full. He dipped his fingers into jacket and trouser pockets, feeling for something substantial, but there was only fragmentary evidence of nights out: receipts, club flyers, wrapped condoms and small change.

A bench press sat in one of the spare rooms. Eliot's DJ

equipment took up most of the other: a small fortune in speakers, turntables and vinyl. A serious hunter would take it apart, but Jim confined himself to leafing through Eliot's record cases. None of the bands whose singles were stored there were familiar. Maybe if he had paid more attention to the music his son liked . . . Jim dismissed the thought.

The bathroom cabinets in the en suites were empty, the shower units transparent, the toilet cisterns boxed in. He looked up at the ceilings, recalling hundreds of movies where dislodged ceiling tiles had revealed a hiding place, but they were smoothly plastered and free of loft hatches.

Jim left Eliot's bedroom until last. The bulb in the overhead light was dead. He crossed the room and turned on the bedside lamp. A large print hung above the bed. A below-the-waist shot, taken from behind, of a long-legged woman, standing with her legs apart. The woman wore red high-heeled shoes and a high-cut red swimsuit, its crotch ridden upwards, exposing her rear.

Jim turned his attention to his son's clothes. Eliot's taste was flashy, but he liked quality. His boxers were Calvin Klein, his T-shirts Levi, suits Hugo Boss. Jim worked his way through them, wondering whether the value of his son's wardrobe could be considered incriminating.

He was feeling behind a shoe rack at the back of one of the wardrobes when he came across a package the size of a brick. Jim sank onto Eliot's unmade bed and looked at it. The wrapping was a plain manila envelope. Jim weighed it in his hands, knowing already that it was a hefty wad of cash. He drew the notes out and saw that they were all fifties. Jim swore softly under his breath. It would take too long to count them, but he guessed he might be holding twenty grand in his hands. Jim slid the money back into the envelope. It was evidence. People might have been hurt, or even killed for its sake.

'Fucker.' Jim cursed his son. He took a deep breath and tried to work through his options.

He could walk away, hope the police didn't find it. But how could Eliot explain it away? Use it as a bargaining tool towards a lower sentence? He could take the money home, hide it and hope it remained undiscovered. That was a move with potential to land Jim in the kind of trouble the university classed as 'bringing the institution into disrepute'. It would be a sacking offence, disgrace, the end of everything he had worked for. He could take the envelope and its contents through to the kitchen and burn it in the sink. But what if Eliot was holding the cash for someone else? People had been murdered for less. *Fuck.* Jim turned the package over in his hands.

There was another option. He could leave the cash on the premises, but hide it securely, somewhere the police – or whoever had left the boot marks on the front door – would be less likely to find it. He wished he could speak to Maggie. The flat conversion had been done with an eye to minimalism, but surely there was somewhere a small package could be concealed.

Jim ran through hiding places in his head: behind the bath panel, under the mattress, taped behind a picture, to the base of the bed or some other piece of furniture. Everywhere seemed obvious. For the first time in decades, he asked himself what his father would have done.

Eliot's kitchen cupboards were sparse. Jim rooted through them and chose a catering-size tin of baked beans. The beans were past their sell-by date, probably bought by Maggie when she still harboured hopes that Eliot and his flatmates might occasionally eat together. Jim applied the tin opener to its lid, half opening it, turning it roughly so the edge became torn and jagged. He poured some of the beans into a bowl and then took some of the notes, rolled them as tight as their bulk allowed, put them in a plastic freezer bag, stuffed them into the tin and covered them with the rest of the beans. His father would have found some way of resealing the tin, but this was the best he could do for now.

Jim stuck the tin at the back of the top shelf of the fridge and arranged some beers he found in a cupboard around it. He half opened a tin of sweetcorn, hotdog sausages and kidney beans, repeated the procedure and added them to the shelf.

He washed his hands, rinsed the bowl and cleaned up after himself. It was 5.30 a.m., the time when joggers began to rise from their beds, but Jim continued his search. He checked beneath the mattress in Eliot's room, worked through the rest of the wardrobe, tipped out drawers and felt his way along the underside of the remaining pieces of furniture, making sure to return things to how they had been. He found nothing beyond confirmation that his son was a feckless waster who had not read a book since he left school.

When he could think of nowhere else to look Jim took a dark suit from Eliot's wardrobe, draped it over his arm and left the flat, taking the black bin bag with him. He dumped it in the communal bins and walked to the Audi, his hood up. The sun was rising, the street bathed in a rosy glow. Jim looked at the pavement as he walked – keeping his head down, hiding his face from the world.

Eleven

LINBARLEY PRISON HAD changed since Jim last visited his father there, over twenty years ago. Then it had looked like an asylum lifted from the set of a Hitchcock horror. Now the front of the building was stucco white, its edges sharp and modern, like an oversized shopping mall that had forgotten to add customer appeal. Jim took Maggie's hand, and they crossed the car park together towards the reception building. Maggie had dressed down in jeans and a dark sweater under a leather jacket. Jim was still in his suit and tie. They had left Sasha with a babysitter. Their reticence about where they were going had plunged their daughter into an excitement of curiosity.

Maggie squeezed his hand. 'We'll have to tell her sooner or later.'

The thought of prison touching Sasha made Jim queasy. 'Let's make it later. Did you remember the passports?'

'Of course.' Maggie touched her handbag and stopped still. 'I'm not sure I can go through with this.'

Jim put an arm around his wife and drew her close. She was wearing a new scent, something sweet and floral he did not recognise. 'You don't have to. Take the car. I'll get a cab home afterwards.'

Maggie shook her head. 'He needs us both.'

'Not if it upsets you, love.'

She raised her face to his, and he was surprised by the anger in her expression. 'I'm not upset, I'm furious.'

'I'm angry too. What the fuck was he thinking?'

Maggie pulled away. 'You're always quick to blame him.'

It started to spit with rain. Other people were making their way to the reception. Heads down, shoulders hunched against the weather, like labourers at the end of a shift. Some walked from the car park, but most came from the direction of the bus stop near the main gate. Jim noticed a skinny lad with overgrown curls making his way alone in a thin hoodie and worn trainers. The boy looked too young to be visiting a prison unaccompanied. It was like seeing his own teenage self.

'Eliot did this to himself.'

Maggie's voice took on the clipped edge she used with city planners and recalcitrant builders. 'Our son made a stupid mistake. He didn't harm anyone. He doesn't deserve to be locked up for months with rapists, murderers and God alone knows who else.'

They were beginning to draw glances.

Jim took Maggie's hand. 'This isn't the right place for this conversation. Eliot's in here, whether we like it or not. The best thing we can do is not draw attention to him, or ourselves.'

They resumed their progress towards the entrance. Maggie spoke without looking at him. 'Eliot doesn't belong here.'

Jim squeezed her hand again. 'I know love.'

Eliot had broken the law, but Jim agreed with her. Their son, who they had loved, nurtured and invested so many hopes in, did not belong in HMP Linbarley. They joined the line of visitors waiting for the doors to open. Jim wondered how many of them felt the same way about the person they had come to see.

It was like going through airport security, except airport security guards did not tell you to lock your phone and other valuables, barring five pounds max in cash, in a locker, ask outright if you were carrying anything you should not be, and remind you again, before you entered the secure area, that it was not yet too late to dump contraband.

The dozen or so toddlers crowding the waiting area were a welcome distraction. Some visitors knew each other and chatted as if bag searches and uniformed guards were a normal backdrop to socialising. Others were quiet, staring at the ground, as if they had discovered a fascination with their own shoes.

Jim watched the young lad he had spotted in the car park. Someone should have told him to cut his curls. The boy had a soft look that would make him vulnerable. His hoodie was too lightweight for the night, the soles of his trainers so thin the coldness of concrete would bleed through. Jim had forty pounds in the wallet he had left in the locker. He wondered if he could give it to the boy on the way out. But it was a gesture that might be misinterpreted. And anyway, he had done a poor job of raising his own son, so who was he to interfere with someone else's?

A guard divided the waiting queue into small groups and called them forward in turn. When their time came, Jim reached for Maggie's hand, but she stepped ahead and entered the visiting hall before him. Jim had expected a modern room, a match to the prison's resurfaced façade, but the hall had the air of a 1970s social club. Beige leatherette benches curved around oval tables scarred with ring marks; everything was bolted to the floor. They were assigned a table and told to wait. Maggie's face was pale, her expression drawn. She fiddled with her wedding band, twisting it around her finger. Jim's nerves tightened with every twist. A metal shutter at the far end of the room scrolled upwards and slammed open, revealing a basic tuckshop, selling coffee and tea, juice, sweets and crisps.

Jim touched Maggie's hand to stop the turn-turn-turn of her wedding ring. A door opened, and the inmates filed out, in tracksuits of dowdy grey, navy and brown that denoted their status. The attention of the room was on the men. A few stepped forward boldly, shoulders pinned back, chests puffed. Others looked bashful, amateur actors, unused to the bright lights of the stage.

Maggie stood up as their son entered. Jim remained seated, feet set apart, hands clasped. Eliot was dressed in grey. His hair lay flat and greasy against his head, his chin stubbled with three days' growth. He was talking to the inmate next to him, a short, middle-aged man dressed in navy.

A prison guard counted the inmates and then gave them permission to break ranks. They dispersed, dissolving the illusion of actors and audience. A rising hubbub of noise and greetings filled the visitor hall. Eliot and the man in blue lingered on the edge, finishing their conversation. The guard said something, and Eliot nodded without looking at him. He touched his companion's shoulder in an unhurried parting gesture and lifted his head to scan the waiting visitors. He spotted his parents, gave a small smile, and loped towards them. Jim saw that Eliot had already adopted a lazy prison gait: knees bending, hips moving in a languid swagger. A man setting his own pace, with all the time in the world at his disposal.

Eliot hugged Maggie. 'Mums.' He let her kiss his cheek and then held his hand out towards Jim, absurdly formal. 'Dad.'

Jim clasped his son's hand briefly and let go. 'Son.'

Eliot eased himself into the seat opposite his parents. 'I suppose I should say sorry.'

Maggie leaned forwards. 'Are they treating you okay?'

'It's not a holiday camp, but I'm fine. Guess the OTC wasn't such a waste of time after all, Dad.'

He grinned at Jim, who had insisted Eliot join the Officers' Training Corps at his final, fee-paying school. Eliot had been predictably reluctant but had attended without disaster. It had been a time of hopes-soon-to-be-dashed.

Jim got to his feet. 'Want anything from the shop?'

'Lucozade Sport if they've got it. Irn-Bru full-strength if not.'

'Okay.' Jim turned to his wife. 'Mags? Coffee?'

Maggie's eyes were trained on Eliot. She shook her head without turning to look at Jim. 'Do you have to share a cell?'

'My celly's all right.'

'Why's he in here?'

Eliot laughed. 'It's considered impolite to ask, isn't it, Dad?'

Jim shrugged. 'I'm not an expert on prison etiquette.'

'But you've got a good working knowledge.' Eliot smiled at his mother. 'Mums, would you be okay getting the drinks? I need to ask Dad a couple of things.'

Maggie looked like she was about to object but got to her feet and walked towards the refreshment hatch where a queue had formed.

Jim glanced at the prison officers stationed around the visiting hall. None of them were close enough to hear him, but he kept his voice low. 'I dropped by your place last night and straightened it up.'

Eliot rubbed his forehead. He looked through his fingers at Jim and gave him a slow, lazy grin. 'That's a welcome surprise.' He shifted into Maggie's seat so that they were sitting side by side, with a good view of the hall. 'I left a bit of a mess. Lots of stuff lying about.'

Jim nodded. 'You could say that.'

'Thanks for having my back.'

Jim looked at his son. 'I'm your father, not your pal. I don't *have your back*.'

Eliot's voice was still low, but it held an anxious edge. 'But you tidied up?'

'As best I could.'

'Did you take any valuables home with you for safe-keeping?'

Jim turned and looked his son in the face. 'I didn't want your stuff getting in your sister's way.'

Eliot shook his head in disbelief. 'You've got a massive house. How would it be in her way?'

Jim looked at him. 'Are we talking about the same thing?'

'I'm guessing you went through the wardrobe.'

'Unfortunately.'

'Then we're talking about the same thing.'

Jim whispered, 'I will not have your shit in our house.' He looked to where Maggie was waiting. The queue was moving at a steady pace, and it would not be long before she was served. 'I hid it as well as I could in your flat.'

Eliot closed his eyes, gathering his patience. 'The money isn't mine.'

'That's your problem.'

'I thought we were family.'

'Families have rules.'

'Christ, do you never let up? You've been using that line since I was six years old. The guys I owe don't mess about.' Eliot gestured to the visiting hall, taking in the prisoners in their coded tracksuits, the uniformed guards, the notices warning that antisocial behaviour could result in termination of a visit. 'See all this? It's nothing compared to the trouble I'll be in if I don't pay up with interest.'

Maggie had reached the top of the queue and was getting served.

Jim said, 'Your mother's been through enough. I can't have her worrying about any of this.'

Eliot hissed, 'I owe more than money. I got a lay-on.'

'A lay-on?'

'Goods upfront. An advance of stuff to sell.'

'I don't get it. You had plenty of cash. Too much cash.'

Eliot's face flushed. 'I borrowed the money from the same team. There was a car I wanted. It was a good deal, but the guy would only hold it for a week. I reckoned if I sold the drugs, I could pay a wadge back, get another lay-on and sell it. I would have been clear in six weeks.'

Maggie was walking towards them, carrying a tray.

Jim whispered, 'You're an idiot.'

'It was a good plan.'

'Aye, masterful. It worked out brilliantly.'

A couple of toddlers ran in front of Maggie, slowing her progress.

Eliot hissed, 'I'm meant to sort them out with the first instalment next week.'

'They'll have to wait.'

'It's not that simple . . .'

'What's not that simple?' Maggie gave a bright smile and set the tray on the table before them. It was laden with two bottles of Lucozade and several packets of Haribo. She gave Jim an apologetic smile. 'Five pounds doesn't go far. There wasn't enough to get your coffee.'

Eliot shook his head. 'You've not got a clue, have you? You think they'd let me take all that back to my cell?'

Jim snapped, 'Don't speak to your mother like that.'

Maggie's smile vanished. 'It's all right, Jim. I can stick up for myself.' She took the seat Eliot had vacated. 'I don't know prison rules, and I don't want to get to know them. We're here because we're your parents and we love you. We'll always love you, but don't think we won't ever walk away.'

Eliot reached for a bottle of Lucozade, unscrewed the cap and tilted it to his lips. Maggie took the bottle from him. A prison officer noticed the gesture. He took a step closer but did not intervene.

'If you think I'm going to grow old visiting you in jail after jail, you're mistaken. I don't know where it is yet, but there's a point down the road you're on, beyond which your father and I will not follow you.'

Eliot looked from one to the other. 'You think I like being in here? I slipped up, okay? It won't happen again.' It was a variation on a speech they had heard countless times before. Maggie put the bottle of juice back on the table. Their son hesitated, as if tempted to ignore it, then put it to his lips and took a long swallow. He wiped his mouth with the back of his hand. The whine in his voice recalled the child he had been, quick to flying fists and tantrums. 'You're meant to cheer me up.'

Maggie gave a small laugh. 'You're an adult, Eliot. It's time you learnt your father and I don't exist for your convenience.'

Eliot ripped open a packet of Haribo. He scooped some into his mouth. 'You think I don't know that? You're the original absent parents.'

Jim helped himself to a gummy bear. It was sticky and tasteless. 'Don't try to guilt-trip your mother and me for your mistakes. You had a good upbringing.'

Eliot chewed with his mouth open. The jewelled sweets glistened between his teeth. 'On paper maybe. You took me to sports clubs, cultural stuff, helped me with my homework, but all you were really thinking about was your careers . . .' He looked from his mother to his father. 'The buildings you were designing, your precious research. I was never your priority. You would have been better off not having kids.'

Maggie whispered, 'Eliot . . .'

Jim sensed a softening in her and interrupted. 'At last, something we can agree on.' He looked across the hall. The young boy he had noticed in the waiting area was sitting with a thin, straggly-haired man who looked like Ben Gunn. There were no refreshments on their table. The man was talking, the boy listening. 'How many of the people in this place have had a fraction of the advantages that were served to you on a plate?'

Eliot chewed his sweets. The tattooed skull on his neck pulsed. 'You're talking about yourself again, Dad. We get it. You were raised by wolves and managed to drag yourself up by your bare knuckles. Good for you, big man.'

Jim looked at his watch. 'I've had enough of this. When does visiting time end?'

Eliot shovelled more Haribo into his mouth. 'Why? Do you have marking to get back to?'

Maggie glanced at the clock above the entrance. 'We don't have much time left. I put some money into your prison account. Apparently it takes a day or two for it to go through. We can't phone you, so you'll have to call, if you want to speak to us.'

Eliot lifted the edge of his sweatshirt and rubbed his face with it. 'What about Eddie?'

Maggie nodded. 'I spoke to Mr Cranston this afternoon. He'll be in touch.'

'He needs to get me out of here.' Eliot looked up, his eyes red, watery, bravado gone. 'Will you talk to him, Dad?'

Jim nodded. 'If you want me to.'

There was a fretful mood in the visitor hall as people tried to fit what they had come to say into the vanishing, last few minutes. Across the room Ben Gunn passed a sheet of paper to the boy.

Eliot stared at his father. 'I need you to help me.'

'I'll do what I can.'

Maggie reached out and took her son's hands in hers, all talk of the end of the road and wasted chances forgotten. 'We both will. Try and use this time well. Go to classes, visit the library.'

Eliot snorted. 'I think you're taking the phrase "University of Life" a bit literally, Mums.'

A bell sounded. The volume in the hall rose as people said their goodbyes.

Maggie got to her feet. 'Use the gym. Exercise will make you feel better.'

Eliot gave his father a look over his mother's head. 'I'll do my best, but this isn't a healthy place. There's not a lot of space. It's easy to get pinned down.' He held Jim's gaze. 'You know what I'm talking about, Dad.'

Inmates were making their way to the far side of the hall, lining up to be counted.

Eliot got to his feet. 'Bye.'

Jim touched his son's arm. 'Keep your head down and stay out of trouble, but don't let anyone push you around. Your granddad always said, if you think someone's going to come for you, get in there first.'

Eliot nodded, 'Thanks, Pops.' There was a glimmer of respect in his expression that Jim had not seen since his son was a youngster.

Maggie hissed, 'Do you want his sentence extended? Ignore your father.'

Eliot said, 'I'll call you about that thing, Dad.'

The bell rang again, and a guard shouted, 'That's visiting time over, folks.'

As Eliot turned to leave, Maggie called, 'Behave yourself and do what you're told.'

A passing guard said, 'Good advice.' But their son did not look back. He joined the waiting inmates. The men's combined impact was less now, as if their individual visits had reduced them. The count was completed, and they filed out, leaving the visitors and a few remaining guards in the hall.

Jim kept his eyes on the young boy with the curls as they trailed through the reception area. The paper Ben Gunn had given him was a drawing of Bob Marley done in felt-tip. He must have got special permission for the boy to take it away.

The guards passing the drawing through the security scanner admired the handiwork. Jim thought how different it was from when he had visited his father. The guards had treated him like a criminal in waiting.

The boy smiled shyly and kept his eyes down. He slid his gift beneath his hoodie to protect it from the rain that had grown heavier while they were inside and stepped into the twilight.

Jim retrieved his wallet and passport from the locker, passed Maggie her handbag and hurried into the forecourt. The boy was not amongst the visitors making their way home. Jim sprinted through the prison gates into the street beyond, as far as the bus stop, but the boy had disappeared. Jim retraced his steps. He could see Maggie silhouetted in the driver's seat of the Audi, her head resting against the side window. He paused for a moment, letting the rain run down his face, then Maggie flashed the headlights, casting the prison car park in bronze and darkness, and the moment was broken.

Twelve

PROFESSOR SIR MALCOLM Lulach poured Jim a cup of coffee from the pot his PA had brought through. He added milk, passed the cup to Jim and took a seat at the long meeting table, beneath a portrait of his predecessor. The principal looked tired. The bags beneath his eyes, which had been a gift to three generations of university magazine cartoonists, were darker than usual, and there was a jaundiced taint to his skin.

'There are processes to go through, protocols to be observed, an election to be won, but you'd be my preferred choice. That counts for something. Our institution has a tradition of favouring internal candidates and, of course, you're a graduate of the university. People like that. One of our own made good. But, most importantly, you've got the ability and experience.'

Jim set his cup and saucer on the table. 'This is a bit of a surprise, Malcolm.'

'It shouldn't be. You've proven yourself a good colleague, loyal to the institution.'

Jim gave a self-deprecating grin. 'You mean I know where the bodies are buried.'

The principal smiled. 'This is an age of transparency. There are no bodies. Not unless there's something you're not telling me.' He laughed, and Jim joined in.

Jim took a sip of his coffee. As usual, the principal had forgotten that Jim took it black. The chalky liquid furred his tongue. He had coveted the top post, but now that his candidacy was being discussed, he was surprised to discover an undertow of reluctance.

'Well, as you say, it wouldn't be a foregone conclusion.'

The principal detected the hesitation in Jim's response. 'Are you turning coy on me?'

Jim smiled. 'Not at all. I appreciate your support . . .'

'But . . .?'

'But nothing. Like I said, I'm surprised — that's all. I thought you might prefer a female candidate. Some might say it's overdue.'

The principal looked towards the leaded windows of his office, out over a view of the quadrangles and the gap of sky where the Adult Education building had stood and where soon a new Learning and Teaching Hub would rise.

'It crossed my mind, but our female vice-chancellors are both recent appointments. Neither of them has the right experience.'

'I imagine you'll want to see the new building to completion before you go. Alice and Kendell are intelligent women. They might well be ready by the time you retire.'

The principal made a face. 'Sounds to me like you're trying to talk yourself out of a job.'

Jim shook his head. 'Not at all. I'm flattered. I'm just surprised to be discussing it so far in advance.'

The principal frowned. 'You must have heard rumours about my retirement.'

'I hear rumours about a lot of things.'

'I'll take that as a yes.'

Jim shrugged. 'I assumed they were a slow build-up to the real thing. You know what the university's like. People get anxious about big changes, but things still move at a glacial pace.'

The principal's voice was hollow. 'The glaciers are melting. Things are speeding up.'

Jim said, 'Are you okay, Malcolm?'

The principal got up and walked towards the window. He stood with his back to Jim. From where he was sitting Jim could see only sky and the tops of the old buildings opposite, but the clock tower had tolled, signalling a quarter past the hour, and he knew that students would be crossing the green, heading to classes. The principal touched the window glass with his fingertips, as if reaching out to the students in the quads below.

'Cancer of the bowel. They're going to treat it with chemotherapy in the hope of shrinking the tumour. If that's successful, they may be able to operate.'

Jim took a deep breath. 'I'm sorry.' He wished he had not joked about knowing where the bodies were buried.

The principal nodded, his back still to the room. They stayed silent for a moment, then he coughed, took out a handkerchief, blew his nose and returned to the table. 'You know the workings of this place and you've proven yourself an effective colleague. Senate will agree that you're a safe pair of hands.'

Jim looked at the portrait of the previous principal. He had died in office, struck down by a heart attack during a senior management meeting. 'We don't have to make any decisions . . .'

The principal gave him a look that made it clear sympathy would be unwelcome.

Jim gathered himself. 'Ron Fergusson won't like it.'

This time the principal's smile was genuine. He was a man of the arts. He and Fergusson had been on opposing sides for over three decades. 'Ron's a good man, but he's got his own agenda. I'm confident you'll put the interests of the university first.'

Jim nodded. It was clear now. Malcolm Lulach would support his appointment in the hope of continuing his own legacy. 'Can I think about it?'

The principal frowned. 'I didn't think you'd need convincing.'

Jim looked down at the table. A faint blur of his face was reflected in the polished wood. 'There are things in my personal life—'

'What kind of things?' The principal's voice was suddenly sharp.

Jim shook his head. They had both sat on enough disciplinary panels and appeals to know there were vagaries in human nature that could not be anticipated. 'Don't worry. I'm not about to confess an addiction to undergraduates. Eliot is in trouble with the police.'

'What kind of trouble?'

'Drugs.'

The principal visibly relaxed. A middle-class boy in trouble with drugs was hardly a scandal. 'Sorry to hear that. I hope it works itself out.'

Jim rubbed his face. 'It's a small problem compared to yours.'

'I've entered a new landscape, but that doesn't mean everything else is insignificant.' The principal leaned across the table, emphasising his point. 'This university has existed for over five hundred years. It was here before you and I were born. It will be here long after we're gone. I have the honour of being one in a line of custodians, and you might too, if you stand.'

The principal's office was almost the size of the room and kitchen Jim had grown up in. A series of watercolours depicting the city in earlier times lined the walls. A carriage clock ticked on the bookcase behind the desk.

'When do you need to know by?'

'My consultant has advised me to begin chemo next week. I intend to stay at my desk for as long as possible, but if it goes badly, vice principals will have to deputise. Obviously, that can only be a temporary measure. I've worked hard to keep this place in good order. The best service I can give now is to make sure it's left in safe hands. That means setting procedures for calling an election in motion as soon as possible. I can give you twenty-four hours, but ideally I'd like to know now. Are you up for it, Jim?'

Beyond the door, in the anteroom to the principal's office, a phone rang and was swiftly answered. The clock ticked on the bookshelf. The bell tolled again, indicating another quarter-hour had passed.

Jim took a deep breath. He should phone Maggie, talk it over with her. He reached out and shook Malcolm Lulach's hand. 'Count me in.'

Thirteen

JIM STEPPED FROM the old building into uncertain sunshine. He walked away from the quads and down a short, winding staircase towards the university gates and the main road beyond, thinking about Malcolm Lulach. Nobody knew what was in store for them. He did a quick mental inventory of his various life insurances, the university pension that would go to Maggie if he was suddenly felled.

There was a bounce to Jim's step as he passed the porters' lodge. He felt more alive, the way he did when a near miss on the motorway quickened his blood. He exchanged greetings with one of the porters, stepped through the open gate and turned his phone on. It buzzed with missed calls and messages.

'Professor Brennan.'

He turned to see the tall figure of his postdoc student Michael Peterson, whose reference he had spent a long night completing. The sun slipped from behind a cloud, bathing the street in a harsh glare. Jim shielded his eyes and raised a hand in welcome. 'Michael, any news from the New World?'

The student had made no concession to the approach of spring. Michael was dressed in a long black coat of the kind favoured by 1930s gangsters. A tartan scarf was wrapped around his neck. He came into focus and Jim saw he looked unwell.

'Just that they didn't receive all my references in time, so my application won't proceed.'

The euphoria of a moment ago was replaced by a shot of pure fury. 'Who didn't submit?'

Michael looked at him. 'You, apparently. They didn't receive your reference.'

There was a bench by the university gate. Jim grasped Michael by the arm and led him to it. 'It was me who suggested the studentship to you. I wrote your reference and submitted it on time.' The student took out his phone and tapped into his browser. Jim strove for a matter-of-fact tone but could hear the panic in his own voice. 'I told them you were one of the most promising students I'd encountered in thirty years of teaching.'

Michael did not reply. He passed his phone to Jim, showing him an email from Harvard in response to his query about his submission.

Jim returned Michael's phone. 'You should have got in touch as soon as you received this.'

'Why? They're clear: there's no appeals process.'

'I promise you, I submitted.'

'Did they send you a confirmation?'

Jim took out his own mobile and opened his university webmail, searching for a response from Harvard. His phone buzzed in his hand and an unknown number flashed on screen. He rejected the call. There was no reply from Harvard, no confirmation that his reference had been received. He thought back to the night he had written it. Eliot had been arrested for the second time and taken to jail. He had fallen out with Eddie Cranston on the way home from the police station and completed the reference in the small hours of the morning, wracked with anxiety about his son. Was it possible he had written but not sent it? He tried to remember filing his details into Harvard's electronic system and adding his e-signature but could not. 'I'll call them.'

Michael James got to his feet. 'I told you, there's no point.'

'There's always a point.'

'You let the ball drop, Professor Brennan. It happens – busy people make mistakes. It's just my bad luck it was me you forgot about. Maybe you weren't as confident of my chances as you said you were.'

Jim face was burning. He tapped open his electronic diary. 'Let's make an appointment to meet properly. There are other opportunities, and, in the meantime, I'll phone Harvard and explain . . .'

Michael was already walking away, head down, shoulders bowed, like a gothic outcast. Jim got to his feet, ready to call after him, but the street was busy with students and colleagues, and he did not want to draw attention to himself. He swore under his breath, cursing his son, the spanner in the works, the fly in the ointment, whose actions were dismantling all the goodness in his life. Jim started down the hill towards town and the multi-storey where he had left the Audi. He checked his phone. Three missed calls from Eddie Cranston, a text from his colleague Grace McCann, a missed call from an unidentified number and another one, number withheld. He turned to Grace's message first.

Anything to suggest your Chinese friend might be a blogger?

There are reports of several recent arrests, including a Li Jie but details are hazy.

Jim felt another cringe of conscience. Li Jie was not his friend. The missing Chinese student was nothing to him, just a handshake and a photo attached to an email. Grace had attached a PDF of a news article from the *South China Morning Post*. He downloaded and glanced at it, getting an impression of a spiral of confessions, too detailed to read on the move. He scanned the list until he found Li Jie's name. The blogger had admitted spreading irresponsible posts online with a view to inciting social chaos.

He typed: *Any way of checking who this Li Jie is?* And pressed send. He felt irritated at Grace for asking a question she must have known he could not answer.

Jim had paused in the street to type the text, students streaming past him, like water around a stone. He called up voicemail and resumed his walk to the car park, his phone pressed to his ear. The first message was from Eddie Cranston: *I've seen your boy. He's doing fine for now, but we need to speak. Phone me back when you get this.*

The message was followed by a hang-up, then a woman's voice he could not place: *Professor Brennan, I'm sorry about the other night . . . I drank too much and was rude. I wondered if you might have time to meet. There's something I'd like to discuss with you.*

The woman recited a telephone number. Jim replayed the message. The caller was Cranston's girlfriend, Becca. He resisted the impulse to delete it. He would ask Maggie to call her.

His phone told him he had one more message, and then his son was in his ear, faint and whispering, a clatter of noise in the background. *Dad, I'm in big trouble. I've screwed up. They're going to kill me.*

'Professor Brennan, are you okay?'

Jim came to, realising he had frozen in the middle of the busy street, his dead phone in his hand. He stared at the young woman who had touched his arm. Then the moment passed and he was himself again. Her name was Lucy; she sat on the student welfare committee he chaired.

'I'm fine, Lucy. Thanks for asking. I was just suddenly struck by a thought.'

The girl grinned, revealing the same perfect teeth all his students seemed to possess these days. 'That's a relief. I thought you'd been taken bad. You didn't look yourself.'

Jim forced a smile. 'I didn't say it was a good thought.'

He wished her a nice weekend and hurried in the direction of the car park.

Jim rang Cranston from the shelter of his car, still lodged on the third level of the multi-storey. The lawyer's recorded voice came on the line, accent curbed, inviting him to leave a message or call the office on . . . Jim hung up, swore, took a deep breath and dialled again.

'I've had a call from Eliot who seems to be in some distress. If there's no chance of an appeal, I want him moved to a vulnerable prisoners' wing. Call me back when you get this.'

Jim leaned his forehead against the steering wheel. The leather was warm against his skin. Eliot had sounded frightened. He thought back to their visit, the line of men in prison uniform.

His phone rang. He snatched it up. 'Hello?'

He expected the clatter of prison, the newly cramped voice of his son asking for help, but it was Becca who answered, her tone warm and consoling, as if they had known each other for years.

'Jim, I'm so sorry about the other night.'

The sun was going down, shadows reaching across the almost empty car park.

'Don't worry about it. These things happen.' His manner was businesslike, designed to discourage further conversation.

Becca did not seem to notice. 'I don't know why I was so rude. My time at uni was probably the best of my life.'

Jim kept his delivery clipped. 'It was good of you to call. I'll pass your apology on to Maggie, but I'm sure she'll agree, there's no need.'

'I was hoping we could meet up. As I mentioned, there's something I'd like to discuss with you.'

Maggie had teased Jim about not noticing when women were coming on to him, but years of teaching young adults and mature students had given him an instinct for lines about to be crossed. He had never been properly tempted, was not now.

'Sorry, Becca, I'm snowed under. Perhaps you should get in touch with my wife. I can give you her email address.'

He wondered how the woman had got his mobile number.

'It's about your son.'

A man and woman carrying bulging carrier bags passed the front of the car, arguing with each other in muted tones edged with bitterness. Jim sank low in his seat, unsure why he did not want to be seen. 'What about him?'

'Someone wants to meet you, someone who could be a good friend to Eliot.'

'Who?'

A cooler tone entered Becca's voice. 'I'd rather not say over the phone.'

Across the car park the couple were loading their groceries

into a silver Ford Focus. The woman put an arm around the man, and they kissed.

Jim rubbed a hand across his eyes. 'We're not living in a police state. Our phones aren't bugged.'

Becca was calm as a stone. 'It's simpler if I introduce you.'

Jim watched the reconciled couple get into their car and drive off. 'Where are you? I could drive over now.'

'They'll be free around ten tonight.'

Jim took a deep breath. 'Okay, text the address and I'll be there.'

'It's easier if I tell you.' Becca recited an address in the centre of town. 'What kind of car do you drive?'

'A red Audi.'

She laughed. 'Not conspicuous at all. There's a gap site off a lane at the side of the building. Wait for me there. I'll find you.' Becca cut the call.

Jim took a small notebook and pen from his inside pocket and scribbled the address down. He phoned Eddie Cranston, but his call went straight to voicemail again. He called Maggie. Her line was engaged.

That morning Maggie had mentioned a shortfall between the design spec and the budget for the Newlands apartments. Her day would have been taken up with consultations between suppliers, builders, clients and planners, but his wife's busy line irked Jim. It was Friday afternoon. The building industry usually knocked off early, eager for the weekend. He called again. Heard the same cool invitation to leave a message or phone back later. Jim set his mobile to hands-free. He started the Audi and swung out of the parking space. The corkscrew of ramps leading down towards the exit made him think of the spirals of confessions in the Chinese newspaper and of his own son, alone and afraid in prison.

Fourteen

BENJI FUSSED AT the door, tail flapping against the floor, wriggling his rear, assuring Jim he was the main man. Maggie's car was not in the drive, but Jim called hello into the empty house anyway. He wondered if she had taken Sasha out somewhere, then remembered their daughter was scheduled for a sleepover at her friend Trina's house. He went to the kitchen and poured himself a glass of water. The dog walker had fed Benji, but the Bichon Frise bustled to his dish, ears cocked hopefully. Jim took a rationed Good Boy chew from the tin. The dog sat on his hind legs, front paws held in front of him, ears flat. Jim tossed it the treat. 'You're a disgrace to the male sex.'

The kitchen clock read 7 p.m., three hours before he was due to meet Becca. Jim rang the prison and asked to speak to someone in charge. The voice on the other end of the line told him to ring back later and hung up. He called Cranston and hung up on his answer machine. Maggie's phone went straight to voicemail. He thought vaguely of car crashes and terrorist attacks, paramedics working on his injured wife at a roadside.

He wished he had not told Eliot to 'get in there first' if he suspected trouble was coming his way. It was bad advice. Jim went upstairs, took a shower and changed into jeans and a dark jumper. He expected to hear Maggie's key in the lock accompanied by the scurry of Benji's claws against parquet, but the house was quiet.

He stepped into his study, leaving the door open so he would hear his wife's arrival. He wrote a brief, formal email to Harvard admissions and an encouraging message to Michael, reassuring the student that he was on the case and suggesting other fellowships he might apply for in the meantime. None were as prestigious as the Harvard position, and the task wearied Jim. He sat with his eyes closed for a moment, then wrote to Malcolm Lulach thanking him again for their meeting and reiterating his willingness to stand for the post of principal. He hesitated over the sign-off, unsure of whether to add some condolence about his diagnosis. In the end he settled for 'kind regards'. Lulach would not want his sympathy.

Jim called Maggie again, and this time she picked up. He heard a blast of music suddenly cut short, Ana Tijoux rapping about 1977, a background of engine rumble and knew he was on speakerphone in her car.

'Hi, love, I was beginning to get worried. Where are you?'

Maggie sounded tired. 'Sorry, I meant to text you, but it's been hectic. I've just left Newlands.'

The site was an hour's drive away. He would have to leave before she was home. 'How come?'

'I told you things were tricky. I had to meet with the client at the site.'

'Is it sorted?'

Her sigh travelled across the miles to him. 'Who knows? I've given them several options. They're going to consider them over the weekend.' She said something else, but the signal cut out and in again.

Jim raised his voice. 'Sorry, love, I didn't catch that.'

'I asked if you'd heard anything from Eliot.'

He lied. 'No, he probably doesn't have any money for phone calls yet.'

'I can't stop thinking about him.'

Benji trotted into the room and sat at Jim's feet. He touched the dog's ears, gently stroking their soft silkiness between his thumb and fingers.

'I know, love, neither can I.' He had already decided not to tell her about his meeting with Becca. 'I've got to head out. I forgot I'd promised to take an external examiner for dinner.'

'On a Friday night?'

The regret in his voice was real. 'I know. Sorry, love. I can't get out of it. It's my turn, and with all this stuff going on with Eliot, who knows when I might suddenly have to schedule time off.'

'I guess I'll order takeaway and snuggle up with Benji.'

'Have you heard from Cranston?'

The signal faltered. There was a moment of fuzz and crackle on the line, then Maggie's voice returned: '. . . months away.'

'What was that? I lost you there.'

'I spoke to Eddie this morning. He said there was nothing much he could do until the trial date is set, and that could be months away.'

Jim knew Maggie would be angry if she discovered he had

kept Eliot's plea for help from her. But it was already dark outside, she had a long drive after a long day, and he wanted to keep her safe. 'Drive carefully, love.'

'Don't worry. You know me – I drive to survive.'

'I know you have four points on your licence for speeding.' She laughed, and he felt his heart pulse. 'I love you, Maggie.'

'Love you too. Dump that examiner and come home early.'

'Soon as I can. That's a promise.'

Fifteen

IT WAS A long time since Jim had ventured into town on a
Friday night. A lane was closed on one of the main drags,
and he was forced to slow the Audi to a crawl, joining a
halting conga of cars and taxis whose sluggish progress was
interrupted by a sequence of traffic lights. The street was home
to fast-food restaurants, bars and upstairs clubs. It was not
Hamburg's Reeperbahn – there were no sex shops, brothels
or live XXXX shows – but local businesses were doing their
best to give an illusion of illicit glamour, investing in bright
neon and LED signs that flashed electric promises of a good
time. Competing heavy beats pounded between clubs and
idling cars. Smartly dressed bouncers stood vigilant in doorways, ignoring the homeless kids panhandling at intervals
along the pavement's edge.

A young girl wearing a fishnet body stocking, stretched
over a string bikini, strutted in front of the Audi, wobbling
on high heels. Less confident friends giggled beside her in

shimmery shorts and miniskirts. Jim caught a glimpse of the girl's exposed bottom and looked away. He wondered if her parents knew about her outfit, or if she had left home cosily clad in a tracksuit. She looked young, only four or five years older than Sasha, he guessed. Exploring a pop-star fantasy and ripe for exploitation. The group crossed the road, still giggling, and disappeared into a pub.

Jim had avoided clubs and bars when he was a student. His social life had been confined to the occasional pint in the union with his flatmate Paddy or post-lecture pub get-togethers, continuations of debates started in the lecture hall. He had been short of money, nervous in mixed company, prone to drinking too fast and blasting flaws in other students' hypotheses. Once or twice, he had got into fights, clumsy, bar-room fisticuffs that barrelled into the street. Maggie had saved him from all of that. She had seen something in him that no one else had marked. Her confidence in him – the fact that she, this good-looking, clever woman could love him – had smoothed the worst of his resentment and brittle edges. In the early days Jim had had to battle with jealousy of every man Maggie came into contact with. He had steadied himself, learned to tolerate her male friends and colleagues, and with time had even come to like some of them.

When she had first mentioned the idea of having a baby Jim had thought of it as something that would bind them closer. He had been surprised by the fierce love Eliot had prompted in him. No matter how much Jim despaired of his son, he would not abandon him.

It was easy to imagine Eliot embracing the street's energy. The boy's flash swagger would synchronise with the half-naked, staggering girls and young men jostling for status. Christ, it was like a wildlife documentary. The hunters and the hunted, sexual instincts on display. The lights changed to green. Jim steered the Audi round the corner, away from the neon and music, down towards the city's business district.

The buildings were higher there, as close as Scotland got to skyscrapers, which was somewhere around twenty floors. By day it was busy with suits, but the servants of commerce were elsewhere, enjoying their profits, and the streets were almost, but not quite, deserted. A woman stepped from a building's shadows into the light cast by a streetlamp. Jim thought of sex workers as desperate people, but the woman looked untroubled, as if time was nothing to her. She met his eyes through the car window. Jim pressed his foot harder against the accelerator. He wondered what would happen if someone were to recognise his car, then dismissed the thought. No colleague drifting through this district on a Friday night would be eager to advertise their presence.

The lane Becca had mentioned appeared on the right, a dark passageway between two office blocks. It was a tight turn. He took it slowly, the Audi's headlights bending across brickwork and cobbles. Jim eased the car down the lane and into a deserted courtyard. High above, at the top of one of the blocks, figures moved, black against the lights of a party. He executed a quick three-point turn, facing the car towards the mouth of the lane. The dashboard clock read 10.05. Jim killed the engine and locked the doors. He wondered how long he was willing to wait. The minutes on the clock rose. Jim resisted the urge to check his phone messages. He could still see the lights of the party reflected in his rear-view mirror. He wondered if Becca was there, doling out corporate hospitality. He felt, rather than saw, her approach and unlocked the car doors. Becca slid into the passenger seat.

She was made-up for a party. Red lips and dark eyes, a touch of sparkle on her eyelids. 'Sorry, I couldn't get away.'

Jim did not return her smile. 'What's this about?'

Becca was wearing a long coat. She wrapped it closer around herself and tightened the belt, though it was warm inside the Audi. 'Your son's out of his depth. There are people who can help him. One of them has asked to be introduced to you.'

'Doing Cranston's dirty work for him?'

Becca shook her head. 'It's nothing to do with Eddie, except I suppose that I wouldn't have reconnected with you if it hadn't been for him. It's a small world.'

'It is if you mix with gangsters.'

'Who said anything about gangsters? And what qualifies you to judge? Last time we met you were fretting about a disappeared Chinese student. You deal with the top country in the world for executions and you deal with them for money. Sounds pretty gangsta to me.'

Jim snapped, 'I work with several overseas universities. I'm involved with education, not the judiciary.'

She looked away. 'Do you want me to introduce you or not?'

'Who to?'

'Someone who wants to help.'

It was no answer at all, but the set of her lips made it clear that Becca was not going to give him a name. He asked, 'Why do we need an introduction? My email and office number are on the university website. I'm not exactly difficult to find.'

Becca shrugged. 'Some people are old-fashioned. They prefer the human touch.'

'And no electronic or paper trail?'

'I'm just a go-between.' She pulled back the sleeve of her coat and glanced at a delicate gold Rolex. 'I need to go.'

'What does this person want in return?'

'He knew you'd ask that. He said to tell you, all he wants is your friendship.'

Jim's laugh was sudden and explosive. 'What is this? *The Godfather?*'

Becca gripped the door handle, ready to leave. 'Do you want to meet him or not?'

'Now?'

She gestured towards the lights of the party. 'No time like the present. He's up there, waiting for you.'

Sixteen

BECCA LED THE way across the courtyard towards an anonymous black door. She punched a four-digit code into a keypad, and they entered a dimly lit basement equipped with barred windows, an old-fashioned Belfast sink and the atmosphere of an abattoir.

Becca smiled at him. 'Not glitzy, but it saves us from having to walk round to the front entrance.'

The building was older than Jim had thought, nineteenth-century offices with a twenty-first-century façade and additions, including a series of extra storeys which extended it higher into the air than its original architects could have dreamt of.

Becca pulled back the grille of a goods lift. 'Like I said, not fancy, but it'll get us there.' She slammed the grille and they travelled upwards in silence. The lift was stuffy. Becca unfastened her coat, revealing a silver dress which plunged almost to her navel. The dress highlighted Becca's athleticism rather than her curves, like a Soviet vision of a woman of the future. The lift juddered to a halt. Becca asked, 'Are you happy to walk the last few flights?'

Jim followed her into a service corridor. 'Will you be okay in those heels?'

Becca ushered him ahead. 'They're more comfortable than they look.'

Jim turned to meet her eyes. 'You used to wear trainers when you were at university.'

'I'm surprised you noticed.'

'I didn't really. I guess I just noticed how much you've changed and that reminded me.'

'I was a sporty girl.'

'And now?'

'I'm what's known as a good sport.'

A thrum of music and laughter echoed from somewhere above.

Jim asked, 'What's this all about, Becca? Seriously? Who am I going to meet?'

'He'll introduce himself.'

'Would you accept his help if you were me?'

She shrugged. 'That's a thought experiment too far, Professor Brennan. I can't imagine being you.'

Jim was out of breath by the time they reached the penthouse. The music was louder here. Black type on a silver sign by the entrance read HENDERS CONSTRUCTION.

'Henders the Builders?'

Becca took her coat off and draped it over her arm. 'Can't slip anything past you, professor.' Her voice was treacled with sarcasm, as if she had decided there was no need to be polite now that they had reached their destination. Jim followed her along a corridor and into a suite of offices. The party was on the balcony ahead. He got an impression of shimmering frocks, dark suits, champagne flutes and outdoor burners warming the chill from the night air.

Jim asked, 'What's the occasion?'

'A fundraiser for one of the theatres. They'll have to close if they don't get a new roof soon.'

'So I'm about to meet a patron of the arts?'

'A patron of a lot of things.'

'Including me, if I play my cards right?'

'That's well above my pay grade.' Becca knocked on an office door. A voice sounded within, and she opened the door. 'I've got Professor Brennan for you.'

Becca ushered Jim inside and left. Jim was not sure what he expected, but the slim, silver-haired man who greeted him came as a surprise.

'Professor Brennan, we've met before – a long time ago at the Association of Architects Awards. I had the honour of presenting your wife with a prize for her work on the extension to the National Museum.'

Jim remembered the awards dinner, but he could not place the man. Maggie had been excited to be nominated, thrilled to win. She had worn a midnight-blue gown with a high collar and plunging back. Jim had been pleased to be her 'plus one'.

'I'm proud of my wife's achievements.'

'So you should be. I took my grandson to the museum the other weekend. It's ageing well.' The man held out his hand and they shook. 'Peter Henders, thanks for coming to me, and sorry about the cloak-and-dagger stuff. I wanted to meet you as soon as possible, but this place is full of theatre and press folk tonight. An entertaining bunch, but prone to gossip.'

Henders was wearing a grey suit and open-necked white shirt, stylish but nothing to frighten the horses. By contrast, his office was vast, and styled as if he had sourced the furniture from a catalogue marked Manly Stuff. A pair of brown leather chesterfields faced each other next to an exterior glass wall with a dizzying outlook across the city. His dark wood desk had its back to the view, as if to emphasise his work ethic.

Jim said, 'I don't move in theatrical circles. I doubt anyone would notice me.'

Henders grinned. 'You're better known than you think. Your face will be even more well-kent if you become principal of the university.'

Jim started. 'What makes you think that's a possibility?'

Henders' grin widened. 'I heard Lulach was considering retirement. The university has a habit of internal appointments. A quick glance at senior management makes it clear you're the obvious choice. Forgive me, can I offer you something? Tea? Coffee? There's a sea of prosecco out there and a wee pond of Veuve Clicquot for special guests. Shall I ask one of the girls to fetch you a glass?'

Jim's voice was just the right side of polite. 'No, thanks, I'm driving . . . and not entirely sure why I'm here.'

'Please, take a seat.' Henders led the way to one of the chesterfields. A series of photographs of buildings, presumably built by Henders Construction, lined the walls. Outside, the city lights twinkled. Henders sat with his back to the window, gifting Jim the view of the city. 'I heard you were having some trouble with your boy and thought I might be able to help.'

Jim sank into the couch opposite Henders. 'Who did you hear it from? Becca?'

The builder's eyes creased with his smile. 'It doesn't matter who I heard it from. I know your son's in prison. It's a rough place for a boy from a good background.'

Jim looked out over the city lights. He considered walking out of the room, down into the darkened courtyard and away, but Henders had brought him here for a reason. He wanted to know what it was.

'My son broke the law. Now we have to wait and see what the law decides.'

Henders nodded. 'Agreed. But there's no reason why Eliot should suffer unnecessarily. In my profession you get to know all sorts of people. If you give me permission, I can have a word in a couple of ears – make sure he's looked after while he's inside.'

Jim noted Henders' use of Eliot's name. 'What do you want in return?'

'Nothing, just your friendship.'

Jim gestured towards the sound of the party. 'You don't strike me as a lonely man.'

'You can never have too many friends.'

Jim stood up. 'Thanks for the offer. I appreciate it, but Eliot's a big boy. He'll have to take his chances.'

Henders got to his feet. 'I respect independence. This is an independent firm, one of the biggest in Scotland. I know the value of doing things your own way, but prison's tough. You of all people will appreciate how tough. I can make life easier for your son.'

Jim stood rock-still. 'What do you mean, me of all people?'

Henders spread his hands and offered an apologetic smile. 'I know about your father.'

Jim's voice was low. 'I don't shout about it, but I've never made a secret of the fact that my father was in and out of prison. He was a petty crook and a violent man. Prison was where he belonged.'

Henders nodded. 'Kudos to you for sidestepping that legacy. All I meant was, you're aware that prison isn't a picnic. People talk about prisoners having TVs in their cells, access to a gym and all that, but anyone who has any contact with the system knows it can be brutal.'

'And you have contact with the system?'

Outside on the balcony someone turned up the music. Henders glanced towards the noise. His expression was irritated, but he made no move to ask for the volume to be turned down.

'Henders Construction is part of a scheme that finds work for ex-offenders. I don't want to give the impression we're overly altruistic. We pay the guys minimum wage and we're pretty strict with them. It doesn't always work out, but when it does, I occasionally get a warm fuzzy feeling.'

Jim remembered Cranston's youth football team. 'I seem to be meeting a lot of people with a social conscience.'

Henders shrugged. 'Social services are being cut back. It's up to men like us, people with money and experience, to plug the gap. If we don't, we'll end up with a society we don't want to live in.'

'And the cheap labour comes in handy.'

'I never claimed to be a saint.'

'Can I ask you a question?'

'Fire away.'

'Is your firm interested in the construction of the new building we're planning on campus?'

Henders grinned. 'It's the largest capital project in the city, one of the largest in the country. There aren't many construction firms in Scotland with the capacity to handle it. Of course we're interested in the contract. We've a good chance of getting it too. I don't need to resort to bribery.'

'And yet here I am, one of the members of the building procurement committee, in your office in the middle of the night, receiving offers of friendship.'

Henders leaned back, knees apart. He stretched his arms along the back of the couch, a man with nothing to hide. 'You're a suspicious man, professor. It doesn't do any harm to be on friendly terms with people who are in a position to influence contracts, but it can also work against you.' He gestured towards the party. 'I'm on the board of the theatre; that's why I'm holding this fundraiser for its new roof. It'll be a nice, not-so-wee job, but there's a clear conflict of interest, so my firm is out of the running. That's close on three quarters of a million in potential turnover we can't be considered for because my wife gets a kick out of tickets to first nights.'

Jim remembered Eliot's voice, strangled with fear. He wondered how his boy was and if anyone had hurt him. He took a deep breath and leaned forward, his elbows resting on his knees. 'You mentioned my dad. If you know about him, then you'll know he had a profile.'

'He was a big man in the city.'

'Not that big, but he did have some influence in a certain stratum of the city.'

Henders nodded, conceding the point. 'He was respected amongst his own kind.'

'And despised by the rest. I've worked hard to escape his reputation. I've forged a good career, kept squeaky clean and stayed away from dubious company. I can't accept offers from you or anyone else to ease my son's way through prison. But you're your own man. I can't stop you if you decide to help a boy who's down on his luck. Especially if I don't know anything about it.'

Henders' smile was gone. 'Understood.' He glanced at his watch. The music was beginning to fade and there were sounds of goodbyes in the hallway outside. 'I'd better get back to my guests.' He got up, ready to walk Jim to the door. 'You never asked how I knew about your father.'

'I assume there's a Wikipedia page on him somewhere – *Scottish Gangsters of the Seventies and Eighties*. I've made a point of not looking.'

Henders put a hand on Jim's shoulder. 'I didn't need to do a Google search. My dad and yours were mates. Your dad talked about you, how clever you were, how you'd make a success of yourself. If he was anything like my old man, he probably never told you, but he was proud of you, for what it's worth.'

'He liked bragging, and I was something he could brag about.'

'He certainly did that. My dad sent me to the Merchant School – hefty fees, hefty expectations. It was wasted on me. My old man kept asking why I couldn't be more like Big Jim Brennan's laddie. I never met you, but I hated your guts. Later, when your book came out and your name began to appear in the papers, I realised you were the same boy and kept an eye open for you. You've done well, Jim. It sounds stupid, and I probably wouldn't say this if I hadn't had a few glasses of bubbly before you arrived, but I want you to keep on doing well.' He reached into his pocket and took out a business card. 'Here, I know you're your own man, but hold onto this. Give me a ring if you need any help.'

Jim hesitated, then took the card and slipped it into his wallet. 'I'm guessing your dad was a bit of an outlaw.'

Henders laughed. 'That's a diplomatic way of putting it. My dad managed to keep on the right side of the law, but he sailed close to the wind sometimes.'

'And you?'

Henders' features hardened. 'Oh, I'm squeaky clean, just like you.'

Seventeen

JIM'S PHONE RANG as he reached the Audi, caller's number withheld. His son's voice was low and raw, a harsh whisper in the darkness. 'Dad, I'm in serious trouble.'

'Has anyone hurt you?'

'Not yet, but it's coming.'

Jim slid into the driver's seat and locked the car doors. There was a tightening sensation in his chest. He pressed the phone to his ear and forced his own voice to calm. 'Take a deep breath and tell me what you can.'

'You already know it. I owe some people, violent people. They're going to get me.' Jim knew prisoners were not allowed access to the hall phone at night. His son was phoning on a contraband mobile. 'Whose phone are you using?'

'I swapped some guy my breakfast and lunch in return for five minutes. We need to be quick.'

'Ask to be put into a VP wing – that's vulnerable prisoners. You'll be safer there.'

Static hissed on the line, beyond it the prison clanked and rumbled, but Jim could hear the fear in Eliot's voice. 'These guys have long arms. They'll get me wherever I am.'

'Don't panic. Have you called your mum?'

'No.'

'Leave it that way. I don't want her worrying any more than she needs to. What about Eddie? I told him to get you moved.'

'I saw him this morning, but things have stepped up since then.'

Jim's breaths were short and uneven. He tried to control it. 'Listen, all that stuff I said about getting in first and using your fists, it was bullshit. Keep a low profile. Try not to attract attention.'

Eliot spat, 'Have you heard anything I've said? It's too late. I'm totally in the shit here.'

Jim closed his eyes. 'You're on your own in there, son—'

Eliot's voice fractured. 'Fuck's sake. You've always been a fucking superior—'

Jim's eyes snapped open. 'For Christ's sake, Eliot, shut up and listen, for once in your life.'

For a moment he thought Eliot had hung up, then he heard ragged breathing and realised that his son was sobbing.

'I've screwed up big-time, Dad.'

'I know you have, son. What I was going to say is, you're alone in there, but you're not alone. Your mum and me love you. We'll do everything we can to make sure you're safe. As soon as I hang up, I'll phone Eddie. I'll ask him what he knows about your situation and what we can do to make it better.'

'There's nothing . . .'

'Trust me, there's always a way. We'll find it.'

Eliot whispered. 'I love you, Dad.'

'Love you too, son.'

The background noise that had rumbled throughout the call seemed to grow louder.

Eliot mumbled, 'I've got to go.'

Jim was about to say that Maggie loved him too, but the connection was cut, and he was left alone.

Men died in prison. Sometimes they took their own life. Sometimes someone else took it for them.

His reasons for walking away from Henders had been sound, but now he slipped the builder's card from his pocket and regarded it. The final decision on who would win the contract to build the Learning and Teaching Hub would be influenced by the architect, with input from the building committee. His own role in the appointment would be small, a cell in a single body that was part of an army.

Jim looked at the office block in his rear-view mirror, and put the card back in his pocket. He could not accept favours from the head of a firm in line for a multi-million-pound contract from the university. The penthouse lights flashed disco-bright. The party was picking up again. Jim thought about phoning Eddie Cranston, but it was after midnight, too late for the lawyer to do anything. He texted: *Had a distressed call from Eliot. Phone me as soon as you get this. I want him moved to a VP wing.*

He started the Audi and steered it slowly out of the courtyard.

Eighteen

JIM WOKE SUDDENLY from a deep sleep, an interrupted dream just beyond his grasp. The room was in daylight. He rolled over, reaching for his wife, but her side of the bed was empty. He opened his eyes. Maggie was rummaging in her jewellery box. She was dressed, her hair freshly styled.

Jim rubbed a hand across his eyes. 'What time is it?'

Maggie found the earrings she was looking for and slipped them on. 'Half nine, I thought you deserved a rest.'

Benji trotted into the bedroom. The dog put his front paws on the duvet and nosed Jim's face.

Jim pushed it away. 'Bugger off, Benji.'

Maggie picked the dog up. She leaned over the bed, putting Benji's face close to Jim's again. 'He just wanted to say good morning.'

Jim gave the dog a conciliatory pat. 'Morning, Benji, your breath stinks.'

Maggie set the dog down and kissed Jim's cheek. 'Yours isn't so fragrant either. I made you a cup of tea.'

'Thanks, love.' Jim got out of bed, shrugged his dressing gown on. He lifted the mug from the bedside table and took a sip. The tea was tepid, a scum of milk settling on its surface. 'Where are you going?'

'I'm giving the keynote at ArchiFringe Festival, remember?'

He did. It was the reason Sasha had stayed at Trina's house. To give them both time to attend.

'You should have woken me. When do we need to leave?'

Maggie glanced at her watch. 'Ten minutes. Don't worry, you don't need to come.'

'I want to.'

Maggie's keynote was scheduled for eleven. He would make it if he shifted himself. An envelope icon indicated a new text from Eddie.

Will call the prison this morning and go in after lunch if I can. Ed

Jim wanted to call him back but instead opened the wardrobe door and flicked through his shirts, looking for one that would fit the cleanly constructed architect vibe Maggie's colleagues favoured. Maggie was applying her lipstick. He saw her reflection in the mirror and knew from her expression that she was reviewing her presentation in her head. He found a shirt and laid it on the bed. 'You go on ahead, love. I'll have a quick shower and taxi over. I'll be there before you start.'

'Are you sure?'

'Certain. I'm looking forward to it.'

Maggie turned the full beam of her smile on him. 'It'll just be boring architect-speak.'

'Bollocks. It'll be great, and you know it.'

Maggie laughed. 'Is that the kind of robust feedback you give your students, Professor Brennan?'

The question made Jim think of Michael Peterson's lost reference. He forced a smile. 'Only the good ones.'

He wanted to tell her about his meeting with Lulach and the chance that he might be in line for the post of principal, but it could wait until later. He would have to tell her about Eliot's phone call sooner or later too. Perhaps by the time he delivered that news, a solution of sorts would be in place.

Maggie took a lightweight black jacket he had not seen before from the wardrobe and pulled it on. 'How do I look?'

'Like Helena Christensen.'

She put her arms around him and brushed her lips against his cheek softly, so as not to smudge her lipstick. 'Helena Christensen's ten years older than me.'

He pressed her closer and resisted an urge to bury his head in her shoulder. 'I meant when she was younger.'

Maggie touched her nose to his. 'Not too much younger though?'

'Exactly ten years younger.'

She slid free of his grasp. 'You're a slippery customer.' She picked up her handbag and checked its contents. 'Will you give Trina's mum a quick call, please? Don't fight it if she asks if Sasha would like to stay another night.'

Jim went into the en suite and turned the shower on. 'I miss her if she's away too many nights.'

Maggie paused in the doorway. 'I know, but the atmosphere here's been grim. It'll do Sasha good to hang out with her friends. And we need space to talk about Eliot.'

The shower stall was beginning to steam up, water vapour drifting into the bedroom. 'Don't think about that just now. Concentrate on your keynote.'

Maggie slung her handbag over her shoulder and lifted her briefcase. 'I can't not think of our boy, but it's no good letting things get on top of us. And we'll need money for his defence.' She gave him a kiss and closed the door gently behind her.

Jim stepped into the shower. If money was all that was needed to set Eliot free and put him on a straight road through life, he would willingly sell the house, their cars and everything else they possessed. But throwing cash at their son had only contributed to his troubles.

He soaped his body and let the needle spray rinse him clean. Eliot's problem could be divided into parts. There were his self-destructive impulses towards shortcuts and get-rich-quick crime. A spell in prison could be the catalyst that reformed Eliot, but Jim doubted it.

Then there was the problem of whoever was threatening his son. Peter Henders might smooth things inside for the boy, but, whatever the builder said, Jim suspected his favours would come at a cost and be easily withdrawn if the price was not paid.

The only way to secure his son's safety would be to ensure the cash and drugs Eliot owed were returned to wherever they came from.

He stepped from the shower and towelled himself dry. Maggie was right. It came down to money in the end. Jim wondered how much it would cost him and how he could pay whoever was owed without implicating himself.

He went through to the bathroom and started to dress. His phone buzzed – a text from his mobile provider informing Jim that his latest bill was available for viewing. He deleted it and saw again the text from Cranston. The lawyer straddled both worlds. He was equally at home in the law courts and the dive bar. He had associates — Becca, his youth team and no doubt others yet unmet by Jim — who might be able to keep transactions at arm's length.

Jim buttoned his shirt, pulled on a jacket and ran a comb through his hair. Was he about to invite the kind of trouble that could dismantle everything he and Maggie had worked hard to achieve? Jim opened the app on his phone and ordered a taxi. Eliot was in the system. He had landed himself there and would have to take the consequences.

Jim checked Benji was not lurking beneath their bed, shut the bedroom door and hurried downstairs. His phone buzzed, letting him know that the taxi was nearby. Jim went into the kitchen. Maggie kept a collection of greeting cards in one of the kitchen drawers. He rifled through them, looking for something plain. Jim's phone buzzed again. He settled for a picture of a fishing boat, beached in a sandy cove he did not recognise, and hurried out, locking the front door behind him.

Nineteen

MAGGIE'S KEYNOTE WAS a coolly delivered mixture of provocations, hard facts and bold solutions. Jim watched from the back of the auditorium, aware of the silence in the room, the number of people taking notes. He knew enough about architecture to follow Maggie's argument, but the finer points were lost on him, and his mind started to drift.

Sasha had WhatsApped during his journey, full of excitement at a treetop adventure walk called the Monkey Run and begging to be allowed to stay over a second night. He had spoken with Trina's mother and agreed. Maggie was right: their daughter needed some fun. But he felt the absence of both of his children weighing on him.

Maggie and he had talked, maybe ten years ago, about the possibility of a third child, but Sasha was barely out of nappies, Eliot a handful, and the miscarriages that had occurred in the interval between their living children's births still lay heavy on them. That ship had sailed, but Jim sometimes wondered what his other children, the dead and the never conceived, would have been like.

Maggie's formal presentation concluded, and the session moved to questions from the audience. Jim watched for a while and then slipped out of the auditorium. The arts centre hosting the festival had a shop and a café. He bought a stamp, ordered a cortado and took out the card he had taken from the kitchen drawer. He wrote, mindful that his words would be read by others:

Dear Son,

You're in a hard place. There may seem like there is no way out, but remember, this time will come to an end. Things <u>do</u> get better. Your mother & I love you and will do whatever we can to support you.

He paused, unsure of what to write next.

Everyone makes mistakes, I've made plenty. What matters is how you deal with them. Remember what I told you, keep your head down and keep out of trouble. All's well here, except that we worry about you. Love from your Dad x

Jim stuffed the card into its envelope and attached the stamp. He knew the address and postcode of Linbarley Prison by heart but had to check his phone to find Eliot's prisoner number. There was no new text from Cranston. Jim was getting to his feet, ready to return to the auditorium, when his phone rang. The university's central number flashed on the display. Jim tensed. No good news came by personal phone on a Saturday morning.

He recognised the university chaplain's voice. 'Jim, sorry to phone at the weekend. Where are you?'

'ArchiFringe, Maggie's giving the keynote.'

'Is she with you?'

The phone trembled in Jim's hand. 'She's still on stage.'

He wanted to ask if something had happened to Eliot but found he could not say his son's name. 'What is it?'

'Find somewhere quiet and take a seat.'

'Just tell me what it is.'

The chaplain's sigh reached across the city and into his ear. 'I'm sorry, but it's sad news. I understand you have a postdoc student, Michael Peterson?'

Foreboding knotted Jim's chest. 'What's happened?'

'Michael took his own life yesterday. His body wasn't discovered until this morning. The police informed us. I'm just off the phone to his father. His parents live in France. The French police broke the news, but I thought I'd better . . .'

Jim felt the blood drain from his body. He sat down. 'Michael had had a disappointment about a fellowship, but I didn't realise . . . I would have put him in touch with student services if I'd known . . . if I'd even suspected . . .'

'No, no, no, Jim. That's not the way to think. Michael left a note. He mentioned you specifically, said what a great help you'd been and apologised for what he was about to do. Whatever was bothering the poor lad, and we may never discover what it was, you helped give him a feeling of self-worth. Michael said your classes and your belief in him were bright spots in his life. He was only sorry he couldn't believe in himself enough to stick around.'

'I let him down.'

The chaplain had served in the army. He'd seen active service in Bosnia and run a parish in the East End of the city before being appointed to the university. He liked to say that he neither suffered nor persecuted fools. 'You did nothing of the sort unless there's something else that you want to tell me about?'

There was a lump in Jim's throat. He swallowed, but it would not go away. 'Michael had his heart set on a Harvard fellowship. I could have been more supportive of his application, but I was busy, and it slipped down my list of priorities.'

The chaplain sounded relieved. 'Perhaps you intuited that a high-pressure American institution such as Harvard wouldn't have been the best environment for a vulnerable person like Michael.'

'He was reserved, but I thought he wanted to concentrate on his studies. I had no idea of any mental health issues.'

'Nobody at our end did. Mr Peterson said he and his wife wanted to inform the university that Michael had a history of depression and self-harm, but the lad threatened not to take up our offer of a place if they did. The poor man's blaming himself of course.'

The doors to the auditorium had opened. Maggie's session was over, and the art centre café was filling up. Jim turned his back on the emerging audience and put a hand to his ear, blocking out their chatter. 'I'll phone his parents.'

'Hang fire, Jim. They'll need time to gather their thoughts and grieve – and so will you.' The chaplain sighed. 'If people knew the effect their actions had, the ripples of emotion they send out, they might change their minds. That young man had his whole life ahead of him. He had talent and people who loved and admired him, and yet he was in such despair that he chose to end it all. I'll never get used to student suicides. Thank God they're a rare event.'

Jim could not imagine thanking God. He glanced back at the busy café. Maggie was by the door, talking with a small group of people. She raised a hand in greeting and gave him a questioning look. He nodded and turned away. 'What can I do?'

'There's nothing much anyone can do at this point. The principal's prepared a statement in case the university's approached by the press, and I'm phoning all of Michael's tutors. Better I break the news than they find out by accident.'

'You're sure I shouldn't phone Michael's parents?'

'Why don't you write them a letter of sympathy? They may want to meet with you later, but for now they need space to absorb the news. Are you going to be okay, Jim? This has been a shock. I can make time this afternoon if you'd like to talk.'

Jim swallowed a horrible urge to laugh. The lump was still in his throat. It choked his voice. 'I'm all right. I've got support.'

'Okay, but remember, I'm available if you need a listening ear.'

Maggie was in the centre of a group of colleagues. She was watching him, a worried expression on her face. Jim shook his head, trying to let her know that the call was not about Eliot. He mouthed 'university'. She rolled her eyes and turned away.

'I'll remember.' Jim hung up.

Maggie saw that Jim had finished his call and waved him over. Delivering the talk had revitalised her. She waved at him again, more impatiently this time. Jim shook his head. It was impossible to cross the room, enter the circle and join in the laughter. His presence would pollute her day. The lump in his throat felt like it was blossoming down past his oesophagus and into his chest. His phone was still in his hand. He texted Maggie: *Sorry, got to deal with a crisis at the uni. You were brilliant. Enjoy the afternoon. Will call you later xxx.* He stepped out of the brightly lit café and into the grey city street. There was a postbox across the road. He took Eliot's card from his pocket, kissed the envelope and posted it.

Twenty

IT WAS GALA Day in the old district. A line of flatbed trucks converted into colourful floats edged slowly down the main street in the wake of a pipe band kitted out in full tartan. Spits of rain gusted on the wind, but the pavements were packed with locals enjoying the spectacle. Jim stepped through the crowd. A flotilla of small girls in pink leotards, fluffy pink ears and painted whiskers flurried past him, carrying silver batons, eager for their turn in the parade. Their mothers followed at a more leisurely pace. One of them smiled an apology, 'Wee bears. High as kites.'

Jim answered the woman's smile, wondering if he knew her from school and hoping no one would recognise him.

A float decorated as the Mad Hatter's Tea Party raised a cheer from the crowd. The skinny hatter chased the white rabbit up and down while Alice, pretty in her blue dress, flapped her hands and an oversized cup and teapot jigged. The name of the float's sponsor was printed in big letters on a blue-and-white banner and across Alice's snowy apron: *Henders Construction*.

A rainbow-festooned float came next, carrying buff boys in silver shorts and sunglasses, accompanied by towering drag queens in high heels and higher hair. In Jim's youth gays had stayed underground or deserted to London. He hoped things had changed and that the boys' features would not be re-arranged by the end of the parade. He scanned the crowd, looking for Eddie or members of his youth team. The squad of little girls dressed as pink bears step-kicked by, part of the parade now, twirling their batons and grinning like tooth-paste commercials. The crowd's cheers grew louder. Jim remembered Becca's remark about wanting to be a majorette when she was a child. His daughter Sasha would also have loved these costumes and the applause. Yet the sight of a parade still had the power to frighten him.

When he was a boy, the neighbourhood's annual Gala Day had intensified the dread that shadowed Jim. The lines of flags fluttering from lamppost to lamppost, the cheerful floats, full streets and fuller pubs excited his father. The district was his stage, and the residents lining the pavements acted as both audience and challenge. Gala Day had been the scene of Big Jim Brennan's last arrest.

Jim had been an undergraduate and estranged from his father by then. He followed the trial via a local broadsheet in the university library's reading room. According to reports, his father had considered himself insulted by an outsider, who ill-advisedly visited his cousin on Gala Day. Big Jim had set about him, not realising the stranger was a promising amateur boxer. His opponent possessed enough street smarts to realise it was not a Marquess of Queensberry situation. He got a good few blows in, bloodying Big Jim's nose and cutting his eye. The stranger came close to winning but made the mistake of underestimating Big Jim Brennan's capacity for violence. Jim's father had grabbed a beer bottle, smashed it against a table, stuck it into the man's neck and twisted. He was still kicking the stranger, who was lying on the ground, bleeding out, when police stormed the pub. It took four officers to subdue him. As the judge noted in his summing-up, only luck saved the beaten man from dying. The newspaper reported that Big Jim Brennan had smiled at that, as if the judge had served him a compliment.

Extra police officers had been drafted in to take him down to the cells, but Big Jim had offered no resistance. Jim could imagine the scene, his father grinning like an unrepentant Droog, adrenaline surging in anticipation of prison.

As a boy he had thought his father was fearless. As a man he wondered if Big Jim Brennan had been fashioned from fear. A Terror Golem sent to bully the district that had formed him.

Metal grilles protected Eddie Cranston's office windows. A locked aluminium shutter guarded its door. A sign declared the office closed on Saturdays and Sundays and offered an out-of-hours emergency number. Jim called, but both it and Cranston's mobile went straight to voicemail. He stowed his phone in his jacket pocket and pushed through the crowds to the Fusilier.

The usual smokers were gathered round the pub door. Something about Jim must have suggested business, because they parted wordlessly to let him through. The pub was rammed. Someone was murdering 'The Boys Are Back In Town' on the karaoke machine, no one joining in the chorus. Jim shouldered his way through the packed bar-room. There was no sign of Cranston or his team. The bar was four deep.

Jim shoved his way to the front and caught the eye of the barman who had served him on his last visit. Billy was pouring Jägermeister shots into a tray of glasses. 'There's a queue.'

'I'm not after a drink, I'm looking for Eddie Cranston.'

Someone shoved Jim from behind. Jim turned and stared at the waiting drinkers. An edge of breathing space emerged around him.

'For fuck's sake.' The barman looked as if he was about to tell Jim to get lost. He held out the card machine to the punter he was serving, who tapped his debit card against it. The machine beeped and the punter ferried the shots away. The barman gave Jim a look and decided answering his question was the easiest way to get rid of him.

'Eddie won't be in till later, if he comes in at all. His boys are on security for Gala Day.' He nodded to a waiting drinker who asked for four pints of lager and a vodka lemonade.

Jim said, 'I didn't see them.'

The barman lined up four pint glasses. He tipped the first one to the Tennent's tap and started filling it with lager. 'Maybe they're on a break.'

Jim was halfway through the throng of drinkers when he felt a hand clutch his elbow. The man was around the age Jim's father would have been had he lived. Shrunken flesh on a large frame, bald head and glasses, coffin-jawed.

'You're Big Jim Brennan's laddie.' Jim pulled free, but the old man's reactions were swifter than he expected. He grabbed Jim's arm again, fingers digging into the flesh. 'Left your manners at the university, did you? No time to talk to an old friend of your da?'

Jim wrenched the man's hand from his arm. It was like detaching a claw. 'I'm in a hurry.'

'You always were. Didn't even spare the time to visit your faither in jail.'

'What's it to you?'

The man leaned close, jabbing a finger in Jim's chest for emphasis. His beer sloshed in his glass.

'You're your faither's son right enough, but you're not a skelf of the man he was. Big Jim Brennan could battle every man in this bar, me included, and still stay standing.'

Jim's phone vibrated in his pocket. 'Aye, he was a great man, my father, one of the best.'

The man shook his head. 'You were aye a spotty wee know-it-all.'

Jim took out his phone. Eddie Cranston's name flashed on the screen and vanished. Jim swore and pressed redial, but the signal had gone. He slammed out of the Fusilier and through the tobacco haze of the doorway. The Gala Day parade was over, the crowds heading home for tea or out and about. Bunting sagged from lampposts. A leaflet blew free of a tumble of litter, scuffed along the pavement caught by the wind and wrapped itself around Jim's shoe. He peeled it off, swearing beneath his breath as he read the words: *Henders Construction Supporting Your Community*. Jim scrunched the leaflet into a ball and threw it into a nearby bin. His phone rang again, and this time he answered it.

Eddie Cranston said, 'I've got bad news.'

Twenty-One

THEY MET IN a fluorescent-bright McDonald's. It was packed with kids who had taken part in the Gala Day. Their fancy-dress costumes and the giant pictures of floating burgers edged with greenery lent the space a surreal 4D-cartoon edge that made Jim's headache zing.

Cranston was dressed down in a Lacrosse sweater, jeans and Nike Airs. He ordered a Happy Meal and a McFlurry. An overweight girl behind the counter asked if he would like to upgrade to a Whopper. Cranston gave her the full-beam smile. 'Tempting, but better not. I'm meant to be on a diet.'

The girl grinned. 'A little of what you fancy does you good.'

Cranston slapped his belly. 'I'll get none of what I fancy if this pot gets any bigger.'

The girl took a wrapped burger from one of the racks of heated trays that separated her from the kitchen, then shovelled skinny fries into a miniature paper bag and set them on a tray. 'Better stick to a kiddy meal right enough then.'

The McDonald's felt airless, the noise of excited children pickaxe-shrill. Jim had missed breakfast and not eaten since, but the news of Michael's suicide had killed his appetite. He ordered a black coffee and a glass of water.

Cranston grinned at the girl. 'Give him an iced doughnut – he needs the sugar.'

They queued for their order and ferried it across the café looking in vain for a pair of empty seats.

Jim said, 'We'll have to sit in your car.'

Cranston scanned the crowded space. 'That's one of the many differences between me and the cops. My car's a food-free zone.' He approached a booth where a young woman and four little boys, dressed in a variety of superhero costumes, were finishing burgers and chips. 'How's it going, Marie?'

The woman was toying with her phone. She looked up and smiled. 'Okay, Mr Cranston. How are you?'

'Good, thanks. How's Lewis?'

The woman made a face. 'Pain in the arse, but behaving himself, I think. Are you looking for a table? We're just about to head.' She started to gather the used wrappers onto a tray. 'Come on, yous lot. Let's see if your gran has any ice cream in her freezer.'

The boys stuffed the last of their chips into their mouths and got to their feet.

Cranston ruffled the nearest boy's buzz cut. 'Don't rush on our account.'

Marie gathered the rest of the debris. 'No worries. We were heading anyway.'

She gave Jim a wary glance. He realised she thought he was Cranston's client and said, 'Eddie's helping my son.'

Marie slid from the booth, herding the little superheroes

together. 'If it can be sorted, Mr Cranston'll sort it.' She lifted the tray of rubbish from the table and slung a bag, heavy with groceries, over her shoulder. 'I'll tell Lewis I saw you.'

Cranston reached into his pocket, took out some change and gave each of the children a coin. 'Be good, and keep the streets safe for auld yins like me, lads.'

The boys took the money shyly. There were no pockets in their superhero costumes, so they clutched it in their fists.

Marie said, 'Say thank you to Mr Cranston.'

The boys whispered, *Thank you, Mr Cranston*, and the family went on their way.

Cranston watched their departure. 'Marie's a saint. Her brother Lewis is a violent arsehole. He'll be in my office on some charge in the next six months, guaranteed. Polar opposites born into the same family. Nature or nurture? If you took Marie and Lewis as an example, you'd come down on the side of nature, but who knows? Maybe there's more to it than that.' He peeled the wrapping from his Happy Meal. The burger looked tiny in his hands. He regarded it with disgust and took a bite. 'Don't worry. I'm not normally indiscreet. I won't plaster your business across town.'

Jim pulled the lid from his coffee cup. The contents smelt blackly of stomach bile. 'You said you had bad news?'

Cranston chewed and swallowed. 'Eliot's pissed off some people he would have been better never getting involved with.'

Jim stared at the plastic surface of the table. It was decorated with tiny flecks of colour that appeared randomly scattered. He guessed that if you zoomed out far enough and looked with the right eyes, a pattern would emerge.

'Eliot told me he owes money. I'm prepared to pay his debts, no questions asked.'

'That's something, but I'm afraid it's not just money we have to worry about.' Cranston took another bite of his burger.

Jim's phone buzzed. A text from the university chaplain informing him that news of Michael's suicide would be in the Sundays. He rubbed his face with the palms of his hands and tried to focus on the problem in front of him. 'What else? Drugs?'

Cranston gave a quick glance around the room, checking no one was tuning into their conversation. 'Last time we met I mentioned that Eliot would get an extended sentence if drugs were found in his flat. You accused me of asking you to collude in a crime.'

'I owe you an apology.'

Cranston finished his burger and started on the small bag of fries. 'Wait until you hear what I have to say before you decide if you want to apologise to me.'

Jim pushed his coffee to one side and took a sip of water. 'Go on.'

'As Eliot's lawyer I have his best interests at heart, but were I to come across evidence that he was involved in a crime I'd be obliged, by law, to inform the police.'

Jim set his cup on the table. His hand trembled, but his voice was steady. 'Is that your bad news? You're going to the police?'

Cranston tore open a sachet of salt and poured its contents over his fries. 'You're jumping the gun. I didn't say anything about reporting Eliot. But I need to make it clear: I can't be associated with covering up criminal activity. Any hint of collusion would result in the loss of my licence to practise.'

Jim let out a deep sigh. 'I don't know what Eliot's asked you to do, but it's his mother and I who are paying your fee. We hired you to manage Eliot's defence. We know he's guilty.

Your job isn't to deny that he sold drugs. Your job is to get us the best possible outcome.'

Cranston chewed and swallowed. 'Eliot hasn't asked me to do anything.'

Jim's phone buzzed again. He glanced at it and saw a message from Maggie. *In Scandi Kitchen. Want me to order for you?* He had forgotten they were joining her colleagues for an early dinner. He texted: *Start without me. I'll be there ASAP x.*

'You're not telling me anything I don't already know. I spoke to Eliot last night. He's in fear of his life. He needs to be moved to a VP wing . . .'

Cranston held up a hand. 'We'll get to that. First, we've got to enter the realm of the hypothetical. Imagine Eliot got an advance of drugs to sell . . .'

'I know about that. He called it a lay-on. It's the reason he's so scared.'

'A very expensive lay-on.'

'How much?'

Cranston shovelled some chips into his mouth, chewed and swallowed. 'Hypothetically, the person who supplied it claims fifty thousand pounds.'

Michael Peterson's death had stunned Jim. This new outrage shocked him awake. 'I'm going to the police.'

Cranston looked up, another handful of fries halfway to his mouth. 'You'd shop your own son?'

It was against the code his father had hammered into Jim. Worse than a book burning or hit-and-run. He leaned his head against his hand and massaged his temples. 'Sometimes you have to cauterise a wound. If Eliot cooperates – comes clean and gives evidence against people further up the chain – it'll work in his favour. Handled right, this could be a game changer.'

Cranston smiled. 'That's one way of looking at things. In a fair world, it might even work.' He picked up the paper bag containing the doughnut he had ordered for Jim. 'Do you want this?' Jim shook his head. Cranston swilled back some coffee, pulled out the doughnut and took a bite. 'Unfortunately, we're not operating in a fair world. Hypothetically speaking, informing the police could sign your son's death warrant . . . Shall I go on, or are you going to walk out on me again?'

Accidents happened in prison. People fell down stairs, slipped in the shower, bashed their head against metal railings, tumbled over landings, hung themselves in despair. Jim's father had spoken admiringly of chibs fashioned from ball-point pens and razor blades; hot oil deliberately spilled; suffocations that went undetected.

Jim increased the pressure of his fingertips against his temples to reduce the tension building behind his eyes. 'I'm not going anywhere.'

Cranston pushed the half-eaten doughnut aside. 'You probably don't realise it, but there are people who take an interest in your progress. People who knew your dad.'

Peter Henders and the old drunk in the Fusilier had told him the same thing in different ways, but Jim said, 'It's almost twenty years since my father died. More than that since I lived here.'

'Memories can be long. You walked away – fair enough, you needed to get out, I understand that – but there are friends of your dad who are impressed by what you've achieved.'

The thought of unseen associates of his father monitoring his progress made Jim uneasy. 'My dad was a low-grade hardman. An occasional enforcer with what we'd now call anger management issues. Back in the day, folk just said he was mental. You're talking about the kind of guys who'd be involved with fifty thousand pounds' worth of drugs? That kind of operation would have been way out of his league.'

'I'm talking about the kind of guys who know those kinds of guys. You underestimate your dad's reach. His pals are getting on, but they're still connected.'

Jim sat back in his seat. He would phone Paddy, ask him to suggest a new lawyer, someone straight who knew what he was doing. 'My father had as many enemies as he had friends. I can't imagine either side would be interested in helping me and mine.'

'You've a poor opinion of your fellow man.'

'I'm a realist.'

'Then you'll know your choice is simple. Leave your son with his arse hanging out or come to his rescue.'

Jim lowered his voice. 'Just to be clear, you're advising me to break the law?'

The lawyer dusted a speck of icing from his jumper. 'It's Saturday afternoon. I'm off the clock. This is a chat between old school friends. We're talking hypothetically, remember? I'm not advising you to do anything.'

The thought of hiring a new lawyer receded. Jim took another sip of water. 'What would coming to the rescue involve?'

Cranston took a last swig of his coffee, scrunched up the food wrappers and stood up. 'Let's get out of here.'

Hi-vis vests littered the backseat of Cranston's BMW. He saw Jim looking at them. 'The footie squad helped with security for the Gala Day.'

'I thought security contracts belonged to the big boys.'

Cranston fastened his seatbelt and turned on the car engine. 'We're talking about a wee gala, not the mean streets of Prohibition Chicago. The team get a lot of support from the community – donations for strips and the like. This is a way of paying some of it back.'

'What goes around comes around?'

'That's a fact. An unfortunate fact in the case of your boy.' Cranston swung the BMW slowly out of the car park, edging around a woman and pushchair. 'Eliot didn't want to keep the drugs in his flat. It's about the only sensible decision he made.' He glanced at Jim. 'Tell me, did you read him bedside stories when he was a tot?'

Jim noticed Cranston had left the world of the hypothetical behind. 'What's that got to do with anything?'

'I'm curious, that's all. I wondered if you read him adventure stories for boys, *Treasure Island* by any chance?'

Maggie had taken it for granted that they would read to the children at bedtime. The concept had been alien to Jim, something from schmaltzy movies he doubted real people ever did. But he had come to relish the closeness and cosy conspiracy that reading aloud to Eliot and Sasha generated. They were good memories, too good to be soiled by contact with this man.

'Get to the point, Eddie.'

Silence sat between them for a moment. Cranston changed lanes and drove towards the city centre. 'Where are you parked?'

'Nowhere. I took a cab.'

'I'll give you a lift home.'

'I'm meeting Maggie in the Scandi Kitchen. It's in King Street.'

Cranston doffed an imaginary chauffeur cap. 'No problem.'

Jim said, 'I'll get a cab.'

'I told you, it's no problem.'

Up ahead traffic lights turned to red. The car slowed to a halt. Saturday afternoon shoppers, laden with bags, crossed the road. A group of young boys ran through the crowd, shoving each other, bent double with laughter. Jim could not imagine ever being light-hearted again.

Cranston's car had the sweet vanilla and watermelon scent of a recent valet. Jim felt his nausea return. 'Why did you ask me about *Treasure Island*?'

The lights switched to green. Cranston drove on. 'I'm about to cross a line. Can I trust you?'

'It depends on what the line is.'

'The one that says I should hand over any incriminating information I have about my client to the police.'

'You barely know Eliot. Even if you did, he's a wee toerag who deserves whatever's coming to him. Why risk your reputation?'

The set of Cranston's mouth was grim. 'I've a debt or two of my own I'd like to clear. You have friends who feel they owe it to your dad's memory to give you a break. If I broker it, they'll wipe my balance sheet clean.'

There was no point enquiring what the lawyer's debts consisted of. Jim asked, 'Would one of these mysterious friends be Peter Henders, the builder?'

Cranston looked surprised. 'Not to my knowledge.'

The car reached the top of one of the city's hills and Jim saw the shopping district laid out before him, drifts of people shaping and reshaping like a human murmuration. In the distance the university tower stood silhouetted against the horizon, small enough to crush between his fingers. The skyline had barely altered over the past hundred years. The new

Learning and Teaching Hub could be a bold intervention. It occurred to Jim that they should name it after Lulach. The thought of the university principal and his desire for Jim to succeed him strengthened his resolve.

'Thank these friends for me and reassure them that having a son in jail won't be an obstacle to my success. What would be an obstacle is getting involved with criminals.'

Cranston said, 'You're a hard man to do a favour for.'

'I'm choosy about the company I keep. You should be too if you want to continue practising.'

'You're being offered breathing space to fix things. If I were you, I'd take it. You told me yourself, Eliot's in big trouble.'

They were nearing the restaurant. Jim took his phone from his pocket and texted Maggie: *Nearly there x*. 'I also told you I want him on a vulnerable prisoner wing.'

Cranston slowed the BMW, looking for somewhere to park. 'It's done. I got him moved last night. But VP status guarantees nothing. The people he owes can't afford to lose face. They're slick as water. Sooner or later, they'll reach him.'

Jim knew Cranston was right. Face was everything to hard men like his father. They would lose their liberty and all hopes of remission before risking a dent in their reputation. 'So what do you recommend?'

Cranston spotted a parking space and deftly manoeuvred the car into it. He switched off the engine and turned to look at Jim. 'You already said you'd pay the cash debt.'

'Yes.'

'They're demanding twenty per cent interest on top of that, non-negotiable.'

'Tell them they can get to fuck. I'll pay back what my son owes, but I'm not paying protection money. Once we start,

it won't stop until they've sucked us dry.' Jim unclipped his
seatbelt and put a hand on the car door, ready to go.

Cranston caught his sleeve. 'There's more.'

Jim leaned back in his seat. 'I haven't forgotten the lay-on.
As far as I'm concerned, they can recover the drugs from
wherever Eliot hid them. I'm having nothing to do with that.'
A sudden, panicked thought struck him. 'He didn't sell them
and spend the money?'

Cranston shook his head. 'There aren't many positive
aspects to this case, but that's one of them. Eliot didn't touch
the stuff. He'd barely taken delivery before things went tits-
up. They're safely hidden, for now.'

'Thank fuck for that.' The strain was showing. The crude
language Jim had schooled himself not to use creeping back.
'I'll get the cash first thing tomorrow and give it to you. I
take it you're willing to act as go-between?'

Cranston held up a hand. 'There's more you need to know.
Eliot wrapped the stuff in plastic and buried them in Galloway
Forest. There's a map. He passed it to me when I visited him
in the court cells, just after he'd been sentenced.'

'Jesus Christ.'

Cranston made a face. 'I know. That's why I asked about
Treasure Island.'

Jim took a deep breath, steadying himself as if he was
about to give an important lecture. 'I don't need to know
the details. I'll give you the cash Eliot owes. You can pass
the map to whoever you wish.'

The lawyer shook his head. 'It's not that easy. These guys
aren't jolly pirates looking for a treasure trove. They don't
give a toss about the map. They don't need the hassle, not
to mention the risk. They just want what they're owed and
an extra bung on top to save them looking like soft touches.'

Jim's headache was full-blown now. It gouged behind his eyes. 'What about these so-called friends of my father's? These old protectors who're so keen to see me do well?'

'Without them your son would already be in the hospital – or the morgue. A couple of disposable wee nyaffs would have been given his map, a pair of spades and shown an after-treatment photo of Eliot as a warning of what happens to light-fingered boys who don't pay their debts. Then they'd be sent to Galloway to dig. Your father's friends are buying you time to get the drugs yourself and deliver them to their rightful owner. You should be grateful. It might not feel like it, but they're doing you a big favour.'

'You're having me on.'

'I wish I was.'

Jim gripped the door handle. 'There's no way I'm going to Galloway Forest on a midnight dig like some fucking resurrection man. I'll pay back the money Eliot owes on condition it can't be traced back to me. That's as far as I'm prepared to go.'

This time, Cranston made no move to stop him leaving. 'You're making a mistake.'

'Thanks for the lift.' Jim opened the door and stepped onto the pavement. He leaned into the car. 'I'll call you later, when I have the money.'

Cranston started the engine. 'There's no point. It's an all-or-nothing deal.'

Jim repeated, 'I'll call you.'

He slammed the door and stepped onto the pavement. The BMW drew away. Jim waited for his stomach to settle and then walked towards the restaurant.

Twenty-Two

SUNDAY WAS A nothing day. Jim got up early, dressed in his sweats and breakfasted alone, searching the papers online for mention of Michael's death. There were three articles, each of them short statements of facts. A twenty-three-year-old man, a student at the university, had been found dead. Police did not suspect foul play. The university principal expressed regret at the loss of a promising young student.

Jim made an online donation to the Samaritans, but it felt like an empty gesture. He brewed himself a coffee. Michael was dead. Jim could not fix the unsent Harvard reference, but he could try to atone for it.

The missing Chinese graduate Li Jie had slipped from his list of priorities. Jim took his coffee to the kitchen island and sat with his laptop, contemplating his options. He considered emailing his counterparts in Beijing but did not want to make a clumsy move that might compromise them. Perhaps someone at his own institution could offer insight into the situation.

Jim searched for the Confucius Institute on the university website. He clicked on their homepage and followed the pages that led from it, noting the way the institute threaded through the university's Chinese language offerings. There were forthcoming seminars, a recently presented conference, invitations to apply for Chinese government scholarships and a major funding stream for technological research. He already knew the institute's work went beyond language instruction, but had not realised how far it extended. An impressive selection of cross-disciplinary scholars contributed to their work. He saw Ronald Fergusson's profile among them and felt a vague sense of jealousy that no one had invited him to participate.

The Confucius Institute's homepage stressed its mission to promote understanding between China and the rest of the world. It was not the right place to take questions about a disappeared national.

Jim returned to his main search engine and clicked on a newspaper interview with a defector from the Chinese Communist Party who had settled in Copenhagen. The defector accused Chinese student and scholars' associations of monitoring and controlling student activity. He was scathing, too, about the Confucius Institute, telling the interviewer, 'None of the gifts given by the Chinese Communist Party are free. Students learn conversational Chinese, but conversations about Taiwan, Tiananmen and Tibet are forbidden.' He recounted an anecdote about an official visit by the Chinese premier Xi Jinping to the UK. The premier had appeared at a British Confucius Institute conference where students performed a song called 'Gratitude' to thank him for all that China had done for them. The defector concluded his story: 'UK Confucius Institute students sang to a dictator.'

The back of Jim's neck tingled, as if some unseen person had stood a fraction too close. He opened a new browser on the Virtual Private Network he sometimes used for research. The defector was working for a Scandinavian democratic think tank. Jim found his email address and sent him a message, saying he had read the interview with interest and asking if they could talk.

He finished his coffee, dumped the dirty cup in the dishwasher and wrote Maggie a note, saying he was going for a run around the reservoir. Instead, he drove to Eliot's flat, where he retrieved the money he had hidden in the fridge. He stashed it in the rarely used safe in their bedroom while Maggie showered.

Jim phoned Cranston at intervals throughout the day. The lawyer did not pick up. Jim called the prison twice, but no one was available to talk to him. Trina's mum delivered Sasha home, late afternoon. Jim had looked forward to his daughter's return, but she was overtired and uncharacteristically grumpy. Only Benji was his usual carefree self.

An email from Malcolm Lulach pinged into Jim's inbox late in the afternoon, requesting he take the principal's place at a meeting with some Saudi visitors the following day and chair the building procurement committee later that same afternoon. Jim swore and rearranged his diary. He drafted a letter to Michael Peterson's parents, full of praise and regret. Anger at himself and at Michael, the bloody, stupid waste of it all, intruded. It was hard to get the tone right, and he set the letter aside to review the next day. Jim worked steadily until five thirty, prepping for the two unexpected meetings, and then helped Maggie and Sasha make homemade pizzas. They ate supper in front of the TV, watching a film they had all seen before. He took Benji for a last walk through the gloaming, thinking again about Michael. Jim wondered what the young man's last moments had been like and wished he had phoned the student in time to halt the vortex of self-doubt that had dragged him under. He checked his email for a message from the Chinese dissident, reviewed his notes again, watched a documentary on YouTube about the detention of minorities in China and went to bed at eleven thirty, full of foreboding.

Twenty-Three

ONE OF THE Saudi visitors was a graduate of the university. His excitement at revisiting the sites of his youth was infectious, and Jim found it easy to enthuse about plans for the new Learning and Teaching Hub. As they strolled through the cloisters and past the quads the Saudi alumnus complimented the lushness of the carefully mown lawns. Jim made the usual joke about Scottish weather. He led the way to the razed site where the new building would soon start to rise, discussing the importance of a lowered carbon footprint, embedded new technology, community engagement and disabled access.

Jim's phone buzzed during coffee in the principal's lodging. Archives had curated a small display of photographs, showing the campus before and after the university's foundation, and he was deep in conversation with the Saudi alumnus about a monochrome image of cows grazing on the lush meadows the university had built over in the 1890s. He turned his phone off, but not before he had seen Eddie Cranston's name flashing on the display.

Next came a meeting of the building procurement committee. They convened in the Dundas Room, a dark, half-panelled office, the opposite of the airy open-plan space he hoped the new teaching hub would be. Jim had not spoken to anyone about his conversation with Lulach, but he sensed a new watchfulness amongst his colleagues. That afternoon's task was to select the winning candidate from a shortlist of three prospective architects. Jim began by reminding the committee of their responsibility to decide the outcome for future educators and students, regardless of their own artistic preferences. Ronald Fergusson snorted, and Jim knew they were in for a long afternoon.

A committee member summarised the results of the staff/ student survey commissioned to help inform their decision or, as Fergusson put it, 'to add an illusory sheen of community to their deliberations'. Coffee, tea and shortbread were delivered, and they discussed the shortlisted firms' proposals, reflecting on the architects' presentations, and the qualities and drawbacks of their designs. When the committee faltered, Jim reminded them of their remit, the budget they had assigned – not all of which was in place – the preferences the staff/student survey had suggested and the different compromises involved in each proposal.

It was a long meeting made longer by Ronald Fergusson's insistence on the most radical design. Jim had hoped they would reach an accord, but was forced to call two separate votes. Fergusson's preferred team were defeated in the first round. The second vote resulted in the selection of Clover Architecture, a firm whose logo featured a four-leaf clover, suggesting a faith in luck that made Jim uneasy. The decision was a compromise. Clover were nobody's outright favourite. Their design had none of the excitement of the rejected proposals. The new teaching hub would be an anonymous tower block that might belong on any campus in the world.

Fergusson slammed out of the Dundas Room, banging the door behind him. No one followed, but the atmosphere was one of frustration, with the remaining committee members subdued. Jim was left with the feeling that his first job as candidate for principal had been a failure.

He waited until he was back in his office before turning his phone on. Three missed calls from Eddie Cranston and four from Maggie. He called Maggie back. Her phone went straight to voicemail, Cranston's did the same. Jim looked up the number of Cranston's office. The woman who answered sounded wary when Jim told her his name, and would give him no information except that Mr Cranston was in court and she could not predict when he would be available.

It was hard to settle down to work after that. A tirade from Ronald Fergusson about the building procurement committee's decision landed in his inbox. Jim deleted, then retrieved and filed it, in case of future disputes, and worked fitfully for the next hour. Shoals of messages sounded alerts as they arrived, building columns of unread requests and communications. An email from Grace McCann headed 'Li Jie' pinged in his inbox.

Dear Jim

Re recent correspondence regarding Li Jie, I do not consider there is enough information to pursue his case. This is frustrating, but not surprising given the current situation in the People's Republic of China. Should there be further developments I will be happy to resume discussions. In the meantime, unless I hear otherwise, I will consider the case closed.

Kind regards

Grace

Jim moved the email to the scant folder of correspondence pertaining to Li Jie. He was tempted to open and re-read the first message he had received, alerting him to the student's disappearance, but he remembered it by heart.

Li Jie who you met at graduation has vanished. He has been disappeared. Please, Professor Brennan, can you help?

Grace had decided that the answer was no. He feared she was right, but logged into his VPN again and checked for a message from the Chinese defector he had reached out to the previous day. A message waited for him there. A link for an online meeting with a time set for midnight two days hence. He wondered at the significance of the time, set on the cusp of one day and another. Villains and spies favoured the night, but what relevance was the dark in the dark of the web? He clicked on the invitation, accepting the meeting, just as his mobile phone buzzed awake.

Maggie's voice was rough with tears. 'Eliot's in Intensive Care in the Royal. I'm there, but they won't let me see him.'

Jim felt as if someone had scooped his heart from his chest. He knew the answer, but asked, 'What happened?'

Maggie gulped for air. 'Someone hurt him. They don't know who.'

He found it hard to catch his own words. 'Take a deep breath, love. I'm coming over right now. Did the doctors tell you anything?'

'He was stabbed, more than twenty times, Jim, all over his body. They don't know if he's going to make it.'

Jim already had his jacket on, car keys in his hand. He

left his desk as it was, not bothering to turn off his computer, and ran into the corridor.

Ronald Fergusson was walking towards him. 'Jim, I have to protest at the way this morning's meeting was conducted . . .'

Jim kept going, running towards the exit. He was aware of the physics professor shouting something at him. The words were nothing but noises bouncing off the brick walls.

Twenty-Four

THE ATMOSPHERE IN Intensive Care was reminiscent of finals exams. A thrum of tension, despair and determination. Jim jogged down the central corridor, looking for someone to tell him where his son was. The only medics he glimpsed were busy tending to patients in the side wards that branched off the hallway. Even in his desperation he knew not to interrupt them. He turned a corner, saw a nurses' station and, beyond it, his wife still dressed in the navy suit and pussy-bow blouse she had worn to work that morning.

Maggie was arguing in urgent whispers with a policeman stationed at a ward door. Jim touched her arm. 'What's going on?'

'He won't let me in.'

The policeman looked uncomfortable. 'It's not up to me. Technically your son's still in prison. You wouldn't be allowed to see him there without a visiting order and you're not allowed to see him here.'

Jim said, 'We're Eliot's parents. You can search us, take our phones away, whatever it is you need to do, but we're going to visit him, whether you allow us to or not.'

A couple of medics were examining documents at the nurses' station. Jim's voice must have carried because they looked towards him. One of them, a short woman in mint-green scrubs, trotted to the door of Eliot's room.

'What's going on?'

Maggie's eyes were sheened with unshed tears. 'He says we're not allowed to see our son.'

The woman's name badge identified her as Dr Darmawan. She addressed the policeman. 'Why not?'

'Strictly speaking he's still in prison. They don't have authorisation. I can get in touch with the station but–'

Maggie interrupted, 'And we can get in touch with our lawyer.'

Dr Darmawan was a foot shorter than the policeman, but she held his gaze in hers. 'This young man is in no position to get up to any mischief. It would be best for all concerned if you allow his parents to sit with him.'

'I'm instructed–'

Dr Darmawan cut the policeman's objections short. 'This is not a prison. It's a hospital, and I am in charge of this ward. My instructions hold sway here.' Her face was stern, but she added more gently, 'And don't worry, I'll take full responsibility.'

The policeman hesitated and then stepped to one side. 'I'll need to stay by the door.'

'You do what you have to.' Dr Darmawan nodded at Maggie and Jim. 'Come through.'

The room was windowless, just big enough for the single hospital bed and the medical equipment that crowded around it. Eliot lay at its centre, cabled in tubes that connected his body to drips and monitoring devices. The machines beeped and burbled. A white cotton sheet covered him from waist to toe. It was folded neatly at the top, as if to make the task of covering his face easier when the time came. Eliot's muscled bulk looked deflated. Gauzed bandages shielded the wounds on his body. There were bandages on his arms too, and another on his left cheek. The tattoos that decorated his chest and neck looked pagan in contrast with the hi-tech equipment keeping him alive.

Maggie made a strange, keening noise and went to his side. Jim turned away, unable to look.

Dr Darmawan followed them into the room, carrying two plastic chairs. 'Take a seat.' She slid a file from a folder attached to the end of Eliot's bed and scanned its contents. Her voice was brisk. 'Your son is extremely poorly. He's fortunate in that none of his major organs – by that I mean the heart, lungs, kidneys and liver – were perforated, but his injuries are multiple. They include a punctured spleen. Eliot underwent surgery on admission. He's currently in a medically induced coma to allow him the best chance of recovery.'

Jim ignored the chair Dr Darmawan had offered him. He forced himself to look at his son. Maggie was sitting by the side of the bed, her hand hovering near Eliot's face, desperate to touch him but scared of causing more harm.

Jim asked, 'What are his chances?'

The doctor's eyes had dark shadows beneath them that told of too little sleep. 'At this stage we can't be certain, but be assured, we give all patients the same high level of care, regardless of their circumstances. Your son is a physically robust young man in otherwise good health, but his condition is serious. The next twenty-four hours will be critical.'

Maggie looked up at Jim, strong yet destroyed, like a vengeful woman from a Greek tragedy or some goddess of war. 'I told you prison was no place for our son.'

Jim went to her side. 'I know you did, love. And I agreed with you, but it was out of our control.' He tried to take her hand.

'You thought he deserved it,' she said, flinching away from his grasp.

Dr Darmawan replaced Eliot's notes in the folder at the end of his bed. 'I'll speak to the charge nurse and make sure that no one prevents you from sitting with your son while he's sedated.'

Jim stared at Eliot's face. His skin was bruised, features distorted by swelling. If it had not been for the stupid tattooed skull, still grinning on his neck, Jim might have asked the doctor if she was sure this was his boy. Instead, he asked, 'And once he wakes up?'

'The prison authorities will insist you leave.'

Maggie said, 'She thinks he's going to die. That's why she's letting us be with him.'

The doctor glanced at her watch. 'I've been honest with you. I don't know if your son will pull through or not. My instinct is that if he survives the next twenty-four hours, he will make some kind of recovery. I could be wrong, but I'm hopeful. You should be too.'

Maggie grimaced. 'It makes no difference whether we're hopeful or not.'

Dr Darmawan squatted by Maggie's chair. Her voice was gentle. 'Your son is under deep sedation, but he may be able to hear you. Let him hear some hope in your voice. It could make a difference.' She looked from Maggie to Jim as if trying to make her mind up about something. 'How long have you been married?'

It was Jim who answered her. 'Twenty-eight years come November.'

The doctor nodded. 'It's none of my business, but you've both clearly got a lot on your plate, so please forgive me for offering you some advice. This is no time to fall apart. You're going to need all the support you can get. That includes the support of each other.' Her pager beeped. 'Excuse me, I have to go.'

Dr Darmawan darted from the room before Jim could thank her.

Maggie looked at him. 'I'd like to kill whoever did this.'

Jim squeezed her shoulder. This time she did not pull away. 'I promise you, I'll find them.'

Maggie whispered, so Eliot would not overhear her words from whatever dreamscape he was floating through. 'Our son could die tonight. He needs both of us. I need you. We both need to be here.'

Jim sat on the chair next to her. 'Don't worry, I'm not intending to murder anyone.'

Maggie nodded, calmer now. 'I'll phone Trina's mum and ask if she can have Sasha overnight so we can both stay here.'

Jim leaned in and kissed her. He lowered his voice. 'Eliot's strong. He'll pull through, but whoever did this did it with the intention of killing him. I'm going to have a word in a few ears and make sure they're told they've gone far enough.'

Maggie raised a hand, indicating the stark room, their son broken and unconscious in the bed. 'Is this not enough for you? Why are you determined to make things worse? What would happen to Sasha if her father and brother both ended up in jail? Or dead? You're an academic, not a thug, Jim. Don't forget it.'

Jim touched the tips of his son's fingers with his own fingertips. 'I'm my father's son, Mags, but with more brains and more connections. Don't worry about me, I know what I'm doing.'

He tried to kiss her again, but she turned away.

'You don't know what you're doing, and neither do I. I wonder if we ever did.'

Twenty-Five

EDDIE CRANSTON'S MOBILE went straight to voicemail. The woman who answered his office phone claimed to have no knowledge of his whereabouts. Jim strode through A&E, out of the building, past ambulances waiting on accidents that were yet to happen. The hospital was only a few years old, a monolithic compound of white cubes and rectangles located on the edge of the green belt that marked the outskirts of the city. Jim had gone hillwalking nearby when he was younger and remembered the village that had lent its name to the hospital. It had been a quiet place, an offshoot of the big estate it used to serve. Whatever dramas the village had experienced, the births, deaths, illnesses and accidents of rural life, were multiplied a million times within the few square miles that now composed the hospital grounds.

Peter Henders' business card was still in his wallet. Jim stabbed the number into his mobile phone as he walked towards the visitor car park.

Henders sounded suspicious. 'Hello?'

Jim did not bother with niceties. 'My son Eliot's in hospital with multiple stab wounds. There's no guarantee that he'll make it.'

There was a pause on the line. 'I'm sorry to hear that. I'm assuming you're phoning because I told you I had some connections within the prison.'

'I'm phoning because you arranged a late-night meeting with me during which you offered to protect my son.'

'I've got someone with me.' Henders said something indistinct to whoever else was in the room. There was a short, muffled exchange, and then Henders' voice was back in Jim's ear. 'Okay, we're on our own now. You're overstating things. I said I could possibly put a word in for him via some of the ex-offenders we support.'

Jim reached the pay machines at the edge of the car park. He fumbled through his pockets, found the electronic parking ticket, fed it into the slot and touched his cash card to the screen. The machine let out a beep and issued him with a receipt.

'I've a good memory. You offered to protect Eliot in return for my friendship, by which I understood you to mean my influence.'

'Memory's subjective, but I do recall that you rejected my offer.'

Jim stopped at the edge of the sea of parked cars, unsure of where he had abandoned the Audi. 'Is that why Eliot was attacked?'

Henders' voice was firm. 'Don't be ridiculous. I heard of your son's arrest and feared something like this might happen. A middle-class kid, out of his depth in prison, is always going to be vulnerable. I was trying to help.'

'Do you recall the reason I turned your help down?'

'You not-so-politely suggested I was touting for favours, an accusation I categorically refute. I hear you went for Clover Architecture, a safe pair of hands. We're in the process of entering a fair and considered tender for the job of constructing their design.'

Jim spat, 'I bet you are.'

Henders' voice was patient. 'Like I said, we're a respected construction company with a good track record. I don't need to manipulate proceedings to win any contract. I hope your son makes a good recovery and that this misunderstanding won't affect whatever working relationship we might have in the future.'

Jim took his car key from his pocket and started to pace the boundary of the car park, pressing the door release, hoping to hear the electronic chirp that would tell him he had found the Audi. He was on the verge of telling Henders that he would do everything in his power to block his tender, but self-preservation held him back.

'I need to know who harmed my son.'

'That's not information I can give you.'

'But you can find out?'

'So you can go looking for revenge? I wouldn't want the consequences on my conscience. Take care of your boy, professor. Leave the rest to the authorities. I'm going to hang up now. I'll forget this telephone call ever happened.'

The line went dead. Jim felt an urge to smash his phone against the tarmac and grind it into nothing with his feet.

A couple pushing a baby in a new pram passed him. They had a shell-shocked proud-terrified look that reminded him of the day he and Maggie had taken their newborn son home from hospital. There was a bench nearby. Jim sat on it. The longing to walk back to the hospital room where Maggie watched over Eliot was almost overpowering, but he had work to do. The people who had come close to killing his boy would not give up and neither would he. He got to his feet and pressed the button on the key fob again. Midway down a row of parked cars the Audi flashed its headlights. He was ready to go.

Twenty-Six

JIM PARKED OUTSIDE the tenement where he had lived with his father until the age of seventeen, when his first student grant enabled him to rent a bedsit near the university. Big Jim Brennan had been a free-with-his-fists bastard whose philosophy of life could be boiled down to 'trust nae cunt', but Jim had not needed Peter Henders to tell him that his father had been proud of him.

Big Jim had mocked his mania for studying. Reading a book was tantamount to coming out as gay. Putting effort into writing an essay was the act of a class traitor. When he entered his teens, Jim began to live between school and the local lending library, only coming home to sleep. He was nervous of taking library books back to the flat, fearful his father would damage them during one of his tantrums.

These were well-worn memories of his younger life, building blocks of the resilience that had built his success. But now, sitting outside their old home, he remembered an evening, not long before he left for university, when his father had returned home with a carrier bag tightly wrapped around a familiar shape.

Jim had been lying on his bed reading a paperback he had bought from Bobby's Book Exchange, when his father pushed open the door and thrust the makeshift parcel at him. 'I got these from a boy in the Fusilier.'

Big Jim had left the room, not bothering to see what Jim made of his gift. Inside the bag was a bundle of long out-of-date schoolbooks, mass-produced primers from the early 1900s. They were too ubiquitous to be valuable, too old to be of practical use. Jim had realised then that, to his father, all books were the same, and now, Jim wondered if his father had been able to read at all.

He had never acknowledged the gift. The books had sat unread in the corner of his bedroom, and he left them behind when he moved out. He had tried to leave his father behind too. But he still heard Big Jim's voice in his head, knew how he would react in any crisis. His father had ghosted, unwelcome, through his life.

Big Jim had been a drunken hardman, but he had done what he could to prepare his son for the harshness of life. And once, when he knew Jim was moving away, to a land of letters where he would be unable to travel, he had reached out with a clumsy gift.

Jim started up the Audi. The reason he always knew how his father would react was that he had been a man of one note – anger. But looking at the flat had reminded him of other things: the cooked breakfasts his father occasionally made for them both, late on Sunday mornings, his sense of humour, harsh but scabrously funny. And for all his violent tendencies, when he was sober Big Jim had negotiated the riven territory of their district with brutal diplomacy. He would not have allowed things to get to this pass.

Jim had been thinking of how his father would act were he in his position, but perhaps he would be better served to imagine Big Jim as his opponent, the man demanding return of the lay-on and reparations from Eliot. Would the beating the boy had taken be considered some form of payment or would it up the stakes? Jim drove through his old district towards Eddie Cranston's office.

The place was locked, but the shutters were up; someone was inside. Jim was about to bang on the door when a face appeared behind the glass. It stared at him for a moment and then unlocked and opened the door. Jim recognised the youth who had driven him home on the night he collapsed. He searched his memory for the boy's name.

'Hi, Marky. Is he here?'

The boy ushered him inside. 'Eddie's in the back. He said you'd be by.'

The front office was utilitarian: a dingy waiting room-cum-reception, decorated in shades of brown and well-stocked with legal aid leaflets. There was no sign of the woman Jim had spoken to on the telephone, but a grey cardigan hung over the back of the desk chair and a pair of women's slippers sat abandoned beneath it.

Marky nodded towards the door to the inner office. 'Eddie's through there. He's not himself. To be honest, I'm a wee bit worried about him.'

Jim gave the boy's shoulder a reassuring squeeze. 'I'll go through and have a word.'

The boy smiled. 'Thanks, prof. Eddie's line of work isn't easy. He has to deal with the dregs of society – and that's only the judges.'

Jim recognised one of Cranston's jokes. He patted Marky on the back and went through to the inner office.

The blinds were drawn. The lawyer sat behind his desk, a dark silhouette outlined in the glow of his computer screen. Jim's anger was replaced by a feeling of deadness, as if his emotions had been Novocained. He pulled out the visitor chair and sat down.

'I've been trying to get in touch with you.'

'I know. I was otherwise detained.'

Cranston switched on the desk light. There was a nasty bruise on his left cheekbone and bags under his eyes that rivalled Dr Darmawan's. The easy affability that had seemed the mark of the lawyer had disappeared. He looked rumpled, his natty suit in need of a dry clean.

Jim asked, 'What happened to your face?'

'Would you believe me if I said I walked into a door?'

A mildewed fish tank burbled between the law books on a shelf behind Cranston's desk. Bubbles rose from an old-fashioned diver trapped on the tank's floor. A melancholic fish swam the length of the tank and back, marking time.

Jim said, 'Eliot's in hospital.'

'I heard.'

'He's in a bad way. The doctors say he might not make it.'

Cranston's expression darkened. 'I don't think that was the intended outcome.'

Jim leaned forward. 'What do you know about intended outcomes?'

Cranston touched his bruised face. 'My impression is that Eliot's beating was intended as a punishment. A warning to pay what he owes, not an execution.'

They sat in silence for a moment. The tank gurgled. Jim stared at the fish swimming left to right, right to left, left to right: a warning to bad boys to mend their ways or end up in jail.

'I picked up the money. If you'd collected it from me, like we arranged—'

'We didn't *arrange* anything. I told you there was no point returning what was owed without the extra on top, plus the other goods Eliot had put out of the way for safety.'

Jim noticed Cranston's guarded language. He took a notebook and pen from his pocket and scribbled, *Is this place bugged?*

Cranston shrugged. He took the pen from Jim and wrote, *Can't be too careful.*

Jim said, 'They almost killed him. They might yet have killed him.'

Cranston shook his head. 'How's Maggie?'

'How do you think?'

Cranston took the pen and paper from Jim. *You need to get the money & drugs & deliver them or . . .* He drew a finger across his throat. He said, 'Maybe there's a nice university in New Zealand you can transfer to, take the family. But it's a connected world. I recommend paying outstanding debts before you go.'

Jim scribbled, *I'll go to the police.*

Outside, a police siren sounded as if to underline the threat. They sat in silence until it passed.

Cranston gave a small smile, acknowledging the irony of the interruption. 'The authorities haven't exactly served your boy well so far. He was in the VP wing when this happened. I'm not sure I'd recommend putting his future in their hands.'

Jim indicated Cranston's bruised face. 'That looks nasty.'

'I've had worse on the rugby field.'

'Is it connected with Eliot's troubles?'

'Like I told you, I've got my own balance sheet to clear.'

'And Eliot paying back what he owes would clear it?'

'I've made no secret of that.'

'It's a conflict of interest. Your advice isn't exactly impartial.'

'Go to someone impartial then.'

Jim had thought again about contacting Paddy and asking him to recommend another lawyer, someone uncompromised by whatever mess Cranston had got himself into. But an impartial lawyer, removed from the old district and its ways, might not have the same raw power to rescue Eliot.

Jim scribbled, *We need to hire someone to do the delivery.*

Cranston took the pad from him and wrote, *It's a fuck of a lot of money.* He said out loud, 'Who could you trust with that kind of responsibility?'

Jim glanced towards the outer office. 'What about one of your youth team?'

Cranston grinned. 'What about one of your students?'

Jim's letter to Michael's parents was tucked inside his jacket pocket. He closed his eyes for a moment. 'It wouldn't be appropriate.'

Cranston said, 'You think I'm a bullshitter – maybe I am – but I'm serious about helping these lads. You consider yourself in loco parentis. So do I.'

Jim closed the notepad and slid it back in his pocket. 'Plus you wouldn't trust them not to walk away with the goods.'

Cranston smiled. 'Isn't that a key part of being in loco parentis? Knowing kids' limitations? Saving them from themselves?'

Eliot was in hospital, Michael in the morgue, Li Jie fuck knows where – a torture cell, work camp or perhaps his grave.

Jim took a deep breath. 'Do you have the map?'

Cranston nodded and pointed to a wall safe.

'We'll collect the goods together.'

Cranston laughed. He let out a groan and his hand went to his ribs. 'That's not the deal.'

Jim had been in enough meetings to know when he had the upper hand. 'There is no deal. I don't know how big your debt is or where it stems from, but you're clearly in trouble, Eddie. You need this package returned as much as I do, and I've no intention of going there on my own.'

'You'd let your son die?'

'You're talking as if I've only got one option, but like I said, I can still go to the police.'

'That would be a mistake.'

Jim leaned back in his chair. 'Last time you told me I was making a mistake, I ignored you. I'm willing to take your advice now, on condition you come too.'

Silence settled again between them. Outside, another siren pierced the air. Some men walked by, talking in deep voices, their words indistinct. Cranston picked up the telephone receiver and punched four digits into its keypad. Ringing sounded in the outer office. It stopped, and Cranston said, 'Marky, has your dad got any off-road vehicles I could have a borrow of for tonight, on the QT?' Jim could not hear the boy's reply, but Cranston nodded. 'Sounds perfect. No, you're a good lad to offer, but I can drive myself. Can you bring it round the back?' Marky must have agreed because Cranston said, 'Cheers, son.' And hung up the phone. Cranston rattled the keys of his computer keyboard and smiled at what he saw on the screen.

He looked at Jim. 'We're in luck. It's a full moon tonight.'

Twenty-Seven

JIM HAD NOT thought that he would sleep, but soon after they left the city he slid into dreamless dark. When he woke there was more dark beyond the window. He rubbed his eyes. 'I thought you said it was a full moon.'

Cranston stared ahead at the road. 'We're in the forest.'

Jim looked out of the passenger window and saw trees, murky shadows on shadows, melting into blackness.

Cranston pulled Eliot's map from his pocket and shoved it at Jim. 'We're going to need this soon. We're looking out for the next car park. It gets tricky after that.'

They had each removed the SIM cards from their mobile phones before getting into the Land Cruiser Marky had borrowed from his dad's showroom. The boy had been relaxed about lending the car to them, asking only that they get it back before dawn, washed and waxed and with a full tank of petrol. His trust had shamed Jim, but Cranston had taken it in his stride.

Jim glanced at his watch. It was 2 a.m. They had added time to their journey by diverting to his house to collect the banknotes from the safe. It did not feel wise to travel into the countryside with his pockets bulging with money, but none of what they were doing was wise.

He opened the torch on his mobile and looked at Eliot's map. He saw again why Cranston had referred to *Treasure Island*. Eliot had drawn the map by hand. He had taken time over the task. Roads snaked and branched through a forest of stylised trees. An extra-large tree stood in the centre of the forest, helpfully labelled *Big Tree* and marked with a cross. Eliot had drawn a compass in the top left-hand corner of the map but had neglected to include a scale.

Jim folded the map away. 'Did Eliot say how far it was?'

'He said it wasn't far, but who knows what that means when you're twenty-three.'

'He was never keen on walking, even when he was a child. If he said it isn't far, it won't be.'

A parking sign appeared up ahead. Cranston slowed the Land Cruiser. 'This looks like it.' He turned off the road into a wooded lane that opened out into a parking area. Two cars were already stationed there. He braked.

Jim looked at Cranston. 'Recognise either of these?'

'Don't think so. But that doesn't mean much. What do you want to do?'

The woodland was densely packed, the path into the forest too narrow for the Land Cruiser to negotiate.

'Presumably anyone who was after the drugs wouldn't park in full view.'

'I make a good living out of the stupidity of criminals. I wouldn't assume anything.'

'Find somewhere else. We'll walk back.'

Cranston drove back to the road. They parked on a verge beneath low-hanging branches and cut through the trees on foot until they reached the edge of the parking area. Jim carried the snow shovel Cranston had taken from his own car.

The two vehicles had been joined by a third. Jim whispered, 'I don't like it.'

'Maybe they're stargazers. This is a designated Dark Sky Park. People come here to look at the firmament.'

Jim glanced upwards. The sky beyond the canopies of leaves was black, the full moon and stars obscured by clouds. 'They chose a crap night for it.'

They crept through the trees alongside the footpath, trying to remain hidden from whoever else was in the forest. Jim led the way, his senses alive. The uneven ground slowed their progress, and the fallen leaves and twigs that coated the forest floor meant every footstep was broadcast by cracks and rustles. After a short while they rejoined the trail. The clouds broke and moonlight lit their way, casting long moon shadows on the path before them. Jim saw their silhouettes, two men in suits, one carrying a spade, and thought at first how ridiculous they looked, walking through the forest in the dead of night. Then, how sinister. He tried to think of a legitimate excuse to use if they were discovered, but the shovel marked them out as men up to no good.

They reached a fork in the path. Jim peered at the map and pointed left. At first he had thought he and Cranston were the noisiest creatures in the forest, but the night was alive with sounds. The treetops capered in response to the lightest breeze, birds screeched and hooted. He thought of Maggie, still in her dark suit, as if already dressed for a funeral, sitting in the white room, watching over their son.

He could not inhabit the possibility that Eliot was dead or dying. His son was made of the same stuff as his grandfather. His wounds would strengthen him.

A bird shrieked, announcing their presence. Cranston stumbled. 'For fuck's sake. How much further?'

'Not far, assuming Eliot kept to scale.'

Jim knew that they would be easy to track, but he doubted that whoever had parked the other cars would be much quieter. The thought had barely crossed his mind when he heard a sound out of sync with the trembling trees, the calls and hoots of the birds. He and Cranston froze. The cry was alive with hurt. It was followed by a deeper, grunting echo, a chorus to the pain.

Cranston put a finger to his lips and crept towards the sound. Jim whispered, 'What are you doing?', but Cranston ignored him. Jim remained where he was, alone amongst the trees, heart pounding. The cry with its grunting chorus sounded again. Now he recognised what it was.

He tiptoed in the direction Cranston had taken and caught sight of him ahead. Jim upped his pace and hissed, 'Eddie.' Cranston turned, his expression half-shocked, half-amused. Jim looked beyond him into a small glade equipped with picnic tables where families on days out could pause for lunch.

There were four or five people in a state of undress. He got a fleeting impression of dimpled white flesh, sagging bellies and naked buttocks. He turned away. A man shouted, 'Don't be shy', and someone else laughed. Jim quickened his pace and retraced his steps. He could hear Cranston lumbering behind him. They did not utter a word until they reached the next turn in the path.

Cranston whispered, 'I guess we don't have to worry about them.'

Jim had an urge to punch the lawyer. He took a deep breath and let it pass. He held the map close to his eyes. 'Left, then left again. Let's hope we know this big tree when we see it.'

The big tree turned out to be a massive Scots pine whose roots fanned outwards across the surface of the soil like arteries. They would stretch downwards too, Jim realised, deep into the earth, forging soundless caverns. He imagined slipping down beneath them into the underworld. Perhaps he would find someone there he could bargain with for Eliot's life.

Cranston was out of breath. He lowered himself onto a toppled log and looked up at the tree. 'Jesus, that's one big fucker. He might have told us which side he buried it on.'

Jim leaned the snow shovel against the trunk. The moon had retreated behind the clouds again. He would have liked to have used the torch app on his phone but did not want to alert the doggers' curiosity. He crouched down, hoping his son had left some kind of marker. The trees gusted above him. It started to spot with rain.

Cranston was holding his side, pressing experimentally at his ribs. 'Aw fuck, rain, that's all we need.'

Jim got down on his hands and knees. Damp seeped through the fabric of his suit. He ran his hands around the tree roots. A rich, loamy aroma emerged as rain pattered through the treetops and onto the leaves that coated the forest floor. Jim's hand touched a large boulder. He brushed dead leaves from its surface and lifted the stone. It was too dark to see them, but he knew woodlice and other bugs would be busying themselves, crawling away from the sudden exposure.

Cranston said, 'Anything?'

Jim dug at the loose soil with his bare hands. 'Maybe.'

There was no need for the shovel; the earth was soft and easily shifted. Well tilled by worms. A vision of his boy, his body invaded by medical apparatus, seized Jim, and he dug harder. The rain grew heavier. Earth gritted his nails. The soil grew more compacted as he dug deeper, and he wondered if he would have to use the shovel after all. His hand touched something soft. He recoiled. When he reached out again, it was still there. He forced the mud from around its sides.

'What have you found?'

Jim was so absorbed in his task Cranston's voice came as a surprise.

'I don't know.' It occurred to him that he was vulnerable, hunkered down like this in the not-quite-deserted forest, and he got to his feet. 'It's stuck. Can you give me a hand?'

Cranston stood up, grumbling about his good suit, the rain, the pain in his ribs, but he lowered himself onto the ground, and together they pulled the object free. It was a square parcel bundled in a black plastic bag.

Jim weighed it in his hands. He undid the plastic bag, revealing a block of resin wrapped in layers of clingfilm. 'I guess this is it.'

Cranston looked at him. 'It would be a fuck of a coincidence if it was some other eejit's gear.'

Jim scuffed the earth from his hands. He tried to brush it from the knees of his trousers and the hem of his suit jacket, but the rain, now heavy, had turned the soil to mud.

Cranston turned up the collar of his suit jacket, like a superannuated rocker. 'Let's get a shift on. We're not through yet.'

The leather soles of Jim's brogues slipped and slid through the mud. By the time they got back to the Land Cruiser their clothes were wet through, their hair plastered to their heads. Cranston turned on the heater and set the windscreen wipers to fast. The dashboard clock read 3.30 a.m.

The parcel was too big for the glove compartment, so Jim slipped it beneath his seat. It was a poor hiding place, but the best he could do for now.

Cranston started the engine. He clicked on the headlights and the forest shone alive.

Jim was impatient to replace his SIM and check his phone for messages from Maggie, but knew he had to wait until they reached neutral ground. He fastened his seatbelt.

'This car's going to need a valet. I'll pay for it if you drop me at your office first. I have to collect my car, go home and get changed before I go back to the hospital.'

Cranston turned the steering wheel, gently bumping the Land Cruiser off the verge and onto the road. 'The night's not over yet, professor. I'm not your messenger boy. You've got to finish the job and deliver these to their rightful owner.'

Twenty-Eight

'YOU'VE GOT TO be fucking kidding me.'

Cranston stared straight ahead, guiding the Land Cruiser round the twists and turns in the road.

'What did you expect, Jim? That *I'd* deliver it? He's your son, not mine.'

The car lost purchase on a tight corner. Jim caught the grab handle above the door and braced himself. 'Slow down. The last thing we need is a crash.'

It was pointless protesting. His humiliation was part of the deal. His father would have loved the idea of ordering a man like himself, a university professor no less, to his door.

Cranston took a blister pack of pills from his pocket and passed them to Jim. 'Get two of these out for me.'

Jim glanced at the label and recognised painkillers he had been prescribed when he twisted his knee at five-a-sides. The injury, he used to joke, that had ended his amateur football career. He popped two pills free. 'These are heavy-duty. You should let me drive.'

Cranston dry-swallowed the pills. 'I've a healthy addiction to being in control, especially when things are out of control.'

They were passing through a small village, a cluster of houses cast in darkness and fronted by neat gardens. Jim wondered what it would be like to live in the middle of nowhere, so close to your neighbours your every activity would be marked by them.

'I'm leaving the drugs with you. You can do what you like with them.'

'Sorry, Jim, you can't macho your way out of this.'

'Then we're both fucked.'

'Not just us. Your boy too.'

They swooped out of the village, back onto unlit country roads. The car's headlamps cast their swift light across fields and hedgerows, then abandoned them to the dark. Jim shut his eyes. What would he do if he lost his job?

People bounced back from disgrace. Only that morning he had heard a government minister, who had spent a year in jail, being interviewed on Radio 4. But no university would want a professor of criminology who had been caught up in a drug deal. Prison would give him time to finish his book, he supposed. His thoughts spiralled to Maggie leaving and taking Sasha with her, Eliot in need of medical treatment beyond the means of the NHS, and himself ending up where he had always been fated to be. In some squalid bedsit, living between the pub and the bookies. A man alone. The bitter taste of self-pity sickened him.

'I should have called the police.'

'I told you, it would have been a bad idea. Anyway, it's too late now.'

They were approaching the city. Jim leaned back in his seat, aware of the drugs, toxic beneath his seat, the banknotes a weight in his pocket. 'How did I get lumbered with the worst lawyer in Scotland?'

Cranston cracked a smile. 'Just lucky, I guess.'

A few minutes later, Cranston pulled into a parking bay outside a row of shops. 'We should be all right to check messages here.'

Jim's fingers were still muddy from the dig, his nails encrusted with dirt. He cracked his phone open and fumbled the small square of plastic into its dock. The phone's silly jingle chimed, and the screen glowed awake. He wanted to step from the car, but the street was deserted, and he was wary of calling attention to himself.

Messages crowded his inbox. He ignored them and called Maggie. She picked up on the third ring. 'Where are you?'

'Taking care of things.'

'What do you mean? What kind of things?'

'Things. How's Eliot?'

Cranston gave a harsh intake of breath. Jim glanced at him. He was staring at whatever was on his screen, his expression grim.

It was a measure of Maggie's tiredness that she did not insist Jim tell her what he was up to. 'The nurse said he's stable.'

Unexpected tears pricked Jim's eyes. 'That must be a good thing.'

'Maybe. When will you be back?'

'Soon. You know I'd be there if this wasn't important.'

Maggie's voice held the deathly calm of a woman who had reached the end of her tether. 'Your son's in hospital. He's seriously ill. It's hard to think what could be more important than that.'

'Nothing, except ensuring his safety.'

Maggie sighed. 'You frighten me when you say things like that.'

Jim stared out of the car window at the row of shops. 'I won't be long.'

Maggie's voice was a whisper. 'Please don't take any stupid risks. It won't do Eliot any good if you get into trouble.'

He whispered, 'I love you.' She told him she loved him too, and the line went dead.

Cranston passed Jim his phone. 'I told you they're slick like water.'

A photo of Maggie sitting by Eliot's bed was on the screen. The photo was timestamped, showing it had been taken less than ten minutes ago. The message beneath the photo read: *Life is short. Time to get a wiggle on* ☺.

Jim felt murder in his veins. He handed the phone back to Cranston and took the SIM from his own mobile. 'Let's go.'

Twenty-Nine

JIM WAS NOT sure where he had expected them to end up, but it was not the anonymous settlement of white apartment blocks by the quayside. He could remember when the land had been reclaimed, almost ten years ago. The goods sheds and industrial buildings that had lined the strip since before he was a boy had been demolished, and billboards depicting the delights of riverside living had sprung up on the cleared scrubland.

Jim had thought more than once that he would like to live there when the kids were grown. He could imagine himself stepping onto the balcony in the crisp, early morning, cradling a cup of coffee in his hands, watching the river flow by. Maggie was sceptical.

Maggie had been right. The posters with their images of blue skies, shapely waterskiers and sea planes had lied. The river proved a barrier, cutting the apartments off from the centre of the city. Promised infrastructure failed to emerge.

Pedestrians trudged via motorway bridges and rape tunnels. The flats were cheaply made. Corners had been cut. People spoke darkly of firetraps, flammable cladding and tragedies waiting to happen. Prices dropped, and investors went bust or scrabbled to find whatever tenants they could. Multiple occupancies, Airbnbs, pop-up brothels and party flats took the place of the slim-smart executives pictured in the developer's schedules. It was rumoured that enterprising asylum seekers had opened an unofficial takeaway restaurant in one of the penthouses, travelling up and down in lifts to deliver their orders.

Cranston drove slowly into the development. It was still dark, but the sky was beginning to lighten in the east. The moon emerged full-faced from behind the clouds. They were too far from the river to see its reflection except as a glimmer on the water. The parking bays outside the apartment blocks were occupied by neatly parked cars. There were no outdoor drinkers hunkered around burning campfires, no billowing litter or rough sleepers in nylon tents. But as they drove between the high-rises, Jim began to notice a dissonance. Gang tags defaced the walls. The clean-edged balconies he had imagined surveying the world from were cluttered with bikes and kids' toys. Dingy washing, left out in the rain, sagged from some of them.

Cranston noticed it too. 'Jesus. Remember when this was going to be the place to be?'

The car's interior was stuffy, but Jim's suit was still damp. He scraped at some of the mud that had seeped into the knees of his trousers. 'Maggie always reckoned it was a bad idea.'

'She's a smart woman.'

'If anyone touches her, I'll kill them.'

Cranston slowed the car and peered at another sign. 'I'm sure you will.' He manoeuvred the Land Cruiser into an empty parking bay, not bothering to reassure Jim that no one would harm his wife. 'This is it.'

It was one of the cleaner blocks, barely marked by graffiti. They were parked between a black Jaguar XE and a soft-top Mini.

Jim said, 'Some people are doing okay.'

Cranston nodded. 'And not afraid to show it.'

A thin shape peeled away from the doorway of the apartment block. A boy aged around thirteen, dressed in a red tracksuit, walked across the tarmac towards them. A football scarf was wrapped around his head, its ends knotted beneath his chin, to keep the rain off.

Jim swore under his breath. 'Jesus Christ, this is all we need.'

The boy reached the Land Cruiser and tapped on the driver's side window. Cranston rolled it down. A faint smirr reached into the car. The boy leaned into the open window, bringing a scent of alcohol and tobacco. 'Which one of you is the professor?'

Jim unclipped his seatbelt. 'I am.'

The boy glanced him up and down, giving the impression that he had never seen a professor before and was not impressed by the specimen before him. 'You've to come with me.'

'Where to?'

The boy jerked his head towards the building. 'Up there.'

'Can they not come down here?'

The boy looked at Jim as if he had requested that God and Elvis manifest themselves in the car park. He repeated, 'You've to come with me.'

Jim pulled off his suit jacket. The white shirt that had been pristine, so many hours ago, was spattered with mud. He reached under his seat, pulled out the package he had stowed there and nodded at Cranston. 'Okay, let's go.'

The boy hugged his arms around his body. He hopped from one foot to the other, trying to keep warm. 'Not him, just you.'

Cranston looked relieved. 'I'll valet the Cruiser and make sure it gets back on time.'

Jim slid out of the car, not bothering to say goodbye. The rain had grown heavier. He tucked the parcel under his elbow and draped his jacket over his head, like a child murderer on his way to a Black Maria. He was wet through, and did not care if he got wetter, but wanted to avoid the scrutiny of the CCTV cameras angled above the door to the building.

Cranston said, 'Good luck.'

His words felt like a jinx. The boy led the way across the forecourt, into the building and along a hallway to where silver elevator doors waited. The boy pressed a button marked *Penthouse*.

The intercom hissed. 'Yeah?'

The boy glanced at Jim, as if to verify that what he was about to say was true. 'He's here.'

The doors breathed open. They stepped inside. The doors closed and the lift began its ascent. The boy untied the scarf from around his head and draped it round his neck. His buzz cut was so short it was impossible to tell what colour his hair was. He leaned against the wall and shut his eyes.

Jim said, 'What's your name?'

The boy opened his eyes and looked at him. 'Why'd you want to know?'

'Usually, people introduce themselves to each other. It's polite.'

'Handshakes and that?'

'Sometimes, if you like.'

The boy's face twisted into a grin. 'You a paedo? You grooming me?'

'Don't flatter yourself.'

The harsh lights of the lift revealed the bags beneath the boy's eyes and accentuated the bone-whiteness of his skin.

'Why'd you want to know my name then?' The lift reached its destination and jerked to a halt. The boy's grin died. 'You don't need to know nothing about me.'

The lift doors opened into high-wattage brightness. The space was larger than Jim had anticipated. An open-plan sitting room-cum-kitchen with a cathedral ceiling and mezzanine. Massive plate-glass windows looked onto a view of the car park and the river beyond. A trio of couches, arranged in a horseshoe around a low-slung coffee table, faced the window. One of the couches was occupied by a tired, thin man with a pallid complexion and a three-day shadow. He looked up, unsmiling, as they entered.

'You took your time.'

The boy's voice took on a nasal whine. 'They just got here.'

'Who they?'

'Him and his driver. I sent the other guy away.'

Somewhere music was playing. The sound of a bass beat thudded faintly into the room, switching between slow and frantic. Jim glanced around the space. There were no obvious cameras, but that meant nothing.

'Are you the person who took a photo of my wife and son in the hospital?'

A mess of tobacco, Rizla papers and tin foil littered the coffee table. The man had been rolling a joint when they entered. He ignored Jim's question and returned to his task. 'You brought what's owed?'

The large windows and panoramic view reminded Jim of Henders' office, but the apartment was over-lit and under-furnished. He took a seat opposite the stranger and laid the parcel, still in its muddy wrappings, on the coffee table between them. A Sunday paper sat incongruous beside the drug paraphernalia, open at the news of Michael Peterson's death. Jim knew it was there for his benefit.

The man sprinkled tobacco along the seam of two cigarette papers, lifted a cube of dark resin from the table and warmed a corner of it with the flame of his lighter. The sweet, burnt scent that perfumed the room intensified. He nodded at the parcel. 'That it?'

Jim watched the clever fingers work. 'Yes.'

The man snuffed the flame and crumbled cannabis into the tobacco. He rolled the papers around their cargo, licked the sticky edge, sealed and twisted the end of the joint. He pointed it at the newspaper. 'Not a good week for you, prof.'

He lit the spliff, sucked on it and offered it to Jim, who shook his head. 'Let's get this over with.'

The man took another long pull and then passed the joint to the boy. 'Piss off upstairs with your mates.'

The boy took a drag and made to hand it back. The man batted him away. 'I don't want your cooties.'

'Thanks, J.' The boy backed away and ran up the stairs to the mezzanine floor, still clutching the joint.

J started to make another spliff. 'How's Eliot?'

'Critical.'

He nodded. 'You know he's a stupid cunt, right?' Jim kept his silence, and the man said, 'It was meant to be a slap. A warning to make him pay his debts.'

'They near enough killed him.'

The man shrugged. 'Your boy has a knack of pissing folk off. I'm guessing once they started on him it was hard to stop.' His eyes met Jim's. 'Did you bring the money?'

'I brought what's owed.'

'Meaning?'

'Like you said, your guys went too far. Eliot's in Intensive Care. He could die. The beating cancels out the interest you wanted on top.'

The man sighed and shook his head. He took a mobile phone from his jeans pocket and pressed a number stored on quick dial. Despite the early hour, whoever he was calling picked up straight away.

J stared at Jim, keeping him in his sights. 'Yeah, he's here. He brought the goods with him and the start-out cash, but he's disputing the interest, says his boy paid it back when he took the beating.' There was a pause and then the man smiled. 'Yeah, he's a cold cunt.'

He nodded. 'Okay . . . yep, okay . . . got it.' The call ended without goodbyes. He looked at Jim. 'Write a letter saying you don't blame the boy that stuck the knife in, and they'll let you off with the excess.'

'You've got to be kidding.'

'We're not kidders. Poor wee cunt's had a hard life, he was leaned on, didn't have any choice in the matter, that kind of thing. You're a lefty liberal. I would have thought this'd be right up your street. Or does it not apply when it's your son at the pointy end of the chib?'

Jim reached into his pocket, pulled out the block of cash and set it on the table. 'That's your lot.'

J made no move towards the package. 'It's a small thing, professor. A few lines to the court saying the little shit's a victim of society. You could probably cut and paste it from something you've got on file.'

'Get to fuck.'

J pushed the package back across the table towards Jim. 'Your choice. One of the boys will see you out.'

'Seriously?"

J nodded. 'Seriously.'

Eliot would feel betrayed, and the world would consider him a soft touch, but Jim had no choice. He would write the letter. 'Okay, I'll send a letter when the case goes to trial.'

'Good decision.' J reached for the money and flicked through it with a cashier's expertise that belied the early hour and the dope he had smoked. He met Jim's eyes and nodded. 'Fine.'

Jim almost asked for a receipt, but he knew that was not how things worked. 'Is that it?'

'Unless you want anything?'

'I want my son to be left alone.'

J tapped the block of cash against the table, squaring its edges. 'We've no interest in your son. Tell him to keep his trap shut and his head down. No one'll bother him.'

A sudden vision of Eliot as he had last seen him flashed into Jim's mind: the oxygen mask over his face, the tubes invading his body. 'He's in hospital. He can't breathe by himself, let alone speak.'

J pulled up the front of his T-shirt, revealing a network of scars across his chest and belly. 'Been there, done that.'

Jim lowered his voice, emphasising his words. 'I'll write your letter, but make no mistake, if my son dies, I'll make sure whoever did this to him is caught. I don't just mean the boy who stabbed him, I mean the people who put the knife in his hands and gave him the order.'

J pulled his T-shirt down. 'You do what you have to, professor. But, remember, we've got long arms. You might think you're safe, up there in your ivory tower, but we're naughty monkeys. We can scale those high walls, nae bother.'

Thirty

JIM WALKED AWAY from the white tower blocks, through
a piss-scented underpass whose walls crawled with graffiti.
A bundle of rags huddled against the wall stirred as he passed.
Jim ignored it and stepped out into a rain-battered no man's
land of dual carriageway. It was pouring. Instead of washing
the mud from his clothes, the rain seemed to hammer it into
the fabric. There were no cars on the road, no taxis in sight.
Jim paused in a bus shelter, trying to decide what to do next,
when to his astonishment he saw a bus crown the hill and
travel towards him. He scrabbled in his pocket for change,
found none and stuck out an arm anyway.

The driver looked as if he had had a long night. When
Jim said he had no cash, he snorted. 'When was the last time
you were on a bus, pal? You can pay by card.' He looked
more closely at Jim. 'What happened? Someone mug you?'

'Something like that.'

'You should call the police.'

Damp, tiredness and the strain of the night were beginning to tell on Jim. His hands trembled as he tapped the card. 'My boy's in hospital. I just want to get home so I can tidy myself up and go and see him.'

'Well, keep off my seats. I don't want them covered in mud.'

Jim stood in the space reserved for wheelchairs and buggies, his sodden clothes dripping onto the bus floor. The driver cast occasional looks in his direction but said nothing. The bus's route was pasted above the exit door. It would pass the university. Jim got off outside the main building and thanked the driver, who drove on without a word.

Jim crossed the campus swiftly, head down, praying he would not encounter any porters or security guards. The space where the new Learning and Teaching Hub would soon rise was a quagmire. He hurried past the sleeping demolition equipment towards his department, let himself into the building and ran upstairs to his office. The room was as he had left it, desk chair thrust to one side, a light blinking on his sleeping computer. Jim clicked on his Anglepoise and unzipped the garment bag where he kept a clean shirt and spare suit for those long days followed by evening functions. He stripped and dressed quickly, stuffed his soiled clothes in a carrier bag, then went to the gents. He ran the hot water until it was scalding, washed his face and muddy hands, and dried his hair under the hand dryer. The reflection that stared out from the mirror looked haunted. Jim slapped his face, the way he used to when he was a student working long hours into the night, studying for his PhD. He went back to his desk and called Maggie.

She answered on his first ring. 'Eliot's awake. He's groggy and in pain, but he's out of danger. They're moving him from Intensive Care into a side room off a general ward. Dr

Darmawan says she's never seen anything like it. We raised a strong boy. He's going to make it.'

Jim whispered, 'Thank God.'

The news had made Maggie breathless. 'I thought we'd lost him, Jim.'

'Thank Christ for the NHS. I've good news too. Eliot was attacked because he owed someone a lot of drugs and a lot of money. I returned what he owed. His debts are cancelled. As long as he behaves himself no one will bother him.'

'Are you sure?'

'Sure as I can be.' He did not mention the humiliating letter he had promised to write defending their son's attacker. 'Tell Eliot that his dad fixed it for him. He's out of trouble.'

Maggie sounded hoarse. 'I'll tell him.' Someone beyond his earshot said something to Maggie. He heard her say okay, then her voice was back in his ear. 'I'd better go. Once they move Eliot out of the ICU, we won't be allowed to see him.'

'I'll call a cab.'

'There's no point, love. By the time you get here he'll be gone.'

Jim leaned back in his chair. 'Tell him I love him . . . Maggie, be careful, love. There are some funny folk out there.'

Normally she would have joked about him being one of the funniest, but now she promised to take care. She told him she loved him and hung up.

Jim laid his head on the desk and wept.

The cleaner's cry woke Jim. He looked up, bleary-eyed, to see Nela standing in the doorway, hand over her mouth.

She gave a startled giggle. 'I'm sorry, you gave me a fright. Are you okay, professor?'

He sat up in his chair, mouth dry. 'Sorry, Nela, I didn't mean to frighten you. I was working late. I must have fallen asleep.'

Nela stepped into the room, dragging the Henry hoover behind her. 'I thought maybe you were dead. You remember last year, one of the girls found a professor dead at his desk? Poor man. Natural causes, but not very nice to find.' The carrier bag containing his sodden clothes sat in the centre of the carpet. Nela glanced inside it. 'You want me to put these out?'

Jim tried to sound normal. 'Don't you worry. I'll deal with that. Do you mind not cleaning the office today, please? I've got a deadline I need to make.'

Nela insisted on emptying his wastepaper basket and then left him alone. Jim got up and stretched his stiffened limbs. He stood by his office window. It had stopped raining. The sun was out, the sky a hopeful shade of blue. Eliot was safe. He was still a prisoner, still suffering from knife wounds, but he would live.

Jim knew he should go home and sleep the night off, but he was too wired to rest. He returned to his desk and woke his computer. An email waited in his inbox from the Saudi alumnus he had entertained immediately before the crisis broke. Jim opened it and read the man's thanks, his gratitude, not just for the enjoyable tour of his alma mater, but for the foundation in life and learning the university had given him. The message ended with a pledge for a significant donation towards the new hub. Jim wrote a warm reply and circulated news of the pledge around the building committee. Now there was enough money in the pot to cover the first and second phase of construction. He wrote an email to the head of strategic philanthropy and another to Malcolm Lulach, hoping the good news would cheer the old man up.

A reminder for that evening's midnight video call with the Chinese defector flashed up on his computer. Jim set an alarm on his mobile. He sat for a moment, staring at nothing, listening to the ping of his email alert as flurries of messages landed in his inbox. He picked up his phone, ready to call Maggie again, but was interrupted by a knock at his office door. Ronald Fergusson entered without waiting to be invited. The physicist's face was stern, but the white-hot anger that had lit it the previous day was gone.

Jim slipped his phone into his pocket. He rose from behind his desk and held out his hand. There was a beat of hesitation, then the physicist grasped it, and they shook.

'Ron, I'm sorry about yesterday. We had a bit of a scare with one of the kids. When you saw me, I was running to the hospital.'

It was the truth, but there was so much unsaid. Jim gestured towards the table where he held informal meetings.

The physicist pulled out a chair and sat down. 'Sorry to hear that. Which one was it? Son or daughter?'

Jim was surprised Fergusson knew his children's genders. 'My son.'

The physicist stretched out his long legs. 'How is he?'

Jim took a seat. 'Not great, but hopefully on the mend.'

'You look like you slept in your clothes. Should you be here?'

'Probably not.'

The physics professor shook his head, as if Jim was a recalcitrant undergraduate who had handed in shoddy work. 'You're a fool, Jim. You've got a good wife, a nice family. You should put them first.'

Fergusson's wife had died of cancer five or so years before. His only son, also a physicist, taught at a university somewhere in the United States. Jim rubbed the point on his temples where a headache was beginning to build. He wished the man would go away.

'You're right. I should sort out my priorities. In the meantime, I'm guessing you're here about the new building?'

'In a manner of speaking.'

The physicist was a man of certainties, not given to shilly-shallying, but he hesitated. Jim let the silence build between them. Fergusson put the palms of his hands on the table, steadying himself for what he was about to say.

'I know you think I've been unnecessarily difficult over the new hub, but you have to remember I'm sixty-two years of age. I've been at this university man and boy–'

Jim interrupted. 'I'm born to this city, Ron. I studied for my undergraduate degree and my PhD here. The university is in my bones too, it's in my marrow.'

The physicist snorted. 'That kind of theatrical overstatement may go down well in the lecture hall, but it's wasted on me.'

Jim glanced at his watch. Its face was spattered with mud. 'What can I do for you, Ron?'

Fergusson looked down at the table, reluctant to meet Jim's gaze. 'I admit I was annoyed by the committee's choice of architect.'

'We realised that when you exited the meeting.'

Fergusson's expression was grave. 'You've known me a long time. I'm quick to anger, but I'm also quick to acknowledge when I'm at fault. I apologise for the email I sent you.'

Jim forced a smile. 'Thanks, Ron, apology accepted. Emails are too easy to send.'

Fergusson nodded. 'A lot of trouble would be solved if we could uninvent email. But that's not what I wanted to speak to you about. You have to reject this latest donation.'

Jim's phone chimed to let him know he had received a text message. 'Excuse me.' He took it from his pocket and went to the window.

Going for a meeting at Newlands. Sasha staying another night with Trina. Home late. Love you xxx

He texted Maggie three pulsing emoji hearts and then turned to look at Fergusson. 'Why?'

'We can't take money from the Saudis for the building. We may as well paint it blood-red.'

Jim sat back down at the table. 'Were not taking money from *the Saudis*. We're accepting a generous donation from a grateful alumnus who happens to hail from Saudi Arabia. There's a difference.'

'Is there? I fail to see it.'

'The difference is between the state and the individual. Okay, we may not agree with some Saudi policies—'

'Mass executions, the war in Yemen, human rights failures on an epic scale, medieval attitudes towards women . . .'

Jim held up a hand. 'Okay, Ron, I do read the news.'

'Then you'll know we'd be accepting blood money.' The physicist leaned forward. 'What do they want in return? A lecture theatre named after them?'

Fergusson was so close Jim could smell the musty scent of rainwater drying on his coat, but he resisted an urge to draw away. 'It's a large donation. Honouring it with a lecture theatre doesn't seem unreasonable. I note you don't have similar qualms about engaging with the Confucius Centre. Don't human rights in China concern you?'

Fergusson shook his head. 'What are you trying to do,

Jim? Weigh suffering? There are problems in China, but however bad the regime is, it is not a static monarchy. Opportunities to advance democratic values exist there in ways that are impossible in Saudi Arabia.'

It was the same argument Jim had made when Becca had challenged him about the university's Beijing campus. He got to his feet, ending indicating the meeting was over. 'It's not my decision to make. I'll submit an application to the ethics committee. Let them decide.'

The physicist's face reddened. 'Your generous donor is a member of the Saudi royal family. If we accept his money, we'll be endorsing a level of cruelty and corruption that I for one do not wish to be associated with.'

The university clock chimed the hour. The long night seemed to be tolling in Jim's head too.

'Are you proposing we boycott Saudi oil as well? That might make it difficult to take your Jag out for a spin.'

Fergusson pursed his lips. 'Sarcasm doesn't help. Your donor wants to buy respectability. You're proposing to sell him our reputation for the price of a few bricks.'

Jim sighed. 'I told you, I'll run it by the ethics committee.'

'A committee you happen to chair.'

The throbbing vein on Jim's forehead quickened its pulse. 'Be careful what you say, Ron.'

The flush on the physicist's cheeks deepened from strawberry to mauve. 'Don't threaten me, Jim. You represent the worst part of this institution. We both know you'll bully the ethics committee into accepting what you want, the same way you bullied the building sub-committee into accepting your choice of architect.'

The old man's age saved him. Jim stepped backwards, putting the physicist's neck beyond reach. 'You're a snob who confuses privilege with worth. The university's doors have always been wide open to you. You can't understand the need to expand access to this place.'

'I understand ambition. Look at you, sitting behind your desk while your son's seriously ill in hospital.'

Jim pointed to the door. 'Get out, Ron.'

The physicist stood his ground, his face now coronary claret. 'I want my objection to this donation formally noted.'

Jim raised his voice. 'Then send a letter to the ethics committee. I'm not your fucking secretary.'

The expletive drew a smile from Fergusson. He looked Jim up and down, from his still muddy shoes to his rumpled hair and dismissed him.

'You've done well, Jim, but you're not the stuff university principals are made of. Your killer instinct helped get you here – watch it doesn't send you back to where you came from.'

Thirty-One

IT WAS MIDNIGHT in Scotland, an hour later in Copenhagen. Jim's office was pitch-black except for the pool of light cast by his desk lamp and the glow of his laptop. The Chinese defector filled the screen, the background behind him a bare white wall. He was a thin man, with a side parting and high hairline. He looked exhausted.

The man listened patiently to Jim's clumsy account of his brief conversation with Li Jie at the Beijing graduation, the email that had announced the student's disappearance and Grace McCann's unsuccessful attempts to uncover his whereabouts.

Jim concluded, 'We only met for a moment, but I would like to help him, if I can.'

The man was wearing a green T-shirt decorated with an image Jim could only see the top of. A fan of brightly coloured feathers, a bird, a Native American headdress, or maybe an abstract pattern . . . He asked, 'You want to help him and him alone? What about others who are missing?'

'Obviously I would like to help all victims of injustice, but that lies beyond my capabilities.'

'If you do not know who or where Li Jie is, then he too is beyond your capabilities.'

'That's why I contacted you. Do you have any suggestions how I might go about finding him?'

In his room, somewhere in Copenhagen, the man smiled. 'Do you read detective novels?'

Jim tamped down a swell of impatience. 'Occasionally, on holiday.'

The man steepled his fingers and leaned closer to the screen. He lowered his voice, as if reading a bedtime story to a child. 'Then you know what to do. You go to his home-town or his university in Beijing and ask questions. Or, if you don't have time to undertake the investigation yourself, you hire a Chinese detective. Instruct them to conduct inter-views with this person and that. They will follow the clues to a detention centre, a work camp or execution ground. Of course, you need to choose the right private eye. Some of these fellows have a habit of getting distracted by beautiful women and hard liquor, maybe even opium.' The man grinned to show he was joking. His smile died, and he resumed his serious expression. 'It may be good that you haven't been able to identify this Li Jie. Amplifying his case won't neces-sarily help him. It could accelerate whatever process he's caught up in.'

Jim said, 'If we knew who he was and why he'd been detained, we could put human rights groups like Amnesty on the case. They could mount a public campaign.'

The man smiled. 'A famous Nobel Prize-winning Chinese poet died in incarceration despite the objections of world leaders and thousands across the globe. A campaign might make you feel less helpless, but beyond that . . .' He let the sentence fade, too polite to say that Jim was naïve.

Jim took a sip from his glass of water. 'What else do you suggest, other than hiring a detective?'

'If you're determined, then there might be something you can do.' The dissident made a face that told Jim he would not like the suggestion.

'Go on.'

'China is vast, but someone knows who Li Jie is and where he's been taken. You're prominent in an influential organisation. That means you might have something to offer in exchange for Li Jie's freedom.'

A bad feeling entered Jim's stomach and spread, like dye melting into fresh water, tinting its hue. He whispered, 'Such as?'

The man shrugged. 'You would know better than me.'

Jim said, 'Are you suggesting I become a spy?'

The man's smile was weary. 'I'm not suggesting anything. You can't bully or shame the Chinese authorities into letting this young man go, and this isn't a detective novel where wrongdoers will be brought to law and justice served. If you want Li Jie freed, you must buy his freedom, not with money, but with influence and favours.'

'I'm not willing to do that.'

The man nodded. 'I am telling you what is possible, not what you should do. You're his professor, not his father. You've already taken a risk for his sake.'

Jim said, 'I haven't risked anything.'

The man's eyes met his, close on the screen, hundreds of miles, and oceans, away. 'You know it is a risk to talk with me about such things, even on a so-called secure platform. They still monitor my movements and who I talk to.'

Jim adopted a formal tone. 'We're merely discussing my concerns for a graduate of our Beijing campus.'

This time the man's smile looked genuine. He stretched his hands above his head. His T-shirt rode up and Jim caught a full view of its design: a phoenix, its feathers tipped by glimmers of red and orange flame. The man completed his stretch and leaned into the computer screen again. 'Talking to me about your concerns has potential to bring you to the Chinese state's attention. If you think they are benign and that hosting satellite campuses in the People's Republic of China is desirable, then you have nothing to worry about.'

Jim stared at the face on the screen, this man who was in his room and yet far away. 'Engagement through education has potential to change lives.'

'You already work with the Chinese authorities. Some might say you work for them. You compromise freedoms in exchange for grants and investment – so-called internationalisation. I wonder if you would offer them any favours in exchange for a young man's life?'

Jim settled his palm on his computer mouse and drew the cursor to the tab that would end their meeting. 'Thank you for taking time to talk with me.'

The man nodded. 'It is always a pleasure to engage in conversation with a fellow scholar. I wish you well in your investigations and I hope our chat does not have any repercussions for you.'

Jim said that he was sure it would not, wished the man luck in his research and closed the meeting with a curt goodnight.

He turned off his computer and walked to the window. The lights in the neighbouring houses were dead, everyone else asleep. He had read a little about the dissident's escape from China, the charges that waited should he be recaptured and brought home for trial. It was no wonder the man was paranoid, but Jim had more to worry about than spies from Beijing jumping out from behind his suburban privet hedge.

He drew the blinds. He had done his best, but Li Jie, whoever he was, was among the lost. Jim turned off his desk lamp and went through to the kitchen to pour himself a glass of milk. He needed to calm the unsettled feeling in his stomach. He was neither Li Jie's professor nor his father. Bad things happened that individuals had no control over. He would settle for the comfort of knowing his own son was safe. He sipped his milk and went up to bed, but the ache in his stomach persisted, and it was a long time before sleep came.

Thirty-Two

THE MORNING AFTER her return from Trina's, Sasha woke complaining of a sore tummy. Her temperature was fine, her colour normal. She managed to eat a bowl of Crunchy Nut Cornflakes and milk without any ill effect. Normally Jim and Maggie would have taken a chance and sent her to school. But Eliot's attack had virtually exiled her from home, and they agreed it would do no harm to let Sasha have a duvet day for once. Maggie phoned the school en route to Newlands. Jim rearranged his diary and told his PA he would be working from home.

Rowan, their twice-a-week cleaner, was hoovering the lounge, Sasha watching a movie with Benji in the TV room. Jim had shut his study door against the noise and was unaware that the doorbell had rung until Sasha trotted into his room, a brown A4 envelope in her outstretched hand, the dog at her heels.

Jim had just received an email from Clover Architecture

outlining the timetable and logistics for the construction of the Learning and Teaching Hub. They had also included a shortlist of builders who they recommended be invited to submit bids for the contract. Henders Construction was not on the list. Peter Henders had been sidelined before his bid was even submitted.

Sasha placed the envelope on his desk. 'Mr Kipper said to give you this.'

Jim looked up, suddenly alert. 'Who's Mr Kipper?'

Sasha shrugged. 'I don't know. I invited him in, but he said he didn't want to disturb you.'

Jim went to the window. The drive was deserted. No unfamiliar cars were parked on the road beyond. He took the envelope from Sasha and turned it over in his hands. It was blank except for his own name, JAMES BRENNAN, printed in capital letters on a white label.

'What did he look like?'

Sasha had lifted a paperweight from his desk and was passing it from hand to hand, enjoying its heaviness. 'Old.'

'How old? Older than me?'

Sasha stared at her dad, taking an inventory of the lines on his face, the grey flicked through his hair.

'His face was younger, but his hair was older. It was all grey and kind of fluffy.' Sasha lifted her long hair with both hands, pulled it up into a messy bouffant. She let go and it fell back into place. 'How old are you anyway?'

'Three years older than your mum.'

'How old is Mum?'

Jim ignored the question. 'Shorter or taller than me?'

Sasha lifted a hand above her head. 'Taller.'

'What was he wearing?'

She put the paperweight back on the desk and stood on one leg, testing her balance. 'I don't know. A black jacket, jeans . . . boring stuff.'

'What kind of boring? Hugo Boss or M&S?'

Sasha laughed. 'Dad, you're being weird.'

'Sorry, love, I just wondered who it was.'

'I told you – Mr Kipper. Aren't you going to open it?'

'I will, in a while.' He sat at his desk, pretending to be indifferent to mystery envelopes delivered by unknown messengers. 'How's your tummy?'

Sasha put her hands experimentally on her stomach. 'Still grumbly.'

'Come here.'

Sasha made a silly face, but she came to him. Jim put his arms around her, and she snuggled into his jumper. 'Are you worried about something?' Jim felt his daughter's head nod against his chest. 'Tell your old dad.'

Sasha's voice was muffled. 'Molly said Eliot's in jail.'

Molly was a classmate Jim had never met but who featured large in Sasha's life. Her father was a lawyer. Word about his son was getting around. Jim wondered if he should tell Sasha more about Elliot's injuries in case she heard about them at school too.

He slackened his hug so he could look his daughter in the eye. 'Molly has a big mouth.'

Sasha laughed. 'Dad!'

Benji jumped up on the visitor's chair and wagged his tail.

'Sorry, sweetheart.' Jim took a deep breath, wishing that Maggie was there to help guide the conversation. 'Your brother got into a bit of bother.'

'What did Eliot do?'

'He broke the law.' Sasha held eye contact, and Jim knew

he had to tell her more. 'He got involved with drugs. The police found out and arrested him.'

Sasha's eyes were wide. 'Can I go and visit him in prison?'

Jim unwrapped his arms from around his daughter. 'No.'

'Why not?'

'It wouldn't be appropriate.' He diverted Sasha's next 'why not?' with 'Your brother's a grown-up. He's made some bad choices. They've landed him where he is. You're still a child. There are places where children shouldn't go. Prison is one of them.'

Sasha reached out a hand and stroked the dog. 'Because it's horrible?'

A memory of an early visit to his father interrupted Jim's train of thought: he and his mother passing through the security check; the prison officials' contempt. He struggled to explain himself. 'Because you're too young to understand it. You can write to Eliot though, if you want. I'm sure he'd like to get a letter from you.'

Sasha took a bobble from the pocket of her joggers and pulled her hair back into a ponytail. 'I don't think I'm too young.'

'That's part of being too young – no one ever thinks they are. You'll understand when you get older.'

Sasha clicked her fingers and Benji jumped down from the chair. 'I'm sick of people telling me I'm too young.'

'You're not too young to go to school this afternoon if you're feeling better.'

Sasha glanced at the clock on the wall. 'There's no point now. Anyway, my tummy's still sore.'

Jim gentled his voice. 'This Molly, are she and the other girls giving you a hard time about Eliot?'

Sasha grinned. 'No, they think it's badass.'

'It's not badass.'

Sasha nodded. 'I know. They're stupid. Will Eliot be all right?'

'Yes. I promise you he'll be fine.'

His assurance seemed to satisfy Sasha. She picked up the dog and carried him, ungainly, to the door. 'Benji likes it when I'm off school. He gets to watch his favourite afternoon TV, don't you, Benji?'

Jim called her name and she turned to look at him. 'What?'

'Don't use words like badass, especially not in front of your mum.'

'Okay.' Sasha let the door swing shut behind her.

Jim looked at the envelope on the desk in front of him. He picked it up. He wondered briefly what would happen if he were to take it through to the lounge, place it unopened in the grate of the wood-burning stove and set fire to it. It was not an option. He lifted the silver letter opener Maggie had given him for their sixth anniversary, slit the seal and slid the envelope's contents out.

They were deftly composed photographs, six in total. The first one showed him walking towards the riverside apartment block side by side with the young boy who had met him and Cranston. The camera had caught Jim in the act of pulling his jacket over his head, his expression hard and shifty. The next two had been taken inside the lounge of the apartment where the transaction had taken place: Jim and J sitting side by side, the wad of money and block of cannabis resin on the table in front of them, J offering the joint in his outstretched hand to Jim. The angle suggested the photographer had been stationed somewhere on the mezzanine.

The first photo was odd – suggestive of something sordid, damning but inconclusive. The ones of him inside the apartment were press-worthy, career-nuking humiliations, but it was the final two photographs that sucked the breath from Jim's chest.

Maggie and Peter Henders were sitting in her parked car, laughing. The shot was tight, focused through the windscreen, but there was a glimpse of greenery in the background, enough to hint they were somewhere rural. The final photograph zoomed in close on the car's interior. Maggie was in the driver's seat, her face turned towards Henders'. They were not kissing, but there was the suggestion of a kiss just ended or about to happen.

Rowan had turned the kitchen radio on. The faint sound of an advertising jingle reached Jim. He looked at the photographs again. The interior shots of him and J in the apartment were enough to permanently derail his career. Jim leaned back in his chair, trying to map the events that had led to this moment. Eliot had screwed up his DJ business by getting involved with drugs. He'd got caught, placed on remand, screwed up again and landed in prison.

The image of Maggie and Henders, their almost-embrace, meant nothing. If they had kissed, or more, the photographer would have captured it on film to torment him. Jim lifted the photograph and stared at Maggie's face. He knew that smile. It was the one he thought she saved for him.

His mobile jangled alive. Number withheld. The voice on the other end was unfamiliar. 'Professor.'

'Who is this?'

'Did you get the photos?'

The kitchen radio was playing an upbeat pop song. Rowan's voice joined in the chorus, high and slightly out of tune.

'I don't appreciate your delivering them to my family home.'

The man's accent was local, the same as his own, but there was no kinship there. 'Relax. I sent Ray – he's good with kids. Would you rather I'd sent them to your office at the uni?'

Jim reminded himself the conversation might be being recorded, though the photographs splayed across his desk made it barely seemed to matter. 'I'd rather you fucked off and left me and my family alone.'

There was a crackled edge to the voice that suggested long years in smoky bars. 'It'll happen. There's a couple of things needing done first, then you'll be free of us. What did you think of the pictures we sent you? Your wife's very photogenic.'

'All I saw was two colleagues having an informal chat.'

'Is that what you call it?'

'What do you want?'

'Clover are going with the wrong builders. Set them straight and we'll delete the photos.'

'If I don't?'

'We'll upload them online, send copies to the press, your employers . . . the usual shite. You'll be out on your arse and up before the judge. Before you know it, you'll be sharing a cell with your son.'

'It's up to Clover which builders they appoint. It's not in my power to set anyone straight.'

'You're the big man at the uni. This is a big contract. You can witter on about focus groups, consultations and the like, but at the end of the day, your say goes.'

'That's not how it works.'

'Then brace yourself for a lifestyle change.'

Sasha must have joined Rowan in the kitchen. The radio had switched to some boy-band ballad. They were both mimicking the singers, stretching their voices out, harmonising in wobbly falsettos.

Jim felt the pain of all he had built and all he could lose. Sasha's goofy confidence, the woman she could become. Maggie's love for him. Eliot's recovery. His own rise from unloved boy to principal of his university. He went to the window and looked out at the neat garden, the Audi slanted on the gravel drive. 'In your opinion, who should be awarded the contract?'

The man on the other end of the line tasted victory. The smile was back in his voice. 'You already know.'

'Henders?'

'You said it, not me.'

Jim pressed him. 'Is it Henders?'

'Fix it, and the photos will go nowhere.'

'I was told everything would be square if I paid my son's debts. Now you're telling me this will all go away if Henders get the contract. Why should I trust you?'

'Because you've got no choice.'

'There's always a choice. I can ignore you and let events take their course. I can go to the police and tell them what I know. Or perhaps I can just threaten to go to the police and trust you'll make the right decision.'

'Have you forgotten what happened to your son?'

'Of course not. Someone nearly killed him. I've no proof it was you though.'

The man snapped, 'The photos of you paying his debts, fuckwit – they're the proof.'

'They're a connection, but they're not conclusive proof you or your associates were the ones who harmed Eliot.'

The man on the other end of the line sighed. 'I heard you were a pedantic prick. I said Ray was good with kids – not everyone is. Some of them are a bit rough.'

A chill entered Jim's veins, the dread of a cancer diagnosis. 'Be careful who you threaten.'

'I'm threatening you. If these photos get into the wrong hands, you're fucked.'

It was true. Jim shut his eyes for a moment. Was this how Michael Peterson had felt before he hung himself? The telescoping blackness of a hopeless future.

'How long do I have?'

'I'll phone you in three days.'

'That's not enough time.'

'You'll make it work.'

'Does Peter Henders know about this?'

'Pete's a good boy. He likes to keep his hands clean.'

'So who do you represent?'

The voice bristled. 'I represent the end of your career, the end of your marriage, if you're not careful. You've got three days.'

The line went dead. Somewhere in the house Sasha called to Benji. He heard the scuttle of claws against parquet as the dog ran to meet her.

Jim lifted his mobile and dialled Peter Henders' number. It went straight to voicemail. He lifted his phone again and called Maggie. There was no reply. He put the photographs back in their envelope and slipped them into this briefcase.

Rowan was on her knees in the kitchen, cleaning the oven, when Jim entered the kitchen. 'The kettle's not long boiled.'

He tried to smile. 'I'm not after a coffee. I've a favour to ask. I've got to nip out for a meeting. Would you be able to stay on for a couple of hours and keep an eye on Sasha? You could put your feet up and watch something on Netflix or read a book, whatever. I'd pay you extra for your time.'

Rowan got to her feet and pulled off her rubber gloves.

'Sasha's no trouble, but I've got to collect Ryan from school in half an hour.'

Jim had forgotten about the cleaner's small son, though he had seen the boy often when he came to the house with her during school holidays.

'Bring Ryan over here. I'll send a taxi to pick him up.'

Rowan made a face. 'He's nine years old. I wouldn't let him go anywhere with someone he doesn't know. And we go swimming after school on Wednesdays.'

'Maybe Sasha could go with you?'

Rowan looked at him strangely. 'I thought Sasha was off school because she wasn't feeling well?'

Jim shook his head at his own stupidity. 'I'm not thinking straight.'

Rowan pulled her yellow Marigolds on again. She sprayed the sink with Cif and started to scrub the porcelain, more to avoid looking at him, Jim suspected, than because it needed cleaned. 'I'm sorry, but I can't help you.'

A scent of bleach and synthetic lemon prickled Jim's nostrils. 'I wouldn't ask if it wasn't urgent. I'd pay you extra.'

Rowan scrubbed harder. 'I only do this job because it fits in with Ryan's school times.'

Jim felt her resolve waver. He had taken to carrying cash with him and had a hundred pounds tucked inside his wallet. He slipped the notes out. 'Maybe one of Ryan's friends' mums would take him home for dinner?'

Rowan stopped scrubbing and looked at him. 'I saw the news about the student who killed himself in the newspaper. Was he one of yours?'

'I was his supervisor.'

'Is this anything to do with him?'

Jim felt the temptation to say he was rushing to intervene

in another student suicide or to console Michael's poor parents, but he shook his head. 'There's nothing I can do for him now. This is something else. Something I need to do.' He held out the money. 'There's a hundred pounds here; it's yours if you'll look after her.'

'It's too much.'

The notes shook in his hand. 'I'm stopping you from having a swim with your son. That's worth more than a hundred quid.'

Rowan ignored his outstretched hand. 'I'll ring my friend. If she can take Ryan, I'll stay. As long as you understand it's a one-off.'

Jim nodded. 'Thanks, Rowan.'

She turned away and took her phone from the pocket of her jeans.

The TV room was empty, the television on, a quiz show Jim did not recognise playing silently on screen. He perched on the arm of the couch and phoned Maggie. This time she picked up. He said, 'Where are you?'

'Is Sasha okay?'

'She's fine.'

'Eliot?'

'I've not heard anything. I'm guessing no news is good news. Where are you?'

'Newlands. I won't be home until later.'

Jealousy pricked him. 'I need to see you.'

'What's wrong?'

'I can't say over the phone.' Jim heard a noise and looked up. Rowan was standing in the doorway. 'I'll call you right back.' He looked up, wondering how much she had heard and if it mattered. 'Everything okay?'

Rowan gave a small nod. 'My friend can take Ryan.'

Jim slipped the money from his wallet and handed it to her. 'You're a lifesaver.'

Rowan folded the notes into her pocket without counting them. 'She'll give Ryan his tea, but he has a bath at six thirty on school nights. I need to be home by then.'

'Don't worry. Maggie or I will be back in plenty of time. We'll get you a taxi to your friend's and home afterwards.'

Jim shouted goodbye to Sasha from the downstairs landing, pulled on his jacket, lifted his briefcase and went out to the Audi.

Thirty-Three

THERE WERE NO guards at the gatehouse that marked the
entrance to Newlands estate. Jim called Maggie on the hands-
free as he passed through the gates and bounced the Audi
over the speed bumps that punctuated the long drive. The
stately home that lent its name to the new development sat
squat on the landscape, dwarfed by glass-fronted apartment
blocks ranged around it. Maggie had initially designed each
block twenty storeys high. After local objections the planning
department had limited them to seventeen. Jim had glimpsed
mock-ups of the development in Maggie's office, but it was
a jolt to see the real thing towering before him. The apartment buildings struck him as ugly – too tall for the site,
composed of white stone that would stain in the rain – giant
monoliths that made him think of ancient stone circles.

Managing the Newlands build had condemned Maggie to
late nights and interrupted dinners for months, but work on
the development was further on than Jim had expected.

Gardeners were landscaping the green spaces between the buildings. The tired stonework of Newlands House had been repointed, and each floor was equipped with modern balconies.

Maggie met him on the steps of the old house, looking tired and vaguely aristocratic, as if she owned the estate and was weighed down by the responsibility. The sun was beginning to set. Light cut across the lawns, lengthening the shadows of the gardeners and the tower blocks beyond.

Maggie shielded her eyes with her hands. 'What's going on?'

Jim tried to give her a reassuring smile. He wanted to tell her there was nothing to worry about, but they had promised not to lie to each other. 'Is there somewhere we can talk?'

'Is it one of the kids?'

'No. I told you, they're okay.'

'Where's Sasha?'

'Rowan's looking after her. They're ordering pizza.' Somewhere inside the old house, a drill started up. Jim said, 'Is there somewhere less noisy we can go?'

The mundane detail about the takeaway seemed to reassure Maggie. She glanced into the building behind her. A chandelier glimmered above carefully restored tiles in the entrance hallway. A workman in dark blue overalls strode past carrying a ladder.

'The car's probably the best bet.'

Jim tucked the briefcase containing the photographs beneath his arm. 'Yours or mine?'

Maggie shrugged. 'Yours.'

He laid the briefcase on the backseat and held the passenger door open. She slid in without looking at him.

Jim started the engine. 'Where shall I go?'

'Follow the drive. There's a pond. We can park there.'

He did as she said and drew in beside a pool overgrown with rushes and pondweed. A heron glowered at them from the other side. Now that they were there, Jim felt reluctant to speak.

He nodded towards the bird. 'He thinks we're here to steal his fish.'

Maggie lowered the window. The sound of birdsong reached in, beyond it the faint rattle and bang of the construction site.

'We are. We're hoping to encourage young families. A secluded pond, walking distance from the flats, is too much of a risk. We're draining it next week.'

The heron hunched over the water, motionless except for wing feathers trembling with the breeze.

Jim watched the bird, its frozen eye and long beak. 'Seems a shame.'

'It'll find somewhere else.' Maggie turned to look at him. 'What's in the bag?'

Jim retrieved it from the backseat. 'How did you know?'

'You were holding it like an unexploded bomb.'

He unclipped the briefcase, took out the envelope and handed it to Maggie. 'An unexploded bomb isn't a bad description.'

Maggie slowly leafed through the photographs of Jim at the riverside apartment. Her mouth tightened 'What am I looking at?'

'I told you I paid off Eliot's debts. Someone photographed the transaction.'

'Jesus.' Maggie stared at the image of Jim crossing the apartment courtyard with the young boy by his side. It showed nothing illegal but was somehow the most damning of the shots. 'You look like. . . I don't know what you look like.' She placed the photos on her lap and took a deep breath. 'Why photographs and not video?'

It was a question Jim had asked himself, but he was struck by his wife's cool. He shrugged. 'For all I know they took videos too.' He thought about the conversation with J. A recording of it would destroy him.

Maggie brushed a strand of hair from her eyes. 'Couldn't you have been more careful?'

'Not really, no.' Jim had separated the photographs of Maggie and Henders from the rest. He took them from the inside pocket of his jacket and handed them to her. 'There's more.'

Maggie looked at the pictures. A flush spread from her breastbone to her face. She bit her lip. 'Why would someone take these?'

'I guess they're meant to make me jealous.'

Maggie looked at the photos again and shook her head, incredulous. 'Someone spied on me?'

Now was the time to tell Maggie about the photograph of her sitting by Eliot's hospital bed, but instead Jim found himself asking, 'Should I be?'

Maggie turned to look at him. 'Should you be what?'

It was as if a portal had opened to Jim's younger self, his confidence stripped away. 'Should I be jealous?'

His wife's voice was dangerous. 'Are you serious?'

'It's a simple question.' Maggie got out of the car and slammed the door. He followed her to the water's edge. The gloaming was coming in, the night descending. There was a scent of rotting pondweed. 'You and Henders look pretty cosy.'

The heron leaned in towards the water. It spread its wings and took flight.

Maggie's voice was hoarse. 'For God's sake, Jim, can you hear yourself? Someone spied on me. They took photographs of me without my knowledge, and your response is to ask if I'm having an affair?'

Jim watched the bird climb beyond the trees, its wings slowly flapping, suddenly graceful. He felt like punching someone, preferably Peter Henders. 'Why would someone send me a photograph of the two of you together?'

'I don't know. To fuck with you? It worked.'

'You look . . .'

'Look what?'

He could not think of the word. 'Cosy.'

'Cosy. Right, I'm not sure that's how I'd describe Peter Henders.' Maggie shook her head. 'I was on a site visit. It was pissing down, so we sat in my car. I guess he cracked a joke and I laughed.'

'Why wouldn't you describe him as cosy?'

Maggie leaned against the bonnet of the car and gazed over the soon-to-be-drained pond. She was still holding the photographs of her and Henders. She looked at them again. 'Cashmere socks are cosy. Labrador puppies are cosy. Candlelit baths and cocoa by an open fire are cosy. There's something brittle about Pete Henders. He's too fragile to be cosy.'

Jim leaned against the bonnet. Their hips touched. He took hold of Maggie's free hand. She did not pull away. 'What do you mean, fragile?'

'I don't know. He has that corporate machismo they all have – the flash suit, big shoulders, swanky office, struts around like cock o' the walk. He was born into the business, knows it inside out, but I got a sense that some of the swagger was a front.'

Being interesting was the kind of ruse men pulled when they wanted to seduce a woman. Jim said, 'Are you sure he wasn't trying it on?'

'For fuck's sake, Jim. I'm not having an affair with Peter Henders or anyone else. Where would I get the time?' Maggie let go of his hand and pressed her fingers to her throat. The dark was coming in, but the diamond eternity ring Jim had given her for their twentieth anniversary glinted. 'Henders is a big firm. Of course our paths have crossed, but I barely know Pete. He was involved with a job I did a few months back. Honestly? I was surprised how hands-on he was, given his seniority, and he was good to deal with, professional.'

Jim wondered how long the plans against him had been in the making. He said, 'Did you get any sense that he was trying to get close to you?'

She shook her head. 'Do you think that in all the years we've been together no one's ever come on to me? I work with men every day. I told you, Pete Henders was professional. If he hadn't been, I'd have dealt with it. I'm too tired, and too busy, to go fucking around.'

His eyes met hers. 'The person who sent these photographs wants me to guarantee Henders Construction will win the contract for the new hub.'

Maggie took a deep breath. 'That doesn't make sense.'

'None of it makes sense.'

'No. I mean threatening you with these photos. It's not how people go about things.' She turned to look at him. 'Corruption's rife in the building industry. Sweeteners, price fixing, bid rigging, blacklisting, unnecessary shutdowns. Think back to how this started.'

'Eliot got caught with drugs, and then he broke his bail conditions and ended up inside.'

Maggie nodded impatiently. 'It's too random. There was no guarantee Eliot would behave the way he did.'

'Eliot's screwed up more times than I can remember. Odds were he'd screw up again somehow.'

Maggie rolled her eyes. 'Think about it. Getting caught might have shocked him into behaving himself for once. Or we could have sent him to some overseas rehab where he'd be kept under lock and key.'

Jim snorted. 'Eliot wouldn't agree to rehab.'

'They don't know that though, do they?' Maggie sighed. 'My point is, it wasn't inevitable that Eliot would end up in prison available to be stabbed by some arsehole. There are too many variables for whoever's doing this to be sure of the outcome. You're suggesting some jailbird almost killed our son as a prelude to forcing you to compromise yourself so that someone could threaten you into giving Henders the contract? It's too convoluted.' She waved the photos of her and Peter Henders in the air. 'And what are these? Sprinkles on the icing on the cake?'

Wind rippled the pond and sent the long grasses at its edge bobbing.

Jim ran his hand over his face. 'So what would you expect? If Henders was dead set on getting the contract?'

Maggie shrugged. 'They could play it by the book.'

'Clover have already set a shortlist of building firms. Henders isn't included.'

They stood silently together. The breeze and the distant sound of construction drifted across the pond. Maggie said, 'Then Henders has various options, if they want to rig things. They could try and bribe you, but you've got a lot to lose and no history of corruption, so there's a good risk you'd report them. They could sweeten the deal for the architects, but Clover's a top firm. They have a lot to lose too. Most likely option? Make a pact with their competitors, agree the Henders bid will be the clear winner and that, in return, they'll fold on the next big deal.'

Rooks heckled each other from nearby treetops.

Jim said, 'That relies on their competitors playing ball.'

Maggie nodded. 'It's been known to happen, but this is a prime capital build. There's not many of them about at the moment. Anyone with a decent shot at the contract will want to take it.'

'So what you're saying is there are several options to swing the bid, but they're either too risky or long shots. Maybe whoever's behind this – Peter Henders or someone else with a vested interest – decided that threatening me is the best chance they have. It doesn't mean they followed a convoluted plan. Perhaps they simply took advantage of circumstances. They didn't know Eliot would end up in prison, but when he did, they made the best of it and put pressure on me.'

Maggie let go of his hand. 'It feels wrong.'

'You can say that again.' Jim glanced at his watch. He would have to leave soon if he was going to get back in time for Rowan. 'Do Henders Construction have any form?'

'I think they were fined for bribing officials in Qatar or somewhere.' Maggie shrugged as if it was no big deal. 'There were rumours. There are always rumours. Not enough to stop us from working with them, but . . .'

'But?'

'This is a high-debt industry. Profit margins are low, tendering processes competitive, supply chains long. A couple of major players went bust not so long ago, owing big money. It's a bit like Jenga. When a firm collapses, it puts their creditors in a precarious position. If there's a hint that someone's in financial trouble, loans and contracts dry up. Loyalty's fine and dandy, but when a big firm goes down, it can take a lot of otherwise sound businesses with them.'

'And that's what happened to Henders? There were whispers that they might be in trouble?'

Maggie nodded. 'Word was they'd over-extended a line of credit to a housing development company who went bust. There were problems with the houses too – substandard drainage, flammable cladding, the usual shit that happens with shoddy builds. I can't remember the details, but it may have gone to court at some point. Either way, Henders were in danger of getting hit from both sides – no payment for work done and sued for work done badly. But then they had a piece of luck. A large council premises they were converting went on fire. The insurance payout was astronomical.'

'With one leap they were free.'

'Not quite. Turned out the fire had been deliberately set. There was a court case. It could have been the final straw, but the court agreed that Henders had taken due precautions and the payout went ahead.'

'Convenient.'

'It saved their arses.' She frowned. 'There's something else.'

'What?'

'It hadn't occurred to me before, but remember the arsonists Eddie won a reduced sentence for?'

Jim said, 'Are you telling me the boys Cranston defended burned down the same building Henders Construction received the arse-saving insurance payout for?'

Maggie nodded. 'This is a small city. It could be coincidence.'

'Could be, but it's another connection.'

It was almost dark. The smell from the pond was stronger, drawn forth by the night air.

Maggie stood up and took out her phone. 'This is ridiculous. I'm going to phone him.'

Jim caught her hand. 'Cranston or Henders?'

'Henders. If he doesn't know about this, he should, and if he does know, I'll report him to the police and the ombudsman.' She tried to pull away from Jim's grip, but he held her tight. She swatted him with her free hand. 'Jim, let me go.'

He loosened his grip but kept his hand on her phone. 'They threatened Sasha.'

Maggie froze. She stared at him. 'When?'

'Before I came here.'

'And you left her alone?'

'I told you, I left her with Rowan. They're not going to do anything so long as they get the contract.'

'How can you say that? They already put Eliot in hospital.'

'Do you think I've forgotten that? I'm not going to let anything happen to Sasha.'

Maggie looked at Jim as if reassessing him. 'You're seriously considering giving them what they want?'

He shook his head. 'It goes against everything I've worked for . . . but you and the kids . . . you're what I work for.'

He was overcome by images of hit-and-run drivers, acid attacks, men who liked to hurt little girls. There was a rustle of air and feathers, and the heron swooped back into position on the other side of the pond. It stared at them from the shadows and then started to preen beneath its wings. They stood in silence for a moment, watching it.

Jim put his arm around Maggie.

She drew closer. 'It feels personal.'

'I know.' Jim kissed the top of Maggie's head.

'If it's personal, it won't stop here. They'll own you.'

His wife was right, but he could not see a way out. 'I've no choice.'

Maggie looked up at him. 'I'll kill anyone who comes near our kids.'

Jim felt a sudden, unexpected stab of desire. He kissed her on the lips. 'I know you will, love. But you won't have to. I'll kill them first.'

It was the kind of thing people said, a turn of phrase, but he meant it. He was prepared to kill for his family. He would die for them too, if that was what it took to keep them safe.

Thirty-Four

JIM CHOSE A seat at the centre of the committee table. He set his laptop in front of him, opened the documents he would need for the meeting and switched his phone to silent. Ronald Fergusson slid into the seat opposite and poured himself a glass of water.

'How's your son?'

Jim glanced through the agenda, though he knew it by heart. The Saudi alumnus's sponsorship offer was item three, after the minutes of the previous committee meeting and the decision on whether to accept Clover Architecture's shortlist of building contractors. He looked at the physicist over his laptop screen and waited a beat. 'On the road to recovery.'

They were due to start in four minutes. Other members of the committee were taking their seats, setting laptops, notebooks and tablets on the table. No one glanced at Jim or Fergusson, but academics were as prone to gossip as anyone else and Jim knew the tension between them had been marked.

Fergusson sipped his water. 'Glad to hear it.'

Jim returned his attention to the screen, but Fergusson was determined. 'I owe you another apology. I shouldn't have insulted you.'

'You said what you needed to say.'

The physicist's brow creased. 'It was a cheap shot.'

Jim nodded to Grace McCann, who had just entered the senate room. He turned his attention back to the physicist. 'You have a problem with impulse control. It might be worth getting a check-up. I can arrange it for you via HR if you like.'

The suggestion was his own cheap shot, but unexpectedly it hit home.

Fergusson's face flushed. 'Have you been talking to my son?'

'I've never met your son. Doesn't he work somewhere in the US?'

Jim hesitated over the word 'somewhere', implying the institution was low-grade, the kind of place inclined to issue doctorates for the price of a stamp.

Fergusson said, 'MIT, Massachusetts Institute of Technology.'

'Impressive.' An article from a few years back snagged in Jim's memory. Student demonstrations against a crown prince's visit, an internal report that dismissed ethical objections to the institute's ties with Saudi. 'No stranger to Saudi Arabian investment, I seem to recall.'

Fergusson flinched. 'I'm afraid that's beyond Alexander's pay grade.'

Jim closed the lid of his laptop and gentled his voice. 'You've always been forthright, Ron, but recently I've noticed a change in you. If your son's also worried about your mental health, it might be an idea to have a chat with someone from support services.'

The physicist took his laptop from his rucksack. 'Have you heard of "gaslighting", Jim? It's a favourite with our students. Named after an Ingrid Bergman movie few of them have seen.'

'I've heard of it.'

'Then you'll know that it means manipulating someone into doubting their grasp on reality. My son has spent too long in America. You, on the other hand, are a gaslighting opportunist.'

Jim glanced at the academics settling themselves at the table, studiously avoiding him and Fergusson. He kept his voice low. 'That's exactly the kind of response I'm talking about.'

Fergusson shook his head. 'You're not the right man for the top job. I'll oppose your appointment with every atom of my soul, but I shouldn't have insulted you.'

Jim smiled, as if the physicist's opposition was a feather on the wind. 'You couldn't help yourself.'

Fergusson met Jim's smile. 'Save your energy. I'm not going to rise to the bait this time.'

The half-dozen members of the committee were seated. Chatter faded to expectant silence.

'Okay.' Jim glanced to either side, a swift sweep of his assembled colleagues' eyes. 'We have a lot to get through. I assume everyone has read the minutes of the last meeting. If there are no amendments, can I have a motion to approve them, please?' A hand went up at the end of the table, the minutes were passed, and Jim nodded his thanks. 'First item on the agenda, approving Clover's shortlist of building contractors invited to tender for the job of bringing our Learning and Teaching Hub into being.'

Fergusson's voice was smooth. 'Isn't this a formality?'

Jim gave an efficient smile, quick as the click of a lock. There was a lump in his throat. He coughed, but it was lodged there. He took a sip of water and swallowed his shame.

'Clover Architecture have submitted a shortlist of contractors they recommend be invited to tender, but given recent disasters involving new buildings, it is incumbent on us to make an informed choice. I've done a bit of research and am inclined to drop one of their suggestions from the list and ask Clover to advertise on the open market for a replacement. We know from our own efforts to decolonise the university the role that nepotism and unconscious bias plays in restricting opportunities for those outside the fold.' He caught Grace McCann's eye. Her expression was neutral, waiting to hear what he had to say. Jim continued: 'Clover, no doubt, has a preferred pool of builders, but that's not to say that their preferences are best for our needs. In fact, I feel distinctly uncomfortable about one of their recommendations.'

He and Maggie had sat late into the night researching Clover's shortlist of builders and had selected one to be dropped to make way for Henders. According to Maggie, the firm's infractions were nothing special, but listed together they looked damning to Jim's eyes. He would have liked to distance himself from the move by getting a colleague to deliver the material, but there had been no time to set things up. He assumed his formal voice and read out some of the choicer disputes the firm had been involved in.

There were a few heavy sighs across the committee table,

but no one objected or requested the document in full. They all knew that Freedom of Information requests made it unwise to commit some material to electronic exchange.

Grace McCann stated that she for one was grateful to Jim for bringing the facts to the committee's attention. Jim repeated his suggestion that they request Clover advertise for contractors on the open market and that a small sub-committee, led by him, be established to assess the resub-mitted shortlist. The motion was passed, the foundation laid in the plot to save his reputation and his son. He felt a now familiar sickness in his stomach, and it flitted through his mind that perhaps this was how ulcers started.

The discussion about the Saudi donation was more heated. Grace McCann and Ronald Fergusson were staunch in their opposition, Jim studiously reasonable in his nudges towards acceptance. The university bell rang the end of their second hour without any firm conclusion being reached.

Jim reluctantly agreed to ask the prince if his gift would remain in place if they declined to call the lecture theatre after him. Grace McCann suggested the name of a recently murdered female Palestinian journalist as an alternative. The meeting broke up in a babble of bitter amusement and discontent.

Grace caught up with Jim in the corridor outside the senate room. 'You're wrong about this so-called gift, Jim. We'd be endorsing a corrupt regime for money. It's immoral, and it'll backfire on all of us.'

Jim glanced at his watch. 'Sorry, Grace, we're going to have to save this discussion for the next meeting.'

He upped his pace. Grace was forced to trot to keep up with him. 'I'll resign if the committee decides in favour of the donation.'

Jim slowed down, and they fell into step. 'You're more powerful inside the tent than outside. If you walk away, you'll have zero influence.'

Grace was cancer-thin, as if she had given up eating in solidarity with the victims of repression who were her field of study. She adjusted the strap of the large bag slung across her shoulder. 'Life isn't a choice between being outside the tent pissing in, or inside the tent pissing out.'

Jim averted his gaze from her collarbone, the ridge of sternum visible beneath the open neck of her blouse. He was tempted to ask how she felt about being inside the tent pissing on her own shoes, but he knew Grace would dismiss him as childish. He said, 'Most people's choices are limited.'

'That's true, but we're fortunate. We do have a choice. We can use it wisely, or we can sell our principles for the price of a fancy lecture room.'

It was like talking to his daughter. 'It's not that simple.'

'Yes, it is, Jim. This is a straightforward choice between right and wrong.'

He stopped walking and turned to look at her. 'Remember the Chinese student I was concerned about?'

She nodded. 'Li Jie. Did you discover what happened to him?'

'No. My point is, you and I were concerned, we tried and failed to locate him. We feel bad about it . . .' He did not mention his sleepless night, the pains that even now were cramping his stomach. 'But neither of us is suggesting the UK cut off relations with the People's Republic of China.'

Grace rolled her eyes, and Jim realised he had chosen a bad example. She said, 'You know as well as I do, the reason universities are interested in hobnobbing with China is a rerun of the old colonial adventure.'

'Again, it's not as simple as that.' Jim looked at his watch again. 'I've got to go.'

Grace's bag, stuffed with books, slipped from her shoulder, and she hauled it back into place. 'I can't work you out. Sometimes, like when you mention Li Jie, or suggest expanding the tendering process, I think there's a decent human being in there. Other times it seems like you're one of *them*.'

'By one of *them* I suppose you mean the enemy, whoever they are?'

'The suits, the corporates, the neoliberal capitalists.'

The uselessness of it all felt like a brick in his chest. He met her eyes. 'Don't you ever get tired of judging people?'

Grace said, 'I'm not judging you, I'm just . . .'

Jim turned his back and walked swiftly along the corridor, not bothering to wait for her to finish her sentence. Grace knew as well as he did that sometimes there was nothing you could do: people got lost, sons went to the bad, buildings required building, money demanded certain actions. She knew that responsibility had to be borne and she stepped aside to let others take the fall. He did not have that luxury.

It was the first day of Malcolm Lulach's chemotherapy, and Jim was temporarily at the helm of the university ship. He sent a message to the Saudi prince, politely enquiring if he would forego naming the lecture theatre after himself, and then worked methodically through his inbox, answering what he could, deferring some queries, delegating others. It was an effort to keep his attention from drifting. This must be what it was like to be a drug addict or an alcoholic, your mind always elsewhere.

Maggie had phoned the hospital that morning. Eliot was

sleeping a lot, but his vital signs were stable, and he continued to make progress. Jim wondered if his son was dreaming, caught in some parallel world between the living and the dead. Trauma altered people. Perhaps Eliot would emerge changed for the better.

The thought was a tug in the guts. Jim knew now that he should have turned his back on his son, sold the warehouse flat and let Eliot take his chances. They had coddled him, pandered to his impulses, kept him a child when they should have been guiding him towards being a man. Jim had done everything to be the opposite of his own father and had ended up raising a boy that might have been Big Jim's shadow.

He realised that he was staring into space and returned his attention to the computer. An email from a representative of the Saudi prince nestled amongst the latest tranche of unopened messages. Jim's hopes for a quick, amicable outcome dimmed. He and the prince had communicated directly until now.

The email was brief. The representative contradicted Jim's impression that the prince had intended the theatre to be named for himself. The honour was a gift to the prince's father, 'whose commitment to education is widely celebrated'. The message was clear. The gift was reliant on the naming of the lecture theatre, Jim's enquiry a slight.

Jim began an email to the building committee and deleted it. A paper trail was unwise. He spent the next forty minutes phoning members of the committee, reiterating the arguments in favour of the donation. He knew each member's special interests and laid it on thick. For one, the bait was the planned 5D lab which would put the university at the forefront of AI research; for another, increased access for disabled students; for yet another, the vaulted glass courtyard that would act as an events and performance space. He implied, without stating it, that each member was the sole, remaining objector, and he felt them cave, one by one, beneath his argument. There was no point in pressurising Ronald Fergusson or Grace McCann – they were lost causes – but Jim knew he had done enough to swing the vote in his favour. He felt more alive than he had in weeks. If he played his cards right, the new building would rise on the hill, and though it would not bear his name, those who mattered would know that it would not have existed without his force and vision.

Jim's mobile rang. An unlisted number flashed on the screen. The good feeling of a moment ago vanished, all his smugness dissolved like smoke. The voice on the other end of the line sounded wheezy and short of breath, but it had lost none of its authority. 'Is it done?'

'These things take time. We're getting there.'

'How long?'

'I don't know. A month tops. I've started the process to get you onto the tendering shortlist.'

The man on the other end of the line snorted. 'A month? We could build it in less time than that.'

'If that were true, you wouldn't have to resort to threats.'

The voice sounded amused. 'You're a gobby wee shite.'

Jim took a deep breath. 'I'm doing my best.'

'You're a clever boy. Do better.'

'Or else?'

'You've already had a demo. Do you want another one?'

'No.'

'So don't ask stupid questions. Get it done.'

The line went dead.

Jim swore. He had made Maggie promise not to contact

Peter Henders, but now he scrolled through his contacts until he found the builder's number. The thought of Sasha stopped him from calling. The builder was somehow entwined in the drugs intrigue and threats. Contacting him might press go on some plan there was no coming back from. Jim tried Cranston's number. It went straight to voicemail. He left a message for the lawyer to call him and put his head in his hands, ignoring the ping-ping-ping of emails landing in his inbox. His diary for that afternoon included a meeting with a conglomerate interested in buying the university's remaining student halls of residence, followed by a Zoom catch-up with colleagues in Hong Kong and a meeting with union reps about alleged staff casualisation. He dialled Malcolm Lulach's PA from his desk phone and instructed her to rearrange all three appointments. If she was surprised, she gave no sign.

Jim walked to the window. The street below was crowded with students. He watched them for a moment, then shifted his gaze to the university tower rising proudly into the sky. He was risking everything, but he had gone too far to back out now.

He returned to his desk and woke his computer. His temporary role gave him enhanced access to the system, and although he was unsure of what kind of trace his searches might leave, he pushed his misgivings to one side, logged into alumni records and found Becca's file. A landline and an address were listed under her details. He typed the address into Google Street View. A substantial lochside house with its own mooring and jetty appeared on screen. He and Maggie had looked at homes there when the children were small, but prices had sailed in at close to a million, way beyond their means. If he was appointed principal, a property like that would be within his reach. Jim was not usually a superstitious man but imagining the future felt dangerous. This was a time for smothering hope and living in the present.

Jim dialled the number from his desk phone. His bet that it was the family home and that Becca had flown the coop was confirmed when an older woman answered and said that her daughter no longer lived with her. Jim confided that he was calling to check on Becca's current address, prior to sending an invitation to a university reunion.

Becca's mother sounded suspicious. 'Don't you usually do these things by email?'

He had his answer ready. 'Our research has told us that people's inboxes are swamped with unsolicited emails. Postal invitations get a better response.'

'Surely it's too soon for a reunion. She only graduated four years ago.'

Jim put a smile into his voice. 'Things move fast these days. No one wants to wait twenty years before catching up.'

'I'll be surprised if you manage to entice Rebecca. She knew some nice girls at university, but I think she's lost track of them all.'

'All the more reason to make sure she gets the invitation.'

Becca's mother recited an address and postcode somewhere in the east of the city. Jim scribbled it down on a scrap of paper, thanked her and hung up. He pulled on his raincoat and left his office, locking the door behind him. Becca was a smart girl who had become careless about her future. She was connected to both Cranston and Henders. Perhaps she had a clue about what was going on and, perhaps, if he asked in the right way, she would enlighten him.

Thirty-Five

BECCA'S FLAT WAS above an Asian grocer on a street busy with other Asian grocers, Indian restaurants, sari shops, wedding jewellers and the occasional pub. Jim parked in a side street and retraced his steps, noticing signs of gentrification. A cold-brew coffee shop with industrial décor that would look at home in Hamburg or Toronto. A vegan restaurant, its windows lush with glossy-leaved plants. A barbers manned by bearded lumberjacks.

He rang the service bell to Becca's building and the door gave onto cool dimness and a scent of floral disinfectant. Her flat was on the top floor. Jim trotted up the stairs, past a couple of expensive baby buggies parked in doorways, tidy bikes chained to stairwell railings, a couple of potted plants on a landing. The oak banister curved upwards. He had thought Becca was slumming it, had not anticipated this middle-class enclave.

The storm doors to Becca's flat were the only ones in the

building shut and bolted. Jim knew the effort needed to drag yourself from bed after a night of heavy graft. The drive to escape had kept him at his books through his kitchen porter and bartending years, but it seemed Becca had lost her ambition. He pressed his finger to the doorbell, heard it ring inside the flat, and then battered the brass door knocker, shaped like a clog, against the door – raising memories again of the police swoop that had been the final straw for his mother.

The door across the hallway opened, and a young woman wearing the same brand of yoga gear Maggie favoured leaned into the lobby. 'Hi . . . what's going on?'

From deep inside her flat, a calm voice gave instructions on how to bend and stretch. A toddler with baked-bean rust stains around his mouth peeked from behind the woman's legs.

Jim moderated his accent, the way he did when representing the university overseas. 'Overdue library fines.'

The woman made a face. 'She seems to get a lot of visits from male librarians.'

Jim smiled at the toddler who ducked behind his mother and then peeked out again. 'Is that right? Like keeping an eye on the comings and goings of your neighbours, do you?'

From deep in the flat the voice instructed: *And lean into the stretch as far as you can without straining. This is your time. You are doing this for you.*

The woman snapped, 'Remind that whore there are families in this building. Keep the noise down or I'll call the police.'

He wanted to ask about the other male librarians who had visited Becca, if they were night or day callers, if they arrived singly or in pairs. If they hurt her. If the woman meant it when she called her a whore, or if it was just a turn of phrase, a yoga thing. But the woman pulled the child indoors and shut the door with a firm click.

Jim rattled Becca's letterbox. He sensed movement inside her flat and slammed the brass clog again. He squatted and called through the letterbox, 'Open up, Becca. I'm not going away, and your neighbours are threatening to call the polis.'

Jim heard the inner door open and knew she had put her eye to the spyhole. He gave a bright smile he did not feel and heard the bolts slide back, the locks turn.

Becca's face was free of make-up except for dark smudges of mascara around her eyes. She was wrapped in an oversized towelling dressing gown, legs bare, her feet in flip-flops, toenails painted a slatey blue. 'Couldn't you have phoned?'

'Would you have picked up?'

'Probably not.'

Becca went to shut the storm door, but Jim inserted his foot and held it open. 'Your posho Mumsnet neighbour's sick of you and I'm ready to make a noise.'

Becca said, 'How would a police caution for making a racket outside an ex-student's door go down with the university?'

'I'm beyond that point. Your friends put my son in hospital. Now they're threatening my daughter, so bring it on, because I'm halfway to calling them myself.'

Becca said, 'I don't believe you.' But she opened the storm doors wider and turned away, leaving the inner door ajar. He followed her down the hallway. The walls had been stripped of paper, and a large tub of undercoat sat unopened on bare floorboards. Jim followed her into the kitchen. Becca took a glass from a shelf above the sink, filled it with water from the tap and took a sip. 'They're not my friends.'

Jim took a seat at the kitchen table. A book lay splayed open. Jim glanced at the cover. *Crime and Punishment*. 'Who aren't your friends?'

Becca tightened her dressing gown, though it was already tightly tied. 'Whoever it is you're talking about. I lead a minimalist life. I don't have any friends.' She took the book from him. 'Don't touch anything.' And left the room.

Jim got to his feet and went to the window. The shared back court had been prettied up with plants and a picnic table. A child's bicycle slumped on the ground and an over-sized trampoline took up most of the lawn. The families in the building had claimed the space as their own.

He sat back down at the kitchen table and looked around. The cabinets were the same style as the ones in the first flat he and Maggie had bought together, almost twenty-five years ago. They had been old-fashioned then and had not come back into style since. Becca had found a good property to turn a profit on.

She returned, dressed in baggy black joggers and a vest, and took a seat at the opposite side of the table. Her eyes met his. 'Did you mean it? When you said someone threatened Sasha?'

Jim had not expected Becca to remember his daughter's name, but now he recalled that her memory had helped to make her a good student. He adopted the firm but gently disappointed tone he used for disciplinary enquiries. 'Someone phoned to say they put my son in hospital and will do the same thing to my daughter if I don't do what they tell me to.'

Becca held eye contact. Her irises were blue, her pupils wide. 'What do they want you to do?'

'Something illegal that would be advantageous to your friend, Peter Henders.'

She looked away. 'I told you, he's not my friend.'

'Your boss, then.'

'I don't have a boss.'

He was not sure what to ask next. 'Your neighbour called you a whore.'

Becca laughed. She had washed her face and tied her hair back in a messy ponytail. It made her look younger, less poised than the party girl shimmering in silver who had delivered him to Henders' penthouse.

'She should talk. She stays home all day. Her husband goes out to work. If anyone's a whore, it's her.'

'Presumably, she and her husband have an arrangement.'

'Presumably, she should mind her own business. So should you.'

'Minding my own business is an unaffordable luxury.'

Becca's expression turned serious. 'I don't know anyone who would want to harm Sasha.'

'But you let me in.'

Her voice rose a pitch. 'Of course I did. You told me someone was threatening your daughter. I don't want anything to happen to her.'

Jim believed her. He lowered his voice, trying not to let his frustration leak out and scare Becca into silence. 'You met Sasha when you were at my house with Eddie Cranston. You phoned me the next day and demanded I meet you. Then you introduced me to Peter Henders. I hadn't seen Cranston for years, but I bumped into him on the night my son was arrested. I'd barely rubbed shoulders with Peter Henders, but suddenly his firm is key to my daughter's wellbeing. Yesterday I found out that Cranston acted for Henders Construction in an arson case. I don't believe in coincidences. What's going on?'

Becca looked away. 'Ask them: it's nothing to do with me.'

Jim broke the puzzle down, the way he did when tackling research. 'How did you end up at Henders' party if you don't work for him?'

Becca's water glass was almost empty. She went to the sink, refilled it and drank. 'It was a one-off. Pete was a friend of my dad's. He knew I was doing corporate events and asked me to make sure his wife's party ran smoothly. We'd had a falling out. I thought it would be a chance to put things right.'

'What did you fall out about?'

'It was stupid . . . Pete didn't approve of my seeing Eddie, which is ironic given we met through him.'

'You said you swiped right.'

Becca leaned against the kitchen unit. 'It was less embarrassing than saying we met at a random party given by my godfather.'

Jim leaned forward. 'Peter Henders is your godfather?'

She shrugged. 'My dad and Pete's dad were business partners. Dad was the money man. Pete's dad did the practical stuff. Pete took over when his dad retired. When my dad died, Pete tried to "show more of an interest", which meant sticking his nose into my business.'

Becca had not been lying when she said Henders was not her friend. He was closer than that. Someone who had known her from childhood and had taken a religious oath to protect her. Jim asked, 'How did Cranston come on the scene?'

Becca boosted herself onto the kitchen unit. Her feet dangled off the ground. 'Eddie acted for Henders Construction in some trial. They won, and Pete gave a dinner to celebrate. Eddie was on good form. We got pissed. Pete got pissed off, then I got pissed off with Pete. Eddie took me home and one thing led to another. I think Pete and Eddie fell out about it, but you know Eddie – he doesn't let things bother him.'

Sasha was more than ten years younger than Becca. It was easy to imagine how he would feel if, in a decade's time, his daughter invited her own version of Eddie Cranston home for dinner. Jim said, 'Last time I saw Cranston, someone had beaten him up. He's getting too old to play the fool. Too old for you.'

Perhaps Becca already knew about Cranston's beating or perhaps she did not care. She got down from the kitchen unit, brushing some dust from her rear, and took a seat at the kitchen table. 'Pete's overprotective, but he's basically okay. He wouldn't get involved in anything dodgy.'

Jim was too up to his own neck in dodgy business to have faith in other men's integrity. 'What makes you so sure?'

Becca looked at her feet. 'Because my dad was crooked. It's ludicrous, Pete going on about Eddie being too old for me. My dad was fifty-five when he hooked up with Mum, almost sixty when I was born. He did well to hang on until I graduated, considering how much he liked his brandy and his smokes.'

Jim had a sense of things sharpening into view. 'Why is the business called Henders and not Henders and . . .?' He paused, realising he had forgotten Becca's second name.

'Henders and Harvey.' Children's laughter drifted in from the back courts. Becca glanced towards the kitchen window and then back at Jim. 'My dad preferred to stay in the background. His name wasn't on the letterhead, but it was on the deeds. Him and Pete's dad founded Henders Construction back in the eighties. Mum and me still have a non-executive interest in the business. Pete visited us when he took over and set things out. He said that under his watch there'd be no more bribes, intimidation or tax dodges. He was going to play everything by the book.'

'Things didn't go by the book when your dad was alive?'

Becca smiled. 'My dad liked to think he wrote the book. Henders Construction probably wouldn't be such a big success if Pete's dad and mine weren't a pair of arsehole gangsters. They were notorious back in the day.' Her eyes shone with amusement, or maybe pride, at their transgressions. 'If they wanted a job, they took it. If the council denied them permission to demolish a building, they burned it down. But I guess there's only so long you can get away with that kind of behaviour. It's a different story now. Pete's straight.'

Jim made a face. 'So why did he make such a cloak-and-dagger production about meeting me?'

Becca shook her head. 'Pete heard about Eliot's arrest on the grapevine. It put him in a temper. I mentioned you used to be my lecturer and that I'd bumped into you. He told me to invite you over, but not to make a big deal about it. He didn't want anyone bothering you at the party.'

The photographs of Maggie and Peter Henders together in the car, smiles stretched, eyes locked, flickered on the edge of Jim's consciousness.

'Why would my son's problems make him angry? He doesn't know Eliot. Boys go to jail every day. It's nothing to him.'

Becca shrugged. 'Pete's got a sensitive side. He has some arrangement with a rehab project. Likes to stand up for no-hopers and losers.'

Eliot was a no-hoper. A loser. Flesh, blood and bone in a hospital bed.

'Is there anyone else in Henders' organisation that might take it on themselves to threaten me?'

Becca shrugged. 'You're asking the wrong person. All Pete asked me to do was invite you to the party and make sure you had a bit of privacy when you got there. I guess I camped it up a bit.'

'Why?'

She took a deep breath, looked up at the ceiling and then directly into his eyes. 'You're always broadcasting how you're a working-class lad made good. You pretend anyone can get where you are if they work hard enough, but your generation pulled the ladder up after you. You got your education for free, bought your houses cheap and saddled people my age with a bunch of student debt. Then you sucked up the good jobs. I know PhDs who've worked for the uni for a decade and are still on zero-hours contracts. Getting fired and rehired, working in a coffee shop over the summer or signing on?' She shook her head. 'Forget it. I respect myself too much to be treated like that.'

Jim cast his eyes around the room. 'Save me the poor little rich girl act. You grew up in one of the most advantaged parts of the city. You've got money, good health, white privilege, middle-class connections. You caved at the first sign of hardship, but you want to blame the system.'

Becca snapped, 'Don't tell me about my life. You know nothing about it.'

Jim remembered Michael's suicide and felt a stab of shame. It was true. He knew nothing about what she might have experienced. He spoke softly. 'Every generation thinks the previous one had it easy. I did when I was younger. The truth is, everyone struggles when they start out.'

Becca raised her chin. 'You were struggling towards something. There's nothing left for us.'

How could he tell her what he had been through?

'There's plenty left if you're bright enough to step up and take it. Old guys like me retire. Sometimes you get lucky, and they drop dead of a heart attack.' He remembered Malcolm Lulach and added, 'Or cancer gets them. There's a whole menu of diseases waiting to wipe out old farts like me.'

Becca muttered, 'Great life plan. Wait for someone to die.'

Her bitterness was comic. He laughed, and after a moment she joined in. The tension between them relaxed.

Jim said, 'All I want to do is protect my children. Eliot's in Intensive Care. The same people who put him there are threatening Sasha. She's eleven years old. If you know anything, please tell me.'

Becca shook her head. 'I told you . . .' She looked away, reluctant to meet Jim's eyes, and he knew she was lying.

'What is it?'

She sighed. 'I don't know what it means – maybe nothing – but the night of the dinner, after they won the court case, it wasn't just because of me that Pete and Eddie fell out.'

'What else was it?'

'I don't know. Something to do with the case. One minute they were best friends, next thing Pete was shouting at Eddie to get out before he kicked him out. I left with Eddie, which went down like a lead meringue. That's all I know, except that Pete wouldn't threaten a child. He wouldn't threaten anyone.'

'You just told me he threatened Eddie Cranston.'

Becca shook her head. Her ponytail bobbed from side to side. 'Eddie's got a big mouth. He probably asked for it. To be honest, I wasn't paying attention. I've heard enough about the ups and downs of the building trade to last me a lifetime, several lifetimes. It bores the bejesus out of me.'

Jim wondered if she had inherited her sangfroid from her gangster father. 'Why did your neighbour call you a whore?'

'Because she thinks I'm a whore.' Becca stared at him. 'Aren't you going to ask if she's right?'

'Is she right?'

Becca shrugged. 'Depends on your definition.'

He got to his feet. 'Hanging out with men like Eddie Cranston and Peter Henders will land you in trouble. Quit while you're ahead.'

Becca walked him down the long hallway to the front door. She unlocked it and paused in the doorway. 'Eliot's a good DJ.'

It was a long time since anyone had said anything positive about his son. Jim felt an urge to touch her arm, but kept his hands bunched at his side. 'You know Eliot?'

'We've been in the same company a few times. He knows how to fill a dance floor. I told him you used to be my professor. I got the impression he hates you.'

He wondered why she wanted to hurt him when he was already hurting. 'All sons hate their fathers.'

'All young people struggle. All sons hate their fathers. In seminars you used to tell us not to draw conclusions from generalities. Do you think he got involved in drugs to get back at you?'

'Maybe. Who knows? Either way he's a fool.'

Becca smiled. 'Having a fool for a son must be a disappointment.'

Jim wanted to tell her that all his ambitions were dead and the best he could hope for now was to keep his children alive, but he left the thought unsaid. It occurred to him that Becca's dad and his might have known each other. Becca's father had been more successful, but they were both outlaws who occupied the same small city in a small country. He felt an unexpected kinship with the girl. He met her eyes. 'Take care of yourself, Becca.'

She nodded and shut the door behind him.

Jim had a sense that another pair of eyes were watching. He wondered if the tense yoga woman was observing him through her spyhole, keeping track of Becca's client list. He resisted the urge to give her the V-sign and loped down the stairs, taking them two at a time. He knew where he was going next.

Thirty-Six

JIM HAD NOT spoken to Eddie Cranston since the lawyer had driven away from the Toblerone flats in the 4x4 they had borrowed for their nocturnal skulk through Galloway Forest. He phoned Cranston from the Audi, and when he did not pick up swung the car into the slow-moving late afternoon traffic, down towards the old district. Jim parked in a lane opposite Cranston's office, not quite out of sight. The metal shutter was halfway down, the office closed, but a light was on in the back room. Jim tried the phone again. This time, the line was engaged; Cranston talking to someone.

He slouched in his seat and googled *Henders Construction Eddie Cranston*. The article he had already read about the young arsonists convicted of burning down Henders' construction site appeared first, followed by similar accounts of their trial in other papers. Jim scrolled beyond them and discovered a series of reports about the social housing dispute Maggie had mentioned.

Eddie Cranston had defended Henders Construction in a court case that had not exactly lit up the media, but whose proceedings had stretched beyond a month. Peter Henders had denied personal wrongdoing. He told the judge that he regretted placing his trust in experts and subcontractors. They had let him down, cut corners, creamed off profits and endangered the safety of residents. The implication was that he was guilty of naïvety rather than deliberate misconduct.

Jim read on. Initially, chances of a positive result for Henders Construction had appeared After Eight Mint-slim, but Cranston had somehow worked his magic, and the jury had unexpectedly found in favour of the building firm. It was an against-all-odds result that should have had Peter Henders toasting his lawyer rather than ejecting him from the celebratory dinner.

The office shutter clattered upwards, and Eddie Cranston stepped onto the pavement. He locked the door behind him and trundled the shutter down. He was squatting, securing its lock, when Jim crossed the road and put a hand on his shoulder.

Cranston almost tipped over, but he made a quick recovery and got to his feet. 'Jesus Christ. You don't believe in giving a man any warning, do you?'

Jim got straight to the point. 'What did you and Peter Henders fall out about?'

Cranston was wearing his habitual pinstripe and brown brogues. He pocketed his keys. 'I wouldn't have thought that was any of your business, but truth is, he didn't like me and Becca getting together. It's moot now. She gave me the heave-ho.' Cranston shrugged. 'Too young and too classy for me anyway, but it was fun while it lasted.'

Jim fought an urge to slap the lawyer's smirk from his

face. 'I just spoke with her. She said Henders wasn't over the moon about you shagging his goddaughter but that wasn't why you fell out.'

Cranston patted Jim on the back. His bruises were beginning to fade, but they were still there, yellow-grey. 'I'll give you a tip: don't believe everything Becca tells you.' He turned and walked away.

Jim started after him. 'Something's happened.'

Cranston kept walking. 'Too bloody much has happened. Sorry, Jim, I've done what I can. You're on your own. Find a new clown to look after your boy.'

Jim caught him by the shoulder. 'Someone's threatened Sasha.'

Cranston shook himself free and kept on walking. 'Who's Sasha and why should I care?'

'Sasha's my eleven-year-old daughter. You met her.'

Cranston halted. 'Ah, shit. The sweet wee skater girl with the ponytail?'

Moisture threatened Jim's eyes. 'That's her.'

Cranston shook his head. 'Fuckers.' He looked at Jim. 'You serious?'

'As cancer.'

'And are they serious?'

Jim remembered the voice on the phone. 'Yes, I believe they are.'

Cranston's smile was gone. 'What happened to the old villains' code: no harming women and children?'

Jim's father had talked about codes and decency, and then gone home and battered his wife and child. 'It never existed.'

Cranston put an arm around him. 'You're right. It was always a pile of self-serving shite, but, still, threatening an eleven-year-old girl is a fucking low. Come on, let's have a pint.'

It was Jim's turn to pull free. 'I don't want a drink.'

Cranston's grin returned. 'Maybe not, but I do, so if you want to talk to me, you'll have to tag along to the Fusilier.'

Jim nodded towards the Audi. 'I've got the car.'

'Good.' Cranston slapped Jim's back. 'It's been a long day – I'd appreciate a lift.' He shoved his hands into the pockets of his suit jacket. 'Don't worry, I won't funnel beer down you. I remember what happened last time.'

The usual huddle of smokers was stationed at the door of the Fusilier and several tables were occupied inside. Cranston stepped up to the bar, ordered a pint of IPA and a glass of orange juice, and carried their drinks to a corner table. Jim sensed the ghost of his father, his wasted life. He took a sip of his orange. It was warm and sour. He remembered that he had not eaten since breakfast and thought about buying a packet of crisps, but the walk to the bar felt like a journey through no man's land.

Cranston slid the tie from around his neck, rolled it up and put it in his pocket. His cheerfulness was gone. 'So what do they want?'

Jim told him the same thing he had told Becca. 'Something that will benefit Henders Construction.'

Cranston took the head off his pint, hiding his expression behind the glass. 'What exactly?'

Jim stared out at the bar, the drinkers squandering the afternoon. His father had favoured the same slate-grey suit and white shirt for years. Fashions had moved on – the men scattered around the bar were dressed in leisurewear and zip-up fleeces – but little else had changed.

'You don't need to know the details.'

'That means you're thinking of delivering.'

'I can't risk Sasha.'

Someone put a Willie Nelson song on the jukebox and someone else shouted for them to get that pile of pish off. Willie told mothers not to let their babies grow up to be cowboys, an overweight woman in black leggings and a red sweatshirt advertising janitorial services got up and began a loose-limbed dance.

Cranston took another inch from his pint, his eyes trained on the dancer. 'I already stuck my neck out for you. It didn't go well.'

'You said you had debts to pay. You weren't doing me a good turn. You were clearing your balance sheet.'

Cranston touched one of the bruises discolouring his cheekbone. 'For a long-time sole trader, I've always been remarkably bad at balancing the books. Apparently I owed more than I realised.'

'You're a lawyer, surely you make a decent living.'

'Not decent enough, as it turns out.'

Jim leaned forward. 'You know all my dirty laundry.'

Cranston drew a finger down the side of his beer glass, leaving a trail in the sweat of condensation on its surface. 'A dubious perk of the job. No need to burden you with mine.'

'Except I'd like to be sure you don't have mixed motives.'

The lawyer gave him a sidelong look. 'Don't you trust me, Jimmy?'

Jim expected Cranston to tell him to mind his own business or make an excuse about failed marriages and alimony, but he closed his eyes for a moment. He took another swallow of his pint and returned his gaze to Jim. 'I got greedy. Went in for a bit of property speculation of my own. Thought I'd make a million and bit off more than I could chew. I ended up over-extended and looking at the kind of bankruptcy that ends practices. An old client offered me a bridging loan, and, against my better judgement, I took it. I should have known better. Out of the frying pan into the blast furnace. Persuading you to deliver the drugs was my get-out-of-jail-free card.'

Jim knew his university colleagues' weaknesses, his allies and his enemies, who could and could not be bought for the price of a favour. Sitting in the bar with Cranston, he could not tell if the lawyer was on the level or revealing his weakness in order to build trust that could be exploited. 'Did you know someone was taking photos of me?'

Cranston gave him a look. 'When?'

Jim lowered his voice. 'When I delivered the stuff we dug up.'

'Of course I bloody didn't.'

A man was reading something on his phone at the corner table where Big Jim used to hold court. Jim looked at him and then glanced away. How could you trust anything anyone said when words meant nothing? Nouns were fine. A table was a table, a chair a chair, a knife a knife, but promises and assurances meant less than the air he was breathing. Sometimes truth lay in what people did not say, the tilt of a head, the squint of an eye.

The barman wandered over. He added a couple of sucked-dry pint glasses left by previous punters to the stack cradled in the crook of his arm and gave their table a wipe. Jim waited until he was out of earshot and repeated, 'Did your fall-out with Henders have anything to do with property speculation?'

'We already covered that. I told you, Pete didn't like me dating Becca.'

'I spoke to Becca. She said you argued with Henders before she got together with you.'

A man roared as a torrent of pound coins clattered from the puggy machine. The puggy played an electronic victory salute and a couple of drinkers sauntered over to admire his jackpot. Cranston raised his glass to the winner and said under his breath, 'Washers and fakes. He'll be lucky to get a decent round out of that.' He turned to Jim. 'You've been too long at the uni. There's no prizes for good behaviour in the real world. Becca grasped that early. I told you already, don't believe everything she says.'

Jim held his thumb and index finger in front of Cranston's face, the digits almost touching, as if gripping an invisible credit card. 'I'm this close to going to the police.'

'You do what you've got to do. Client confidentiality is sacrosanct.'

'Not when it involves corruption, arson and threatening children.'

Cranston's smile vanished. 'You're on the wrong trail. I'm a gun for hire. Defending people in trouble is my job.'

Jim touched his orange juice to his lips and wished it was malt. 'Strange for you to act in two cases connected with the same firm. First time on their behalf, the next time against them.'

Cranston placed a hand on the table. His gold watch peeked from beneath his shirt cuff. 'The arson case wasn't against Henders Construction. Sure, the lads burned down one of their buildings, but I acted in their defence against the Crown. There was no clash of interests.'

'Strange coincidence though.'

'Shit happens. It's all part of life's merry carousel.'

'You did well in both cases.'

'The lads went to jail.'

'And received unexpectedly low sentences.'

Cranston muttered. 'Not that low, if you're the one in the big white hotel at Her Majesty's Pleasure.'

'Henders Construction looked like they were in deep shit before you came to their rescue.'

Cranston tipped the dregs of his pint down his throat. 'Did you ever consider going into the law?'

'I didn't fancy hanging around with lowlifes.'

Cranston laughed, unoffended. 'Aye, I expect you had enough of that growing up. You would have been good on the prosecution side though. You're relentless. Myself, I like to see the good in people. I'm better suited to defence.'

Jim looked at him. 'You don't have kids, do you?'

Cranston caught the barman's eye. The barman nodded, angled a pint glass under the beer tap and started to pour. 'I know the script. You'd do anything to save your daughter, same way you used to think you'd do anything to save your son.'

'Eliot's old enough to . . .'

Cranston held up his hand. 'You don't have to justify yourself to me. You put your life on the line for that waste of space. I believe you'd do the same for your wee girl. Maybe that's the right thing to do, but it's not my fight. All I can say is, I'm pretty certain Peter Henders isn't your man.'

Becca had told him the same. The barman delivered Cranston's pint. Cranston fumbled in his pocket and passed him a fiver. 'Thanks, Billy, keep the change.'

The barman nodded towards Jim. 'What about your pal? Would he like another Britvic?'

'Nah, the prof's a family man. Got to get back for his dinner before the wife feeds it to the Labradoodle.'

Jim waited until the barman was gone. 'I'm not after you, Eddie. Tell me what you and Henders argued about, and I'm out of here.'

'Trust me, it's nothing to do with your problem.'

How could he explain correlations between dissonances? Jim lifted his glass of warm orange juice, but the thought of it made him set it down without taking a sip. 'Corruption doesn't happen in a vacuum. Maybe I believe you when you say that you believe your row with Henders and the threats against Sasha are unconnected, but you're wrong. If they benefit the same organisation, odds are they share a root. I'm asking you nicely to tell me what the argument was about. It's your choice, but, remember, I have enough influence to make your life a misery.'

Jim did not specify whether the influence he referred to was professional or under-the-radar connections, remnants of his father's fiefdom.

'I wondered when you'd start with the threats.' Cranston pushed Jim's abandoned glass to the edge of the table. 'Have a real drink?'

'I can't.'

Cranston made a face. 'I'd feel better if we were both drinking.'

'I'm not here to make you feel better.'

'That's for sure.' Cranston raised his pint to his lips and took a deep swallow. 'It can't get out that we talked about this. You're not the only person in town with enough influence to make my life a fucking misery.'

Jim nodded. 'Understood.'

Cranston looked dubious. 'I mean it, Jim. My mother used to say, you make your bed, you lie in it. I'm getting too old for dollybirds and beatings, but they're burdens I made for myself. I'm not getting shoved in the shit for the sake of someone else's big mouth.'

'No wonder Becca dumped you if you use words like dollybird.'

'She likes unreconstructed men. Maybe they remind her of her father.' Cranston grimaced. 'That's a gruesome thought.'

Jim said, 'You have my word. I'll keep whatever you tell me to myself.'

'You better. I'm between a rock and a concrete overall.' He drained his beer until the level sank to midway and placed it on the table. 'When I agreed to defend Henders Construction I thought the chances of winning were slim to non-existent. I came in suspecting that Pete had been caught bang to rights, but, after our first interview, my opinion changed. Pete isn't corrupt; he's sloppy.'

'What do you mean?'

'You know sons of the elite. They get promoted beyond their skill set. Nice guys, some of them – the ones that aren't spoilt gits – but they don't have the drive to succeed. Why should they? Life's been good to them. They're already a success, and nine times out of ten they think it's because of something they've done rather than the silver spoon in their gob. That prick Prince Charles is a prime example: a god-anointed accident of birth who thinks he's a fucking political and architectural genius.'

'Flabby ambition doesn't mean someone won't bend the law. If anything, it might incline them to cutting corners.'

'True, but that's not Pete's style. He uses phrases like "the disinfectant of sunlight". He was scared – you could see it in his face – but he was willing to step up and face the music.

I started to worry he'd be too cooperative on the witness stand and start confessing to all sorts.'

'What kind of thing?'

'The Kennedy assassination? Buying Georgie Best his last pint? Leaving the cargo doors open on the *Titanic*? I don't know. It was like he'd always expected there to be a reckoning and now that it was here, he welcomed it.'

'I read the reports in the paper – seemed to me like he shoved the blame onto the contractors.'

Cranston nodded. 'Sure, he told it like it was. He didn't personally manage the project, but what the papers failed to mention was Peter Henders was clear that the buck stopped with him. From where I was standing it looked close to self-harm. And, as if that wasn't enough, I knew we were fucked as soon as I looked at the jury.'

'How could you tell anything just from looking at them?'

'It's not Derren Brown territory. I've been doing this for over thirty years. You can tell by the way they look at the defendants. The way they're dressed. The man who was a cert to be the jury foreman was staring at Henders as if he was the Antichrist.'

'Sounds like the perfect storm.'

'You got it, and Henders welcomed the storm with open fucking arms. Instead of lowering the sails, he lay down on deck and waited for a big wave to pull him under.' Cranston shook his head, reliving the memory. 'Then, halfway through the trial, something changed. It was like an old love song – "clear blue skies where there used to be grey". It was nothing to do with my efforts. My defence was consistent, but it was going nowhere fast until, hallelujah, I sensed that the balance had shifted. My nemesis on the jury's body language changed. He started leaning forward, paying attention. There was even the occasional smile.'

'You're saying someone got at him?'

Cranston shrugged. 'I'm saying nothing, but it bothered me. Not enough to ask for a retrial, mind you. We were on the winning side after all.' His eyes met Jim's. 'I may be an arsehole who has an occasionally complex relationship with the law, but I believe in the sanctity of justice. I prefer to know when I'm crossing the line. The night Henders and I fell out, the same night Becca and me got together? I made a joke that wasn't totally a joke about jury nobbling. Pete lost the plot and threw me out.' He shrugged again. 'Now you know as much as I do, and I'd prefer you don't share it with anyone else. If what I told you reaches the wrong ears, I could be disbarred.' He touched the bruise on his cheekbone again. 'Or worse.'

Willie Nelson was crooning about blue eyes crying in the rain. The woman in the red sweatshirt kept on dancing. The bar was getting busier, but no one offered to partner her.

Jim kept his voice low. 'If Henders didn't fix the jury, who did?'

Cranston drained his glass and patted his pockets. He got to his feet, ready to leave. 'Someone who cares enough about Henders Construction to resort to corruption. Sound like anyone you know?'

'It sounds like whoever threatened my daughter.'

Thirty-Seven

IT WAS DARK when they left the pub. Jim offered Cranston a lift home, but the lawyer turned him down.

'I'm meeting the boys up at the pitch. Football practice.'

'I thought that was for show.'

'I meant what I said. I'm sick of seeing idiots go to jail. Football isn't the cure, but knowing someone gives a damn might make them pause before they throw their life away.' Cranston looked embarrassed at revealing he cared, or maybe he remembered that Jim's son was in jail. 'And it helps keep me out the pub for a few hours.' He slapped his stomach. 'I'm in danger of losing my girlish figure.'

They were crossing a small gap site to the roadside where Jim had parked the car. Cranston paused and pointed back at the glow of the Fusilier. 'It might not look like it, but things are changing around here. See this waste ground? We're breaking soil on a community garden next weekend, somewhere folk can meet up and grow veg. I'm going to get some of the fat lumps from the Fusilier to give a hand.'

The pub's windows shone orange. Its flat roof was outlined by the light of the streetlamps. Jim was reminded of Edward Hopper's paintings of lonely roadside diners. Stories waiting to be told.

'Good luck with that.'

'We don't need luck, we've got drive. Come back here in a year's time, I guarantee it'll be transformed.' Cranston's voice brightened with the energy of a good idea. 'You should get the university to sponsor it. Fuck it, you should sponsor it. You can afford it, with a professor's and an architect's salary coming into the house. Give something back to the place you came from.'

Jim turned and resumed the walk to the car. 'It's good what you're doing, but Maggie and I already give to charities associated with education. No offence, Eddie, but we have different memories of this place. I walked away and never looked back.'

'And yet here you are. Maybe the old place isn't as easy to escape as you thought.'

Jim laughed, unexpectedly caught by the truth of Cranston's words. 'Christ, it's like a horror movie. Just as you think you've got away, a hand reaches out from the grave in the final frame and grabs you by the ankle.' A thought struck him. 'Speaking of succession, did Becca resent not taking over her dad's side of the business?'

'You'd have to ask her. I guess she was too young when he died. I got the impression she and her mother were happy to sit back and take the dividends, but you never know with Becca.'

'What do you mean?'

'Ach, nothing really. She's young and disaffected, a bit

spoilt. Only just discovering that the world hasn't been holding its breath waiting for her genius.'

'You're just bitter at being dumped.'

'It was a bloody relief, to be honest.' They had reached the road; the Audi was parked up ahead. 'Becca sees the world as a series of plots and intrigues.'

'I'm not sure she's wrong about that.'

'Maybe, but it's exhausting.'

'She's young and ambitious.'

'Aye, but she doesn't know what she's ambitious for.'

'Did you at her age?'

'Of course I did. I wanted to be Petrocelli. And here I am, twenty-plus years later, living the dream. You knew what you wanted too.'

'I wanted to get out.'

Cranston slapped Jim on the back. 'Keep your eyes on the prize, pal. You escaped once; you can do it again.'

'Here's hoping.' Jim looked beyond Cranston, aware of the dark stretch they had travelled, the shadows obscuring the waste-land between them and the Fusilier and those yet to be crossed. He felt an urge to ask the lawyer to walk with him to the Audi but was too proud to admit his unease. 'I'll see you later.'

Cranston turned away. 'Not if I see you first. No offence, Jim, but you're not exactly lucky white heather. Best you find a new lawyer for your boy. Call me when all this is over. We'll go for a pint, and you can tell me how things worked out.'

'Aye, maybe.'

It was impossible to imagine a future when he could look back on the mess his life was currently in. Jim pressed his key fob, and the Audi gave an answering blink of its head-lamps. He breathed in and breathed out, and kept on walking until he reached the shelter of the car.

Thirty-Eight

SLEEP WAS A brief pause, a stoplight on a long journey. The alarm woke Jim early. He slid from bed before snug bedclothes and the scent of his wife's sleeping body could lure him back to blessed unconsciousness. It was still dark outside. Across the city others would also be slipping from warm beds or stepping into the chill at the end of long shifts, but it felt as if he was the only person afoot in the world. He showered, fed Benji and left the house before Maggie and Sasha were awake. Jim had worked late into the night, but an afternoon of playing hooky had set him behind. His inbox was swollen with emails, his diary full.

The porter on duty at the gatehouse nodded as he raised the barrier. The wooden sign marked PRINCIPAL, at the head of Malcolm Lulach's parking space, looked like a grave marker in the half-light. Jim slid the Audi into the adjacent space. The slam of the car door, the electronic chirp of its lock sounded loud against the stillness of the morning. Jim took the long way round to his office, aware that it might be hours before he breathed fresh air again. He wondered if his son was still asleep or if he had been woken by the doctors' dawn rounds. Eliot had been a good sleeper as a child. It was the one area where he had given his parents no trouble. Jim paused on the rise by the university flagpole and looked out over the city. Here and there windows were illuminated, bright squares of light in the wakening darkness. Necklaces of car headlamps shimmered slowly along the main arteries towards the motorway.

It was becoming difficult to conjure happy memories of his son. The sweet baby and toddler had been crowded out by the surly teen and surlier adult. Jim allowed himself the thought that he had been trying to suffocate for a long time, possibly years. He wished that his son had never been born. It was not the same as not loving the boy. Not caring would be a release.

He turned his back on the view and took the path towards the main building, reviewing the day's priorities in his head. He was almost at the entrance when his name reached him, hoarse and angry, carried by the wind. '*Brennan!*' He turned up the collar of his coat and walked faster, hoping to outrace the summons. '*Jim!*' There was no escaping it; he might as well try to outrun time. He swore under his breath and turned to greet Ronald Fergusson. 'You're an early bird, Ron.'

The wind caught the physicist's dandelion-fine hair, casting it in a white aureole around his head. He looked pale in the shadows, a ghost of himself.

'You've been scheming again, Jim.'

Fergusson's gaberdine was unfastened. It blew open, fanning his body like a cape. Jim noticed how thin he was, and it struck him that the man looked unwell. He smiled and tried to stall the confrontation with a joke. 'No more than usual, Ron.'

'I know you're trying to manipulate the committee.'

Someone must have spoken about the phone calls he had made the day before, promoting the benefits that would accrue from the Saudi donation. Jim faltered, playing for time. 'I'm not sure where you got that idea from.'

Dead leaves, caught on the wind, birled along the pavement. The physicist stepped closer. 'These aren't the streets, Jim. This is a respected institute of higher learning.'

'I'm well aware of that.'

'You've been plotting behind the backs of the committee. Bullying and bribing people into accepting blood money.'

It was too much. Jim took a step towards the physicist. 'I completely and utterly refute that.'

Fergusson's hair danced around his head. 'I'm sure you do, but you're a liar.'

The wind was speckled with rain now. It hit, cold needle stabs, against the back of Jim's neck. 'And you're way past your sell-by date, Ron.'

Fergusson snorted. 'Take a good look at yourself. You're a gangster, a poor man's Stalin, ready to cull anyone who opposes you.'

Jim raised his voice. 'Are you seriously comparing me to a mass murderer? The fact that you're still alive and kicking is testament to my patience. Stalin would have sent you to the gulag on day one.'

'Are you threatening me?'

Jim's laugh sounded like a machine-gun rattle. 'Don't be ridiculous.'

Fergusson's pallor was flushed with red. He looked ghastly. 'You just told me I deserve to be exiled and murdered.'

'For Christ's sake, Ron . . .'

There was the sound of footsteps swift and military on concrete. Jim turned and saw two security men hurrying towards them. He flicked through his mental Rolodex but only managed to remember one of their names.

The older of the men – Bob – called, 'Everything okay?'

Jim took a deep breath. His lungs hurt. 'Professor Fergusson and I are having a slight disagreement on policy.'

Fergusson raised his chin. His voice wobbled. 'Professor Brennan thinks I should be sent to a death camp. I disagree.'

Jim said, 'That is an absurd distortion–'

Fergusson raised an arm and pointed at him. 'Yesterday you insinuated I was losing my mind. This morning you suggest I should be exterminated. Thank your lucky stars I'm not a member of the snowflake generation. They'd have you up before HR before you could say, "Education is a weapon."' He smiled, pleased with himself. 'You can bluster and bully all you like, Jim, but you're not getting your way on this one. The Saudi donation will not be accepted.' Fergusson nodded to the security guards. 'Thank you for your contribution, gentlemen. Things were getting out of hand.' He gathered his coat around him and stalked in the direction of the physics block.

Jim turned to the security guards. 'I'm sorry about that. Professor Fergusson's been under a lot of strain recently. I can assure you, I didn't threaten to put him in a death camp.'

The younger security guard, the one whose name he could not remember, said, 'To be fair, he didn't say you'd threatened to put him in one, just that you'd said he belonged in one.'

Bob touched his co-worker's arm, shutting him up. 'We have to record this type of incident in our logbook.'

Jim gave him the man-to-man-laced-with-threat grin

which had served him well in his years at the university and
tempered his voice with the authority befitting a professor
in line to be principal. 'Debate is at the heart of universities.'

Bob nodded. 'And I'm required to take note of any act of
aggression on university grounds.'

'We had a brief dispute about a high-level university initia-
tive we disagree on. I'd hardly call it an act of aggression.'

The young guard said, 'You were pretty loud, sir. We heard
you from the other side of the quads.'

Bob gave a grim nod. Jim saw that it would be easier to
shift the old building's stone walls than this man's course.
He reached into his inside pocket for a business card. 'Then
I advise you to put your report in an email and send it to
me to sign off.'

Bob waved the card away. 'It's all right, sir. I know who
you gentlemen are. I'll make sure you both receive a copy.'

It was just after lunchtime. Jim was halfway through reading
a funding application that required his approval. His back
was stiff, and his neck bones felt like they were fusing
together. He locked his office door, lay down on the floor
and stretched his spine.

He was returning to the application when a handwritten
letter peeping from his to-be-read pile caught his eye. He
picked it up, noting the neat script and French stamp. The
sender's name and address were written on the other side:
Mr & Mrs Peterson. Michael's parents.

Jim sat down at his desk and took a deep breath. He felt
an urge to bury the unopened letter beneath a pile of paper
or to hide it in the depths of a book he would never read.
He took a sip of water, lifted his letter opener and slit the
envelope.

The letter was handwritten in black biro. Its style suggested that Mr Peterson was a man more used to business letters than to personal correspondence, but somehow its correctness underlined the emotion behind the words. Michael's father addressed Jim as Professor Brennan and stated his and his wife's gratitude for the care and kindness that he had shown towards their son. They knew that Jim would also be mourning their boy's loss and wanted him to know, in case he was in any doubt, that he bore no responsibility for the death of Michael. The letter concluded by saying that they were Christians who were seeking to find comfort in their Church and their God. They included Jim and his family in their daily prayers. Jim was surprised to find that he was crying. He lay his head on the document splayed open on his desk and closed his eyes.

He was not sure how long he had been asleep when he was disturbed by the sound of distant commotion. He cocked his head, unsure at first if he had heard anything. Perhaps it was just the hazy roar of far-off traffic. But there was something fracturing the air, a jumble of noises that might have been music, a sports crowd or a parade. He rubbed his face as he went to the window, feeling the sense of doom he had carried for weeks darkening.

A crowd of students were streaming down the hill from the student union and assembling on the roadway, blocking the traffic. They carried hastily constructed placards. Their slogans were too far away for him to read, but even at a distance he could see that many were spattered with red, as if they had been carried through a massacre.

Another persistent sound interrupted the horror. It took him a moment to realise that it was his desk phone. The display showed the caller was Robert Cameron, head of security.

Jim took a deep breath and tried to expel the panic from his lungs. 'Hello, Robert.'

'We've got a problem, professor.'

'I know. I can see it from my window. What is it? A protest?'

'The student representative council didn't give us any warning. I've got my guys out there trying to cool the situation, but you know how it goes once these things get started.'

'Any idea what it's about?'

There was a pause on the line, and Jim got a sense of Cameron looking out of the window of the gatehouse trying to decipher the protest slogans. 'Something to do with blood money.'

Jim swore under his breath and grabbed his suit jacket from the coat stand. 'I'll be right down. See if you can find any student reps willing to talk to me. They'll be the ones with the loudhailers.'

It was cold outside. He realised he should have worn his heavy coat over his suit, but the noise was growing, car horns now mingling with the chanting and singing. He could make out the words now, a simple call and response.

Say NO to blood money!
NO! NO! NO!
Say NO to blood money!
NO! NO! NO!

Cameron met him before he got to the main gate. The head of security had served time in Northern Ireland and Iraq. He was shorter than Jim, compact and muscular beneath his suit with the scrubbed-clean, close-shaven look of a particular breed of soldier. Successions of students had nicknamed him Andy McNab.

'It'll be rush hour soon. Work on the new building's already reduced Mitchell Street to one lane, so this could cause a back-up into the city centre in one direction, and towards the motorway in the other. Someone must have tipped off the press in advance. They're already here.'

Jim said, 'Did you manage to pin down any members of the SRC?'

'Appears it isn't their show. This lot aren't up for negotiation. It's a simple yes or no. Give in to their demands, or they'll block the roads and cause chaos.'

Cameron's military cool was not infectious. Jim muttered, 'Jesus Christ. Okay, I'd better try speaking some sense into them.'

Cameron said, 'No offence, professor, but is there anyone else who could have a word? Maybe one of the other vice chancellors? The students seem to blame you for this blood money thing. We don't want the situation to escalate.'

The noise of chanting and car horns was growing. Jim resisted the urge to curse Ronald Fergusson out loud. He said, 'I'll speak to them. If that doesn't work, we'll call the police and have them dispersed.'

Cameron looked towards the gate and the throng of placards and protesters. It was midweek, classes were over for the day, and more students were swelling the crowd, which was taking on the frenzied holiday atmosphere of a seaside fairground. Transgression was in the air.

'Sure that's the way you want to go? It might ramp things up.'

Jim grimaced. 'It's not going to improve things if I go into hiding.'

Cameron nodded. 'I take your point. I'll walk with you. I suggest you stay at the gate. That way we can get you away quick if things kick off.'

Jim snapped, 'I don't need protection from my own students.'

The crimson-splashed placards bobbed up and down, like extras in a puppet show, and the crowd hissed and booed as Jim stepped from the university gates into the street. But they were students, and he was a vice principal, so no one jostled him. He approached the lanky white boy who had possession of the megaphone and gestured for him to hand it over. The boy raised it high above his head, beyond Jim's reach.

Jim said, in a voice sharp as a Glasgow kiss, 'Are you scared of me?'

Cameron was at Jim's side. He put a steadying hand on Jim's shoulder and told the boy to give the professor the loudhailer.

The boy muttered something under his breath and handed it over. It came to life with a shriek. Someone in the crowd shouted, 'Fucking murderer!' Students were holding their phones in the air, recording him like he was on stage at a concert.

Jim raised the loudhailer to his mouth and said, 'I am Jim Brennan, one of the vice principals of this university and a citizen of this city that you are casually disrupting.' The students booed, but he noticed people stepping from their stalled cars into the road to hear him better. Jim recalled Ron Fergusson's phrase of that morning and continued: 'This is an institution of higher learning, a place of debate. It is also an institution that is a proud part of this city.' He spotted a TV camera in the crowd, trained on him. The demonstration was more organised than it appeared. 'Whatever it is you're protesting about – and we can discuss that in a civilised manner – I must object to your anti-democratic disruption of the workers of this city and demand that you step down and let the women and men whose lives you are holding up go about their business.'

One of the drivers who had got out of his car, leaned in and beeped his horn. Others joined in. Jim was pitting town against gown, and the town was on his side. The lanky boy who had handed over the loudhailer tried to take it back, but Jim gave him a discreet dig in the ribs, one that was designed to hurt. The boy pulled back his fist, but Cameron caught his arm, bent the boy close to him and whispered something in his ear that made the boy look at him in disbelief and call him a 'fascist fucker'.

A student shouted, 'Get your hands off him.'

Cameron raised both hands in the air. 'Take it easy.'

A police helicopter came into view. Sirens were shrieking in the distance. One of the drivers must have called the police.

Jim shouted, 'This is an unlawful and grossly uninformed demonstration. I am here and willing to talk with representatives of your choice, but now I am asking you to disperse and let people go about their business. Allow them to go to work, collect their children from school, keep hospital appointments, attend to caring duties, or whatever it is that they need to do.'

Car drivers pressed their horns in support. The sirens were coming closer. Some students on the edge of the demonstration started to slip away. The stalwarts resumed their chanting.

Say NO to blood money!
NO! NO! NO!
Say NO to blood money!
NO! NO! NO!

The ringleader grabbed the loudhailer and shouted, 'Jim Brennan is taking money from the Saudi royal family to fund a vanity project for the university . . .'

Robert Cameron cupped Jim's elbow. 'You've done your best.'

Jim stood his ground. The sirens blared to a halt and blue lights flashed across the stalled line of traffic. The ringleader was intoning a toll of Saudi crimes: *war in Yemen, anti-LGBTQ+ laws, denial of women's rights, murder, capital punishment, murder, torture, murder* . . .

Police officers were now pushing their way through the crowd amidst the din of car horns blaring and students chanting.

Jim Brennan, Brennan!
NO! NO! NO!
Jim Brennan, Brennan!
NO! NO! NO!
Jim Brennan, Brennan!
NO! NO! NO!

Jim wanted to shout back that he had never condoned murder, that his career had been focused on expanding access to education, that the new building would have enhanced disabled facilities – and what the fuck did students think would happen to the Saudi money if it did not come to the university?

He kept his head high, aware of the cameras on him, as Cameron escorted him through the gate towards the main building. His phone was buzzing in his inside pocket. He ignored it and looked back at the demonstration.

The protesters had linked arms and were sitting down on the road. Two uniformed policemen were handcuffing the boy with the loudhailer. As Jim watched, a big man in a business suit abandoned his car and started to manhandle a couple of youths. A policewoman went to intervene and was knocked to the ground. One of her colleagues grabbed the businessman's arms behind his back and cuffed him. More sirens sounded the approach of reinforcements, and a scuffle broke out.

Jim started back towards the demonstration, but Cameron grabbed him by the shoulder. 'Best keep out of this, sir. You'll just be providing fodder for TikTok and Twitter. I'll call you when it's over.'

Jim's phone resumed its buzz-buzz-buzz, like a bluebottle against his heart. 'Okay. Update me in fifteen minutes. And tell whoever's in charge of police on the ground that I want to speak to them when it's over.'

'I'll pass that on.' Cameron broke into a quick jog, heading towards the melee.

Jim walked past the gatehouse of the old campus, away from the commotion, in the direction of the main building. His phone buzzed again. He fished it from his pocket: *caller's number withheld*. He answered, and a crisp English accent he did not recognise said, 'Am I talking with Professor Brennan?'

A few weeks ago, Jim would have cut the call, but now he knew the power of anonymous voices to wreck lives. 'Who is this, and how did you get my number?'

The man ignored the question. 'I'm phoning on behalf of the father of one of your students . . .'

Jim resisted an urge to swear. When he was an undergraduate, students left home, lived in cold-water bedsits, survived on cornershop noodles and considered themselves adults. Now they clung to their parents' purse strings, infants clutching the hems of their mothers' skirts. 'This isn't the best time.'

The voice was unapologetic. 'This is a time-sensitive issue. I have a client with a daughter at your university—'

'More than thirty-five thousand students are enrolled here.'

'My client's daughter is not thriving in the way her previous academic grades suggest she should.'

Jim felt a flood of relief. It was merely the lawyer of an overzealous parent. A father like himself, but one still naïve enough to think their offspring was perfect. 'That's unfortunate, but there are channels—'

The voice cut through his. 'My client is not inclined towards normal channels. There is a matter he can assist you with. He would be pleased if in return his daughter might receive extra tutoring.'

Jim heard his own name, tainted and hateful on the wind. 'Brennan! Brennan! Brennan! Out! Out! Out!' A helicopter buzzed above. He looked up at the sky and took a deep breath. 'Extra tutoring is available.'

'Tutoring which will guarantee a first-class degree?'

Had the concerned father seen news of the Saudi donation and thought he might solve the problem of his daughter's grades with a gift of his own?

Jim said, 'We don't sell degrees, first-class or otherwise.'

The voice was devoid of an accent, indifferent. The kind that delivered orders. 'You are looking for a student named Li Jie?'

'Who told you that?'

'My client can guarantee his release.'

'Release from where?'

'Is that relevant?'

Jim realised he did not want to know where Li Jie was being held. It would only make things more difficult. 'What you're asking is beyond my reach. I can't grant your client's request. If, on the other hand, he can guarantee the freedom of a young man—'

'Achieving Li Jie's release would not be effortless.'

'Did your client jail him with the express purpose of manipulating me into helping their daughter?'

'His sentence has nothing to do with my client, but they have contacts. They're confident they can help him.'

'Can I speak directly to your client?'

'They prefer to remain anonymous.'

'So how can I . . .?'

'They prefer to remain anonymous until their daughter's extra tuition is guaranteed.'

Beyond the gates, on the main road that separated the old campus from the new, police were trying to corral the protesters. Car horns blasted.

Jim said, 'I can arrange extra tuition. Our academics are eager for students to thrive.'

'Extra tuition that will result in a first-class degree?'

'That would depend on the work submitted by the student. A first-class degree is not my gift to give.'

'My client's offer is genuine.'

'So are our degrees.'

The voice retained its neutrality. 'Is that your final word?'

Jim wanted to put the voice on speakerphone, step into the student protest and demand they listen to the way the world worked. 'I can't be any clearer. If your client has the influence he claims, he has a moral duty to help free Li Jie.'

'Thank you for your clarity.'

'Surely we can resolve this. Li Jie is a young man with his whole life ahead of him. Your client is a parent – he must feel some compassion . . .'

'That's beyond my field of knowledge.' The air of formality

slipped, and a note of warmth entered the voice. 'Don't feel bad, Professor Brennan. You stuck by your principles. My client will respect that. Honour is dearer than life.'

'If he can respect that, then surely . . .'

But the line was dead, the voice gone. Jim swore out loud. His chest felt tight. He inhaled deeply and resumed the walk to his office, counting the intervals between breaths. The shadow of the main building touched his face and he looked up. The windows were full of people, admin and support staff, janitors, cleaners, academics and a few stranded students, all watching the action beyond the gates. They looked down at him, observing his progress as he crossed the square, a big man knocked down to size.

Thirty-Nine

THE REST OF the afternoon dissolved into a mess of police interviews and meetings with comms and student reps. Four students and one member of the public had been arrested. There was a request for an interview from the *Guardian*, who were writing a feature on unethical university investments, and an invitation to comment from the *Daily Mail*, who were running an article on disruptive students. Jim drafted sober replies, which were modified by comms, who then began a damage limitation exercise on social media.

Murray Deacon, director of communications, phoned at around three o'clock to let Jim know there was the possibility of an interview with Radio 4's *Today* programme at 7 a.m. the following day. Jim hoped to God it would not happen, but they sat down together and worked out a strategy that denied the Saudi gift had been accepted and emphasised the many humanitarian projects undertaken by the university. It felt flimsy, but it was all they had.

Jim asked IT to update the anti-malware on his mobile phone, desktop computer and laptop. He emailed Grace McCann, briefly filling her in on the phone call and asking her to get back in touch with Amnesty and their sister university in Beijing about Li Jie's case. He did not expect an answer that day, but Grace's reply landed in his inbox not long after four. Neither Amnesty nor the university had any information about the missing student. Jim wondered what he would have done if it was his own son's release that had been promised. What was one more concession? A crooked degree or ten? Rich kids already had the advantage. Why not acknowledge it and scatter first-class honours like confetti?

Murray all but pushed Jim out of the door just after five, with instructions to watch the six o'clock news, keep his phone charged and get an early night. 'Have a whisky if you think it'll help. Just the one. One helps, two hinders.'

Jim phoned Maggie on the hands-free. He let her know he would be home earlier than expected and suggested they get a takeaway. She had been at Newlands all day and had not heard about the demonstration. He decided not to mention it. There would be time to talk later.

Sasha met Jim at the front door with Benji at her heels. She gave him a hug. 'Dad, you're a hero.'

Jim kissed the top of her head, breathing in the fresh shampoo and outdoor smell of her hair, her aliveness. He hung his jacket in the vestibule. 'I'm glad somebody thinks so.'

Sasha was wearing cut-off denim dungarees over multi-coloured stripy socks and a matching T-shirt. She held Maggie's phone in her hand. 'Lots of people think so. You're trending.'

They had forbidden Sasha her own phone. A decision she

railed against, but which, mindful of Eliot's dependence on the digital world, they stood firm on. As a consolation she was allowed occasional monitored use of his and Maggie's phones.

Jim took the mobile from her. 'I thought you weren't allowed to look at Twitter.'

'I know, but Trina WhatsApped and said you're trending. Look.' His daughter slipped the mobile deftly from his hand and brought up a video. 'You're a working-class hero, Dad.'

The phrase sounded old-fashioned in her mouth. He said, 'A what?'

'A working-class her*ooo*.' Sasha held the phone's screen towards him and pressed play.

A video showed him addressing the student sit-in. *I am Jim Brennan, one of the vice principals of this university and a citizen of this city* . . . His accent was broader than it sounded in his head. The camera scanned the road, the stalled traffic, drivers stepping disgruntled from their cars to hear what he had to say . . . *I object to your anti-democratic disruption of the workers of this city and demand that you step down and let the women and men whose lives you are holding up go about their business. Allow them to go to work, collect their children from school, keep hospital appointments, attend to caring duties, or whatever it is that they have to do.*

The tweet was from an address he did not recognise. It was headed 'Working Class Hero' and had attracted over 5,000 likes. He watched it again, bemused at the image of himself on the small screen.

Maggie came through from the kitchen. 'What's going on?'

Sasha grinned. 'Dad's trending.'

Jim held up the phone, and they watched together, his

wife's chin resting on his shoulder, her breath warm against his neck.

Maggie whispered, 'Well done, Jim.'

The clock in the hall struck six. Jim handed the phone to her. 'I've got to watch the news.'

They squashed together on the couch in the TV room, Jim and Maggie each cradling an Auchentoshan, Sasha between them, Benji sprawled across their knees. The newscaster relayed that day's political failures, environmental disasters, wars, health reports and celebrity slip-ups. Jim assumed that his section would fall in the Scottish segment, but it came at the end of the national news. The newscaster slipped into a relaxed smile, signalling to viewers that the worst had passed. She sparkled, her voice warm. 'Today, a university head reminded student protesters that they are a part of wider society.'

The clip of Jim standing outside the university gates came on screen. His voice was the voice of the city: working-class lad made pillar of the establishment. His suit was smart, his expression earnest and strained with concern. A reporter had gathered some vox pops from the protesters blocking the road. The university had plenty of students born and raised in the city, but the reporter alighted on a duo with upper-class accents who struggled to articulate why their sit-in was worthy of disrupting hard-working citizens. The scuffle between the police and the students was briefly shown on screen, followed by a short interview with a woman who had been on her way to visit her husband in a hospice. The woman praised Jim's intervention and then broke down with the stress of it all. A man in overalls said that in his opinion the students hadn't done a hand's turn in their lives. The report was partisan, biased and failed to mention the reason the students were objecting to the donation. Jim looked like a strong, compassionate leader. He looked like a decent man. A good man.

Sasha wiggled her toes. 'They were mean stopping that lady from visiting her husband.'

Jim felt sick. 'They didn't mean to stop her. They just didn't think things through.'

Maggie set her barely touched whisky on the coffee table. 'Actions have consequences. Those kids got a free life lesson today.'

He hugged his daughter. 'Their intentions were pure.'

Maggie blew a raspberry. Sasha giggled and joined in. Benji jumped off the couch and started barking.

Jim's phone rang. He flapped his hands. 'Shh.'

Murray Deacon was jubilant in his ear. 'Ten–nil to us.'

Jim disentangled himself from his wife and daughter, and sat forward on the edge of the couch, whisky glass still in his hand. He had loosened his tie. It hung away from his body, like an abandoned leash. 'It's not about sides, Murray.'

The comms director dialled his enthusiasm down. 'Of course not. But it went well. Really well. *Today* want you on first thing. Same angle – the man who knows the city stands up to ill-informed disruption.'

Jim sipped his drink. 'Tell them I appreciate the invitation but politely decline.'

'I strongly recommend you accept. The student newspaper will put the demo front page, and their spin's not likely to be sympathetic. The story's not dead yet. The Saudi connection can still sit up and bite us. This way we have a chance of controlling the narrative.'

Jim wondered how Murray would react if the truth about his last few weeks emerged. He said, 'I'm not interested in making our students look like arseholes.'

Sasha giggled, and Maggie whispered, 'Jim.'

He mouthed, 'Sorry.'

Maggie shook her head, but she was smiling. She got up, pulling Sasha with her, and left the room. Benji trotted after them.

Murray sounded exasperated. 'The *Today* programme could set a positive tone for the rest of the press. If we don't give them something, they might come up with a less flattering take on things.'

Dishes clattered in the kitchen. Maggie had decided against takeaway.

Jim injected a note of finality into his voice. 'I don't want to become the story.'

'Even if it's supportive?'

'I'm a university vice principal, not a celebrity. I don't need to be loved. Let's just put a lid on it.'

Murray tried to persuade Jim, but the comms director had been a seasoned journalist before he joined the university and knew when he had reached a dead end. He concluded on a warning note. 'I hope we don't live to regret this.'

Jim downed the dregs of his whisky: 'I'll settle for living to remember it.'

They ate dinner – vegetarian sausage and bean stew with mashed sweet potatoes – at the kitchen island. They were halfway through the meal when the landline rang. Maggie rose to answer it, but Jim was quicker. His voice was wary, the way it was these days when he did not recognise the caller's number. 'Hello?'

'Dad?'

'Son, are you all right?'

Maggie came to his side. 'Is it Eliot?'

'Your mum's here, son. Everyone's fine at this end. How are you?'

Jim moved the headset, and they pressed their heads close, so they could both hear him. It was like an old-fashioned phone call, the connection faint, time ticking down. Jim turned to give Sasha a reassuring wink. She scowled at him and forked a slice of veggie sausage into her mouth.

Eliot sounded tired. 'I'm getting better too quick. They're moving me tomorrow morning.'

Maggie said, 'To another ward?'

'No, Mums, back to prison.'

Jim put his arm around his wife's waist. 'We knew it was on the cards. They'll put you in the healthcare wing. You'll be safe there.'

'I'm safe nowhere, not unless you do what they're asking. They'll get me again, and next time they'll do a better job.'

Jim shut his eyes, aware that others might be listening in. 'Don't worry, son. You're going to be okay. Just concentrate on getting better.'

There was a sob in Eliot's voice. 'I don't want to get better. I told you, they'll kill me next time.'

Maggie said, 'When can we visit?'

'I don't know. I'll ask for a visiting order.'

Jim repeated, 'Concentrate on getting well. We'll do what we can from this end.' He hoped it was enough to reassure his son without putting whoever might be listening on his scent. 'There are people looking out for you now. You're going to be okay.'

Eliot whispered, 'You promise?'

'I promise.'

Maggie said, 'Remember to get a visiting order for us.' But the line was dead. Maggie looked at Jim. 'You know what you need to do.'

He nodded. 'I'm putting everything in place.'

Maggie smiled for the sake of their daughter. 'I know you are, love.'

Sasha said, 'What does Dad need to do? What are you putting in place, Dad?'

Maggie took her seat. 'He's going to arrange for us to visit your brother.'

Sasha made an unconvinced face. Jim joined them at the table and tried to regain the jollity of a moment before. 'It's true. I'm the man with the paperwork plan.'

Sasha ferried a forkful of mash to her mouth and chewed, staring at Jim. 'Are you frightened, Dad?'

Jim wondered what had given his fear away. 'Why do you ask that?'

Sasha shrugged. 'I don't know. You just looked funny.'

Maggie put an arm around their daughter and squeezed. 'Your dad and I wish your brother wasn't in prison, but we know he's safe there. He'll be all right.'

Sasha was still staring at Jim, her smooth forehead creased with concern.

Jim felt a rush of love that was close to violence. He would protect his family. He and Maggie would grow old together. Their daughter would grow up and mature until she had her own family to etch creases permanent on her brow.

He reached across the table and touched his fingertips briefly to Sasha's cheek. 'Don't worry, sweetheart. I'm not frightened of anything.'

Forty

THE LASERPRINTER IN Maggie's studio churned out the confidential building specifications and previously tendered bids for the Learning and Teaching Hub. Jim worked in the small pool of light thrown by the Anglepoise. The room beyond was shadows and not quite darkness. Sasha was upstairs, tucked safely in bed, Maggie in the back garden supervising Benji's final outing and smoking a cigarette they would pretend had never happened.

Jim had taken a pair of disposable plastic gloves from the cupboard under the kitchen sink. Fingerprints were less important than they had been in his father's time. There were surer ways to snare wrongdoers these days: DNA, archaeobotany, invisible spores, gait analysis and fuck knows what else. But there was no point in taking needless chances.

Maggie came into the room. She had sprayed herself with perfume. The lingering smoky cigarette smell reached through the scent, reminding him of the early days of their courtship. She nodded at his gloves which glowed, whitely in the lamplight. 'Are they necessary?'

Jim took the pile of paper from the printer tray and tapped it against Maggie's desk, aligning the edges. 'Probably not.'

'They make you look like a criminal.'

He glanced at her. 'And your point is?'

'You're not crooked, Jim. You're protecting your family.'

'I'm not sure that would count as a defence in a court of law.' He scanned the top of Maggie's desk. 'Have you got any envelopes?'

'Third drawer down.'

Jim took an A4 buff envelope from a neatly ordered pile, slid the pages inside and sealed it with tape from the dispenser on the desk. Benji trotted into the room. Maggie picked the dog up and held him to her chest, his paws resting on her shoulder. 'You should post it somewhere central.'

Jim leaned against the desk, holding the envelope in his gloved hands. 'I'm not posting it.'

His wife's eyes met his. 'Don't be stupid.'

'I don't want any misunderstandings. This ends here.'

Benji snuffled against Maggie's ear. She pushed the dog's nose away. 'Stick a first-class stamp on it. I'll drive into town and post it at the sorting office. I'll even wear plastic gloves, if it'll make you feel better.'

'I need to deliver a personal message.'

'You're not Charles Bronson, Jim.'

He graced her with a smile that was no smile at all. 'Guys like this, they push until they hit a wall. I've got to let them know this is as far as I'm willing to go, or they'll be back.'

Maggie shifted Benji from one arm to the other,

redistributing the dog's weight. 'Wait until tomorrow when Sasha's at school. I'll cancel my meetings and come with you.'

'It has to be done tonight, and anyway . . .'

'Anyway, what?'

'This way, if something happens, we can say you knew nothing about it.'

Another woman might have clutched at his chest or begged him not to go. Maggie put the dog gently onto the floor. 'Off you go, Benji – dinnertime.' The dog wagged its tail and trotted obediently from the room.

Maggie straightened up. She looked Jim in the eye and snatched the envelope from his hand. The action was quick and unexpected. Jim moved to grab it, but Maggie gave him a shove to the sternum that knocked the air from his chest and sent him backwards against the desk. She slung the envelope into her filing cabinet, locked the drawer and flung the key behind it.

Jim rubbed his chest where the heel of her hand had made contact. 'For fuck's sake, Maggie. We agreed I'd do this. You knew it was risky.'

Maggie leaned against the filing cabinet, blocking it with her body. 'I've changed my mind. My son's in prison. I won't have my husband there too.'

He took her hand. 'It won't come to that. Maximum I'd get would be a slap on the wrist.'

Maggie stood firm against the cabinet. 'You don't know that. What if things go wrong?'

Jim raised his wife's hand to his mouth and gently rubbed her fingertips against his lips. 'They won't. I promise.' He tried to pull her close, but she resisted. He whispered, 'They threatened Sasha.'

Maggie pressed her forehead to his chest. Her breathing was uneven. They stood like that for a moment, then she raised her face and looked at him. 'Can't you ask Eddie to do it for you?'

'He's made it clear he wants nothing more to do with us. This has to be done properly. I've got to do it myself.'

'Maybe, but you don't have to do it alone. You need a witness. Promise me you'll ask him.'

'I promise.' Jim buried his face in Maggie's hair, smelt smoke again and clasped his hands around her waist. 'You know I can print off another copy, no bother?' She gave a small laugh, leaned into him and raised her face to his. They kissed, and he pressed his still-gloved palms to her bottom. The filing cabinet was too high, so he steered her towards the desk. She moved with him, her hands inside his shirt, skin on skin. He was about to lift her onto the desk when the door opened and light sliced into the room from the hallway.

Sasha said, 'Dad, why are you wearing gloves?'

He and Maggie pulled apart. Jim tucked his shirt into his trousers. Maggie smoothed her hair. 'I've told you before, knock before you come in here.'

There was a whine in Sasha's voice. 'You said to knock if the door's shut. It wasn't properly shut. Were you sexing?'

Maggie put her hand on their daughter's shoulder. 'No, luckily for you. What are you doing out of bed anyway?'

'I couldn't sleep.'

'Why not? Are you worried?'

'Maybe.'

Maggie knelt level with Sasha and hugged her. 'There's nothing to worry about. I'll come upstairs and tuck you in again. Say goodnight to Dad.'

Sasha gave him a sleepy smile. 'Night, night, Dad. Love you.'

Maggie said, 'I love you too, Jim.'

He blew them a kiss. 'Love you both.'

Maggie shut the door. The bright light receded, and he was alone again in the shadows.

Forty-One

JIM TOOK PETER Henders' card from his wallet. It was late to be making business calls, but he dialled the direct line. Peter Henders picked up straight away.

'Hello?' The builder sounded impatient.

'This is James Brennan.' Jim let the sentence hang, not bothering to explain why he was phoning.

There was a pause, and then Henders said, 'Has something happened to your son?'

'A lot has happened to my son, but that's not why I'm calling.' Now it was Henders' turn to let the silence work for him. After a moment Jim continued: 'It's about your bid to build the Learning and Teaching Hub.'

'Don't tell me you're bringing the deadline forward.'

'The deadline's the same. I was told you needed some extra information.'

Henders was all business now. 'Not that I'm aware of. My accountant's in the next room. Hold on, I'll ask her.'

The line went silent. Jim stared out of the window. Beyond the hedge that marked the back garden's boundary, he could see the faint glow of the neighbouring house. He wondered if things would ever return to how they had been before Eliot's arrest. If he survived, he would try to be less busy, make more time for Sasha while she was still a child.

Peter Henders came back on the line. 'Thanks for taking the time to call, but I've checked. No one put in any requests.'

'Are you sure?'

A chill entered Henders' voice. 'Are you asking if I need extra information or offering to give me some? It's a big contract. We'll take all the data you can give us.'

Jim kept his tone noncommittal. 'There are strict guidelines.'

'You didn't strike me as a flirt, Professor Brennan. If you have some information to impart, impart it; if not, let me get back to my accounts. I'd like to get home before midnight.'

Jim detected a blast of the same quick temper that had led to the breach between Henders and Cranston. Had he rattled the builder, or was the man simply tired?

'I guess someone somewhere got their wires crossed.'

Henders sighed. The ice left his voice. 'It's been a long day. I'm guessing it's the same for you. I saw you on the news.'

'Never a dull moment.' Jim wanted to end the call and think about what Henders had or had not said. But he added another turn of the screw. 'I'll give you a tip: the university won't support a bid by a construction firm that doesn't have clinker-built finances. We can't risk a key player going bust before the project's complete.'

'We're solid.'

'Good, I heard you'd had some troubles.'

'Everyone has troubles, Professor Brennan. The thing is to find a solution.'

'Yes, that does seem to be the thing.' Jim apologised for bothering the builder so late at night and ended the call. He stared into the darkness, weighing the odds between involving the police or following through.

The police were incapable of solving the simplest break-in or car theft. They relied on CCTV and blundering criminals. Seeking their help might land him in deeper trouble. Jim's research had confirmed what his father had often told him, that there were ranks of friendly officers happy to take a bung in return for intel or turning a blind eye.

Jim was the son and the father of felons. He had long had what could be considered an unhealthy interest in crime. He had made, some might say, 'a nice little earner' of it. There was footage of him in the quayside apartment, delivering drugs and money to J. People would easily believe he had crossed the line and become the outlaw he was always destined to be. It was too late to turn back now. His course was set.

Something moved in the shadows of the garden. His heart quickened when the security light flashed on, illuminating the lawn. A fox froze in the sudden brightness, then bolted back into the darkness and was gone.

Jim hauled the filing cabinet away from the wall. He retrieved the key Maggie had thrown there, unlocked the drawer and took out the envelope that would buy his son's safety. He stepped into the hallway, clutching the envelope. Upstairs in Sasha's bedroom, Maggie was saying something to their daughter. He took his keys from the dish on the hall table, shrugged on his coat and stepped into the night.

*

Jim cast frequent glances in the rear-view mirror as he drove, wary of tails, feeling like a screen detective approaching the end of the movie. He parked by the wasteland that edged the Fusilier and phoned Cranston. There was no guarantee the lawyer would be in the pub, but a sixth sense told Jim he would favour places where he felt comfortable. He picked up. Jim heard the rumble of bar-room chatter and knew he was there.

'I'm outside. Any chance of a quick word?'

'It's never a quick word with you, Jimmy.'

'I've a final delivery to make. I need a shadow.'

'Find somebody else.'

'There isn't anyone else.'

'Not my problem.'

'Maybe not, but it was my problem that got you a beating.'

'In a roundabout fashion.'

'Was it Peter Henders?'

Cranston sounded incredulous. 'I already told you. Henders has nothing to do with it.'

'He keeps coming up.'

Jim saw the door of the Fusilier open and Cranston step out. He walked past the smokers loitering there, and vanished into blackness.

'It's nothing to do with Henders. Not even at arm's length. I took a loan from an ex-client. He got into a bit of bother and was persuaded to sell it on. I got a kicking and instructions to make sure you paid back what your son owed.' Cranston sounded bitter. 'They didn't need to give me the kicking, but they did. That's the way some guys operate. They want to make sure.'

'Is that why you hang around with the football team? Ready-made bodyguards?'

'You've met them. They can scarcely kick a ball.'

'Aye, but there's safety in numbers.'

'So what am I doing out here on my own?'

'Making sure.'

'I am sure. My debts are paid in full. My continued health relies on casting you adrift. Sorry, Jim. I already told you nicely – you're on your own.'

The phone died. The light of the doorway illuminated Cranston for a moment and then he disappeared into the safety of the pub.

Knuckles rapped against the window of the Audi. A white face appeared at the car's side window. A threatening grin. Other faces emerged from the darkness. One of them pressed against the glass, stuck their tongue out and licked it. Leaving a saliva smear. They were shoved out of the way. A sober face appeared and gestured for Jim to wind down the window. He lowered it half an inch.

'Hi, professor.'

Jim recognised Ally, the member of Cranston's youth team who was destined for the army. 'What do you want?'

Ally's expression was serious. 'Leave Mr Cranston alone.'

'I'm not interested in him.'

'Yeah? Why do you keep on phoning him then? You think you're a big man, but Mr Cranston's worth ten of you. We hear you've come near him again, we'll boot the shite out of you.'

'Don't worry.'

'We're not worried, but you should be.'

Ally nodded to the other boys. They surrounded the Audi and started to rock it – gently at first, but with growing force. Jim's phone tumbled into the seat well. The car alarm blasted into life. Its blare added to the boys' excitement.

They hooted and laughed as they shoved the car to and fro with increasing violence. Jim gripped the sides of the driver's seat and stared straight ahead. He would not give the boys the satisfaction of his fear, though he did fear they were about to tip the car upside down onto the waste ground. Just when it felt as if they were pitching into madness, Ally called a halt. The team gave the car a few half-hearted shoves, a couple of kicks and catcalls, and wandered off.

Ally rapped on the window again. 'That's all the warning you're getting.'

Jim was still holding onto the seat. He let go and turned to look at the boy. 'How far would you go for Cranston?'

Ally looked confused. 'We're not fucking queers.'

'Would you kill for him?'

The boy considered the words and then met Jim's eyes. 'Better you don't find out.'

Forty-Two

JIM PARKED IN sight of the junction that would take him either to the city centre or towards unlit, twisting roads and lonely countryside. He took out his phone and dialled the number that would connect him to the voice that had threatened his daughter and ordered the beating that had almost cost his son his life. There was a swell of chatter and atmosphere in the background, and then the voice said, in playful tones that suggested boozy Christmas lunches and singsongs around a piano, 'Hello, hello, it's the boy they've all been waiting for.'

Jim slumped in the driver's seat. The humiliation the football team had delivered was still on him. He felt dizzy, as if the rocking car had dislodged his centre of gravity. Cranston had won his squad's loyalty with a few football lessons, but the sea of love Jim had poured into his son had been wasted.

He swallowed. 'I've got it.'

'Good lad. Gonnae drop it off?'

'Where?'

'Let's do it at your place.'

Jim bridled. 'You're not getting anywhere near my family.'

The voice sounded amused. 'Relax, I meant the university. You can give me a tour.'

'It's shut.'

'Doesn't matter. It's a nice night. Full moon, if I remember rightly.'

Locating the exchange at the site of his hopes and previous triumphs was another move to demean him. Jim glanced at his watch. It was late: the student unions would have closed, the students weaving their way homewards. By the time he arrived on campus, even the stragglers should be gone.

'Not the old campus. They light it up like Sunset Strip, and there are security guards on patrol. We can meet at the new-build. It's not much more than a hole in the ground. Watch out for the CCTV cameras focused on the union.'

'None on the building site?'

'Not yet.'

'No night watchman?'

'No point paying someone to guard rubble.'

'Your dad never laid out a cent more than he needed to either.'

It was the first time the voice had mentioned his father. Peter Henders had talked about him too, the first time they met. Was it a coincidence or a connection?

Jim felt in his pocket for his office keys. Work would be his alibi, if anyone spotted him. 'What does my dad have to do with anything?'

The voice said, 'Twenty minutes,' and hung up.

Forty-Three

JIM ARRIVED AT the site with five minutes to spare. He slid between the metal barriers that guarded its perimeter and descended a slope slick with scree. The rough ground of the demolition site reminded him of the decades-old bomb craters and ruined slums that had been the playgrounds of his childhood.

He was right about the site being not much more than a hole in the ground. It was pocked by deep sockets, where huge concrete pegs, braced by steel spines, had previously sunk deep into the foundations, securing the old building to the ground.

An occasional car went by on the main road that bisected the campus. Jim saw the distant sweep of headlights, but their beams stopped short of the demolition site. He was alone in a landscape of mud and brick dust, a sole survivor on an urban battleground. An engine grumbled nearby. He heard the rise and fall of indistinct voices talking in accents he recognised as his own. A car door slammed. Jim turned into the darkness and retraced his steps.

A short, broad-shouldered man in a leather jacket was waiting with his back to the perimeter fence. Jim paused, taking in the way the man stuffed his hands into the pockets of his jacket, a glimpse of white hair escaping from beneath a tweed cap. He had a sense that he was witnessing the shrunken version of a once powerful frame. Age might have diminished the man, but he retained the confidence to come alone. Jim wondered if it was justified.

His father would not have caved the way that he had. Big Jim would have put his hands around the old git's neck and squeezed, given the man something to think on, a kick or two to the guts, and then sent him home empty-handed.

Jim's stomach clenched with shame. He started to climb the incline that led out of the site. Rubble crunched beneath his feet, and the man turned to look at him: a white face, round and owl-like, features lost in the gloom. He waited until Jim pushed his way through the perimeter fence before speaking. 'After your bedtime, Jimmy?'

There was something familiar in the older man's delivery, the way he cocked his head to one side.

Jim said, 'Who are you? The Wizard of Oz? The wee squirt behind the big machine?'

The man bristled. 'That's you, son. You're the one in charge of the broken levers.'

'Better than being a big man who threatens wee lassies.'

The stranger looked away. 'You got what I told you to bring?'

The envelope was folded safe in Jim's inside pocket, but he shook his head. 'I don't think so.'

The stranger's gaze returned to Jim's face. His voice was steady. 'We had an agreement.'

Jim wondered if their conversation was being recorded. He said, 'I had a chat with Peter Henders before I came here. He's happy they have all the information they need to make their bid. I'd say the firm stands a good chance.'

Jim's eyes had adjusted to the dark. He could see the blackmailer's features now. He was somewhere in his early seventies, with a plump, clean-shaven face and an expression that was hard to read.

'You don't want to cross me, Jimmy.'

'You can't please all of the people all of the time.'

'I'm one of the guys you want to please.'

Jim straightened his back. 'You're a chancer. You knew my son was beaten up and pretended you'd made it happen. You stalked my wife, threatened my eleven-year-old daughter and tried to intimidate me.'

The stranger grinned. 'I'd say I did a pretty good job of intimidating you, Jimmy. You're here after midnight when you should be tucked up tight in your cosy bed with your cosy wife.'

The phrase 'cosy wife' irked Jim. He said, 'I'm guessing this is something to do with a grudge against my dad. Maybe you think wrecking my career will even things out, but I'm not going to let that happen. My dad's dead and gone. Whatever problem you had with him was burnt to ash, ten years back, in Minehill Crematorium.'

The stranger smiled. 'You always had a good way with words. Not so big on logic though – what about the photos of you at J's place?'

'People talk. They take photographs and sell them to interested parties. I'm not frightened. They prove fuck all.'

A trio of young men appeared at the end of the street. Jim and the stranger fell silent. As the young men drew closer Jim saw that they were Chinese; he heard their voices, talking animatedly in their own language. He ducked his head, hoping not to be recognised. The trio were absorbed in their conversation and passed by with barely a glance.

The stranger followed them with his eyes. 'Sometimes it feels like the city doesn't belong to us any more.'

'Overseas students contribute a lot of money to the city. They come here, work hard and go home with new skills. These guys probably came from the library. It's open twenty-four hours.'

The stranger snorted. 'Jesus, youth is wasted on the young, right enough.' He focused his stare on Jim. 'Where were we?'

'I was in the process of telling you to fuck off.'

'You sure?'

Jim turned to go. 'Certain.'

The stranger stayed where he was. 'I was hoping not to have to do this.' He took out his phone and tapped at its keys. It lit up, and he raised its screen to Jim's eyeline.

Jim froze. His house was captured on screen. The living-room curtains were drawn, but he could tell from the glow beyond them that lamps were lit inside. The upstairs rooms were in darkness. As he watched, a light went on in their bedroom, and he saw Maggie's silhouette briefly at the window as she drew the curtains.

Cold tentacles wrapped around his heart. He said, 'So what? You videoed my home. All that proves is you're a creepy bastard. I knew that already.'

The stranger shook his head. 'You're a difficult customer, Jimmy.' He put the phone's mic close to his lips. 'Arno, say hello to the prof.' The man held the phone in front of Jim's face again. The focus of the video switched. Jim caught a brief glimpse of dark beard and grinning mouth on the small screen. Pale skin and wide eyes, a hint of madness, beneath a black knit cap. His own house still in the background of the shot. Maggie and Sasha nested inside, like victims in the first frames of a horror movie.

The stranger told Arno, 'Show the prof your watch. I want him to know we're in the same time zone.' Electronic numbers shone on Arno's watch face. Jim glanced at his own watch. The times matched. The stranger turned the screen to face himself. 'Ta, Arno. Sit tight. I'll give you a shout if you're needed.' He looked at Jim. 'Satisfied? Or do you want me to get in touch with the prison so you can have a chat with your lad? I've a couple of boys on standby just in case.'

In the street beyond the building site a drunk started to sing. His mates joined in. The sound of their voices reached across the flattened ground, careless and boozy.

Jim whispered, 'Who the fuck are you?'

'An old pal of your da's.'

'My da's dead and gone.'

'I know that. Poor bastard that he was. You treated him like he was shite on your shoe.'

'My dad was a violent headcase.'

'Your da knew that life is fucking tough. He tried to harden you up, so you'd survive. And look at you, you survived.'

'His foot was on my neck my whole childhood. He beat my mother until she lost her mind. Whatever I am, I am despite him.'

'He was a man of his place and time, and you're a whinger.' The stranger's voice was calm, as if it was no odds to him. He nodded towards the demolition site. 'Let's take a walk. Show me where we're erecting this new building of yours.'

Jim said, 'Don't think it's a done deal.' But he pulled the barrier aside and let the man go first, down the steep incline that led to the site. This would be the perfect moment to trip him up, roll his body into rubbled darkness, knock him unconscious and stave his brains in with a rock. Jim still had the plastic gloves in his pocket. He could slip them on quickly before the act, avoid detection. Men like this had enemies. The list of suspects would be long.

Jim followed him onto the rough ground. They walked side by side in silence to one of the unplugged sockets and stared into it. The stranger kicked a loose stone into the depths. 'All that stuff you put in your fucking textbook? You wouldn't have had any of it without your da. You wouldn't have your precious job if it wasn't for him.'

Jim looked at him. 'You read my book?'

'I can read.'

Jim had met criminals who had read his book before, inmates in prison, impressed with their own intellectual prowess. He asked the man the same question he asked them: 'What did you make of it?'

'You really want to know?'

'I'm curious.'

The stranger took a step away from the unplugged socket. 'You gave away stuff that didn't belong to you. I read the reviews. Academics going on about your great insights into the criminal underworld. The dogs in the street could have written what you did, but they know better. Some things are private. You're lucky no one kicked your head in.'

'Is that what this is all about? My book?'

'Don't flatter yourself.' He held out his hand. 'Give.' Jim hesitated, and the stranger took his phone from his pocket. 'You want me to give Arno the go-ahead?'

Jim tried again. 'I told you, I spoke to Peter Henders. He's happy with the information he has.'

The stranger snorted. 'Pete's like you. Thinks the world's a fair place and everything'll be fine if you play by the rules. He doesn't realise there are other rules, and he wouldn't be where he is now if certain things hadn't been done.'

It was the way the stranger said 'Pete', with a mixture of pride and frustration, that made Jim realise. He whispered, 'You're Peter Henders' father.'

The man grinned. 'Penny's dropped.'

The world came into focus, bringing the past with it. 'I remember you. You came round to the house for a drink.'

'A couple of times maybe. Your dad and me weren't exactly close, but I noticed you. You were hard to miss. Snooty wee swot. Nose either stuck in a book or stuck in the air, like there was a bad smell under it.'

'You gave me a fiver.'

He laughed. 'Did I? Must have been three sheets to the wind.'

Jim grinned, though nothing was funny. 'You were.'

Henders' smile vanished. 'Okay, so we've had a nice trip down memory lane. You know who I am, and that means you know I don't fuck around.'

The wind was getting up, grit rising on the air, clouds gusting across the moon, but the letter felt warm against Jim's chest. 'You don't think your son could get the contract without cheating?' He took out his own phone. 'What do you think he'd say if I told him what you're up to?'

Henders gestured at Jim's mobile. 'What's this? A Mexican stand-off? Don't worry about Pete. We should have called him Nelson. He turns a blind eye, pretends he doesn't know what's going on.'

'He didn't like it when you rigged the jury.'

Henders stepped closer. 'I wonder who told you about that?'

Jim silently cursed. 'I worked it out for myself. Like you said, I'm a clever boy.'

'Likely story.'

'You hooked my son into selling drugs.'

'Your son did that all by himself. I take nothing to do with drugs, but we're all connected, Jimmy. Like the natural world, our roots run deep. Sooner or later, those that survive rub up against each other. I let it be known I was interested in you, and lo and behold, I came into possession of a lovely set of photos.' Henders glanced at his watch. 'It's getting late, almost time for my Horlicks. That means it's time to cut the gab.'

The man was right. They had reached the end of the road. Jim reached into his jacket. 'Anyone filming this?'

'Think I'd tell you if there was?'

'That was a dirty trick.'

'Boo-fucking-hoo, says the man who's happy to take cash from murdering Arabs.'

Now was not the time to defend the Saudi money. Jim took a deep breath. 'If I give you this, it has to be the end.'

'I decide when things start and when they finish.' Maybe Henders saw the look of resistance on Jim's face because he added, 'Don't worry, Jimmy. You don't have anything else I want. I'd like to retire, truth be told, but you know how it goes. You've got a useless specimen for a son too.'

Jim said, 'Tell your man Arno to get the fuck away from my house.'

'Soon as you pass it over.'

'Now. Make it a video call.'

'Jesus Christ, fine.' Henders stabbed at his phone and Arno's face appeared, bearded and wild, on screen. 'Okay, son, you can stand down now.'

Arno said, 'Cheers, boss,' as if it was all the same to him, and the screen went black.

Jim whispered, 'Know this. If anything happens to my wife or my kids, I will kill your family and then I will find you and slit you from your navel to your chops. I am my father's son. The only reason I've not done it already is I have more to lose than he ever did.'

'Aye, you're a big man.'

'I mean it. Touch a hair on their heads, and I will kill you and go to prison a happy man.'

Henders smiled. 'I already did. I put your boy in the hospital, remember?'

'I'm still not convinced that was you.'

Henders' voice sank to a whisper that was threatening in its softness. 'Oh, it was me all right.'

Somewhere along the perimeter fence, the metal barriers rattled. Jim looked in the direction of the noise, but clouds were obscuring the moon and he could not see far in the darkness.

Henders said, 'C'mon, time to get moving.'

Jim took one of the plastic gloves from his pocket. His hands were cold, and he fumbled for a moment before snapping it on. He pulled out its partner, but the wind snatched the glove and whirled it, white and gleaming, up into the air. Jim started after it, and Henders muttered, 'For fuck's sake.'

Close by, someone shouted something that was caught on the same gust of air. The rogue glove landed on the ground. Jim bent to pick it up.

Henders spat, 'Stop fucking around. Someone's coming.'

Jim followed the other man's gaze and saw a figure, tall and thin, dressed in something pale that was flapping in the wind. The newcomer pushed their way through the gap in the barriers, slipping slightly as they negotiated the incline. The garment gave them a ghostly aspect, but Jim knew it was a flesh-and-blood spectre that had come to haunt him. He pulled the other glove on.

Henders gripped his arm. 'We've been out on the lash and came down here for a quick slash, two old pals who can't hold their booze.'

The figure was close now. White hair fanning out like a dandelion clock, raincoat agape. Ronald Fergusson shouted, 'What are you doing down here, Jim?'

The envelope was in Jim's gloved hand. He held it by his side. 'I could ask you the same question.'

The physicist drew closer. 'I was at the library. I saw the fence had been moved and thought I should check it out.' He nodded towards the open pits where the foundations of the demolished building had been pinned. 'These holes are an accident waiting to happen. I said we should have security keeping an eye on things, but I was shouted down.'

Henders receded into the darkness, but the moon was out again and the demolition site offered no cover. Fergusson nodded to him before turning to Jim. 'Aren't you going to introduce us?'

'Mr Henders and I were just taking the air.'

Henders threw Jim a murderous look. 'We got caught short. Happens to the best of us after a couple of pints.'

Fergusson's briefcase was tucked under his arm. He adjusted it and peered at Henders. 'Be careful. This ground is uneven – easy to trip and break something.' He looked at

Jim. 'I'd have thought you'd be keen to keep a low profile after this afternoon's theatrics, but it's not my business how you spend your evenings. Enjoy yourself while you can. It's only a matter of time before the students cancel you.'

Jim said, 'Fuck you, Ron.'

Henders hissed, 'Let it go.'

The physicist stared at Jim, as if his eyes had just adjusted to the dark. He whispered, 'Why are you wearing latex gloves?' His gaze flitted from Jim to Henders. 'Did he say your name was Henders?' The builder did not answer. Fergusson glared at Jim. 'You just added Henders Construction to the shortlist.'

Jim said, 'It's not how it looks.'

Fergusson shook his head in wonder. 'I knew you were up to something, but I never imagined . . . it's corruption, pure and simple.'

Jim took a step backwards, still clutching the envelope. 'You're out of line, Ron.'

'What do you have there?' The physicist lunged for the envelope. The move was quick and unexpected. There was a moment when they each held an edge, but the plastic gloves made Jim's hands slip, and Fergusson snatched it. He ripped the envelope open and whipped out its contents.

Henders turned away. Jim dived for the documents, but the physicist stepped nimbly sideways, his eyes on the text. 'Jesus, Jim, what are they paying you?'

Jim grabbed Fergusson's arm. 'It's nothing to do with money.'

'Get your hands off me.' Fergusson was stronger than he appeared. He pulled free. 'Forget becoming principal. This is the coffin nail in your career.'

Jim started towards him. 'Give me a chance to explain.'

Fergusson struck out with his briefcase. Its metal buckle smacked Jim on the mouth, splitting his lip. Jim swore and caught hold of the physicist. Fergusson tried to wrestle free. He kicked Jim on the shin, lost his footing on the uneven ground and grabbed hold of the lapels of Jim's coat, steadying himself. Their faces were close enough for a kiss. Fergusson's breath smelt stale. He whispered, 'You're scum, Brennan — always were, always will be.'

Jim said, 'And you're to the manor fucking born with a silver spoon up your arse.'

He could see Henders walking away across the waste ground towards the road. Everything he had worked for was fucked: his family, his job, his future.

Fergusson hissed, 'You're a foul-mouthed ned and you're finished.'

'Ach, who gives a fuck.' Jim gave the physicist a hard shove to the chest and turned his back on him.

Later, he would wonder if he had meant to do it, if he had been possessed for a moment by the spirit of his father, or the ghost of the man he might have grown into. Fergusson fell backwards, arms flailing for balance, and hit the ground. There was a crack, the sound of bone on stone, as his head hit the sharp rock that pierced his skull.

Clouds gusted across the sky. Fergusson lay motionless on his back. Jim stood over him and then sank onto his haunches. Henders looked back. He paused, and then slowly retraced his steps until he was standing by Jim's side. 'Is he dead?'

'Yes . . . I don't know . . . maybe . . . I think so.'

'Fuck.' Henders leaned stiffly down and felt for a pulse in Fergusson's neck. 'Jesus.' He lifted the physicist's arm, pressed his fingers to the inside of the wrist and then let it drop. 'As a fucking dodo.' His breath sounded laboured. After a moment he squeezed Jim's shoulder. 'Okay, son, what we do next matters. Who's waiting at home for him?'

'No one. His wife died two years ago. He's got . . . had a son in America. Maybe he'll phone.'

'And what if his dad doesn't pick up? Straight onto the polis?'

'I wouldn't think so.'

'Here's hoping you're right. How about his job?'

'Tomorrow's Friday, research day. Soonest he'd have a class is Monday.'

'That's good. Gives us a bit of breathing space.' Henders gripped Jim's shoulder and pushed himself to his feet. 'Okay, as far as I'm concerned, this is your mess. I was here about other business, things took a bad turn, and you killed this guy.'

'It was an accident.'

'Doesn't matter. He's dead.' Henders gripped Jim under the armpit and drew him to his feet. 'Focus. We have to make up a wee story here. And that story is, your man was wandering around, who knows why, fucking eccentric fucker, thinking about the meaning of life or some such, missed his footing and fell down one of the dangerous holes he warned everyone about. Ironic and tragic. These things happen. Case closed.'

Jim looked towards the empty sockets where concrete stanchions used to hold the old building in place. 'I'm not doing it.'

Henders squeezed his shoulder. 'Fair enough. Give me time to get clear before you call the polis and keep my name out of it. I'll put a word in for you at the prison. Maybe they'll let you share a cell with your son. It's been known to happen.'

Jim rubbed his face with his hands. The plastic gloves rustled against his skin. 'I'm not sure I can carry him on my own.'

'You're gonnae have to. Your DNA's already on him. We're hoping no one feels the need to check and I'm guessing you're not on the police database anyway. It's a different story for me. I'm not getting anywhere near that.' Henders gave Jim a slight shove. 'C'mon, shift it. Sooner done, sooner gone.'

It was easier than Jim had expected to drag the physicist's body to the edge of one of the holes. It was his idea to throw the rock that had pierced Fergusson's skull in first, in case a forensic investigation matched its contours to the dent in Fergusson's skull. Henders nodded grimly. 'You're your father's son, right enough.'

Jim pulled the body upright, slid the briefcase beneath its arm, securing it with one gloved hand, while his other arm circled its waist, and then toppled Fergusson headfirst into the pit. The old gaberdine raincoat briefly fanned out like the wings of a bird, there was a wet thud, and everything was done.

Henders bent and retrieved the envelope from the ground where it had fallen during the scuffle. He blew some dust from its surface. 'Not a word. Not to your wife, your therapist or your fucking dog. Do not *Dear Diary* this or write a hint in your memoirs. Put tonight from your mind. It never happened. And when they find the poor bastard's body, don't overdo things. Remember, you didn't like each other. No need to go all chief mourner.'

Jim looked at him. 'Is this the end of it?'

Henders nodded. 'If we're lucky. The end of this, and the start of the rest of your life.'

It started to rain as they crossed the demolition site. Henders held his hand out, testing the weight of the shower. 'We already got lucky. This is what we needed. A good rain to wash away the traces. Soon it'll be like we were never here.'

Semester One 2018–19

One Year Later

THE NEW PRINCIPAL leaned back in his chair and stared at the large abstract painting – a gift from Maggie. He tried again to detect a resemblance between the garish acrylics splattered across the canvas and the gleaming new tower block he could see beyond his office window.

The Malcolm Lulach Learning and Teaching Hub, nicknamed MalcoHub by the students, had officially opened three months previously. Lulach had lived long enough to see the cornerstone laid and had joked that the decision to name the building after him confirmed his cancer was terminal. *You know you're on the way out when they start sticking your name on muckle great buildings.*

A red apple was balanced on the edge of his desk. Jim picked it up and walked to the window, polishing its skin against his sleeve. The university tower clock had stalled a few weeks ago at half past midday, or half past midnight, no one was certain which. Engineers brought in to repair it were waiting on a hard-to-locate component. Jim missed the clock's chimes punctuating the day. He glanced at his watch. In two hours, he would welcome the Saudi alumnus back to the university and escort him to a reception to celebrate three new scholarships in genocide studies that his family's foundation was establishing. They had graciously agreed that the new building's lecture theatre be named after a much-respected physics professor who had died too soon and in unfortunate circumstances.

Jim had cut the ribbon on the Ronald Fergusson Debating Forum himself and made a short speech announcing the newly established Fergusson Prize in Physics. Fergusson's son had attended virtually from MIT and, later, sent an email thanking Jim for his kind words about his father. Jim knew the final words of the message by heart.

My father's untimely death is a tragedy, but it is fitting that he met it on the campus where he spent so much of his life. I am pleased that the university is honouring his services to physics and to his institution.

Classes had ended, and students were streaming across the quads below Jim's office. He barely knew any of them by name these days, except for members of the SRC, rogues and future leaders. It was an inevitability of his new role. The teaching and research that had saved him as a young man must be set aside, for a while at least. He was the captain of the ship, keeper of the keys, the man with access to the dead levers.

Jim breathed in through his nose and held his breath, counting his heartbeats. It was an exercise that Maggie had taught him to displace spiralling thoughts. He breathed out and repeated the process. Replacing the noise in his brain with numbers helped him get to sleep at night. It was easy, except for the memory of bone cracking against stone, the wet thud of Fergusson's body hitting the bottom of the pit.

There had been a brief police investigation into Fergusson's death. The University Bedellus informed the inquiry that the physics professor had taken to wandering the campus grounds in the early hours. The security guards' report of Jim and Fergusson's dawn shouting match had also come to light, and Jim had testified that his colleague had been increasingly prone to verbal outbursts. The statement felt like a risky strategy, but it contributed to the impression that Ronald Fergusson's behaviour had become erratic, that he had been losing his grip. The Procurator Fiscal declared a verdict of accidental death.

Jim placed the apple on his desk, shiny and whole. He sat down and returned his attention to his inbox. A professor of epidemiology had forwarded an email she had received, warning of a new virus detected in Wuhan in China. Nothing to worry about for now, but something to be mindful of, if they had students on exchange in the region or travelling from there to study at the university. Jim forwarded it to his vice chancellors.

He had received a final email about Li Jie six months ago. This time there was no photo attached. The message stated simply: *Li Jie is in a room without windows*. Recently, he had begun to wonder if the whole episode had been a phishing attempt, a move to tip him into an unwise, undiplomatic exchange. The People's Republic was a place of human rights abuses, but there were worlds within worlds, truths beneath truths.

Jim printed out the speech Murray Deacon had written for him, for that afternoon's reception. He selected a red pen and started to work through the text, inserting changes that would make the communications director's words sound like his own. He read the welcome out loud, practising injecting warmth into his greeting.

Eliot had arranged a visiting order for early that evening. Jim would have to leave the reception early if he was to make it to Linbarley on time. Maggie had told him to skip the visit, take the Saudis out for dinner, but Jim felt uneasy about how well their son was adjusting to prison life. He wanted to remind the boy that, even though it was four years before he would be due for probation, there was a world waiting beyond the prison gates. Eliot should start preparing for it.

He returned to the printout and repeated his greeting out loud: 'It is my great honour to welcome Prince . . .'

The telephone on his desk rang.

Jim looked at the display and saw an outside number he did not recognise. *Li Jie is in a room without windows.* He repeated the phrase in his head, and felt the sense of dread that was never far from him now as he reached out a hand to take the call.

Acknowledgements

What is a university? A place of learning and research, city of enquiry, fellowship of scholars, centre of artistic and scientific creativity, influencer of policy, protector of public health, international community, challenger of complacency, safe shelter, repository of the past, herald of the future, home of dreamers and pioneers, books, lands, buildings and estates, explorer, guardian, enterprise, business . . . A university, as Jim Brennan and I both know, is many things and requires more than academics to stay afloat. I want to thank my colleagues across University of Glasgow for their ongoing support and friendships.

Special thanks are due to my colleagues in Creative Writing. Working with a team of dedicated writers from a range of genres continues to enrich, challenge and expand my relationship with literature and the world. Our Monday lunchtime literary events series Creative Conversations, brilliantly led by poet Dr Colin Herd, is a weekly delight which helps to open the doors of the university to a wider community. Like Jim Brennan, and many of my colleagues,

I am the first person in my family to go to university. Pushing the doors wider matters to us and to the future.

Thanks too to my editor Francis Bickmore who encouraged and embraced this slice of campus crime and improved it with his insights and rigor. Alison Rae is a copy editor extraordinaire who has saved me many a red face and whose sense of humour added energy to the process. Sam Copeland's knowledge of literature and industry have once again been invaluable in keeping me on the road, when I might have headed for the hills. The Canongate Art department have given me a Caspar David Friedrich gothic delight of a cover. Massive thank you to Jamie Byng and the wider Canongate team. I am honoured to be published by a great independent publishing house.

A special thanks to Anne Goldrick and Alex Reedijk who many years ago organised a dinner so I could discuss architectural practice – here's the novel at last!

Writing a books is nice work if you can get it, but sometimes lonely and isolating. Thanks to my friends and family who make life fun and keep my boots on the ground. My dad John, sister Karen and niece Sophie. David and Cathy Fehilly, Clare Connelly, Laughlin Bell, Paul Sheehan and John Jenkins keep the good times rolling. Composer Stuart MacRae continues to expand my musical, artistic and ecological horizons. Thanks too to Val McDermid and Professor Jo Sharp for their support, great sense of humour and kindness.

As always my first reader and most constructive critic is my partner in life and love, Zoë Strachan without whom none of this would matter.

Louise Welsh

Glasgow, 2023